"This is the end of the

A wall of water sluiced over the foredeck and swamped the cockpit, drowning out Josh's words. As the wave swept past, Libby clung to the sleeve of his coat as if it were a lifeline.

"I won't make it to the island, Josh."

"You have to, Libby. It's the only way."

"Don't you understand? I can't swim."

"You what?"

"I can't swim."

"You'll be okay. Take my hand," he instructed, and she laced her fingers through his.

"Promise you won't let go . . ."

Seconds after they hit the water, a breaker tore them apart. Even as Josh floundered to the surface he reached for Libby, striving to recapture her hand, but his fingers closed around frigid water. He thrashed around, scanning the darkness. *This can't be happening. Libby trusts me. I can't let her down.*

"Libby!" he howled. "Liiibbeee!"

His only answer was the banshee wind and the incessant roar of the sea . . .

Another Silhouette Sensation by Robin Francis

Taking a Chance

ROBIN FRANCIS
The Shocking
Ms. Pilgrim

Silhouette Sensation

First published in Great Britain in 1990 by Silhouette Books, Eton House, 18-24 Paradise Road, Richmond, Surrey TW9 1SR

© Rose Marie Ferris 1989

Silhouette, Silhouette Sensation and Colophon are Trade Marks of Harlequin Enterprises B.V.

ISBN 0 373 57906 3

18 – 9006

Made and printed in Great Britain

Chapter One

Elizabeth Pilgrim had worked her way through college with a variety of jobs. She'd been a tutor, a tour guide, a barmaid, a typist. She had clerked in gift shops and galleries, and one semester, on a work-study grant at a living-history museum, she'd dug clams and harvested blueberries and knitted heads for lobster traps.

During her senior year at the University of Maine she'd gotten into modeling. She'd done print ads, mostly for local department stores, but one of her photographs had made the mukluks section of the L. L. Bean catalog.

She'd done a lot of things in her twenty-six years, but she had never kidnapped anyone.

Until today.

Elizabeth swallowed, easing the dryness in her throat, and watched the Rum Key marker buoy slide away to stern.

Six weeks ago, at the height of the season, Frenchman's Bay had been buzzing with runabouts, speedboats and skiffs; with yacht tenders, excursion boats and sailboats of every size and description, but on this cloudy October morning most of the summer people were gone. Only an occasional lobster boat chugged down the channel, escorted by squadrons of gulls.

The harbor was quiet. The growl of the cabin cruiser's engine seemed deafening in the predawn stillness, and Elizabeth had an eerie, unshakable feeling that from the rock-bound shores of Mount Desert Island a hundred pairs of eyes were trained upon her, charting her arrival.

A sprinkling of lights off the starboard bow marked the village that was her destination, and she eased back on the throttle as the familiar outline of the Windlass Inn took shape in the dusk. She cut the engine, and the vessel's forward momentum carried it into a berth at one of the floating piers.

The moment the boat nudged the landing, a man crossed the gangway from the quay, oilskins crackling in the breeze. The brim of a battered slouch hat was pulled over his eyes, and a flashlight bobbed in one hand.

"Mr. Trask?" she inquired in a nervous whisper. "Is that you?"

"Ayuh."

To confirm his identity, Homer Trask shone the beam of his torch toward his face, and reassured by the composure she saw in his blunt, grizzled features, Elizabeth made her way to the foredeck and tossed him the bowline, which he looped about a piling.

"You're late," he said, stepping into the cockpit with a spryness that belied his sixty-eight years. "Not havin' second thoughts, are you?"

Elizabeth secured the stern line and did not reply.

"No reason for cold feet," said Homer. "We've done nuthin' wrong."

"Not yet," she said. "Not unless you count conspiring to commit a felony."

Homer switched off the flashlight and stuffed it into a pocket of his slicker. "To my way of thinkin', it's fellers like Joshua Noon who're the criminals."

"But kidnapping seems a bit extreme," said Elizabeth. "Perhaps if we talked to Mr. Noon—"

"Tried talkin'," said Homer. "Tried writin' letters, too. Didn't do a particle of good. Noon wouldn't see us."

"But if we tried again?"

Homer shook his head. "No, Miss Libby. Time for talkin's past. But you've done your share, providin' this fine boat. If you're scared, walk away. I can take it from here."

"I'm not scared, Mr. Trask. It's just that I have a few reservations."

"Such as?"

"Well, how can we be sure that Mr. Noon will listen to reason? I know he's in advertising, and I suppose that implies he's open to persuasion, but I can't help wondering— What if all he understands is force?"

"If it is, 'twon't hurt to give 'im a taste of his own medicine. If 'tisn't, today'll be an eye-opener for him."

"Do you think, once he's met with the committee, he'll see things our way?"

"Mebbe," said Homer. "Never can tell which way a cat will jump. He might think we're doin' him a favor."

"What if he doesn't?"

"Then we're no worse off than we was before. Way I see it, what we got to lose?"

Quite a lot actually, Elizabeth thought. If her brother found out she had taken his boat, she'd never hear the end of it. And if Joshua Noon chose to make an issue of his abduction, she could wind up in jail.

"It'll never come to that," Margaret Ogilvie, president of the Down East Environmental Protection Coalition had predicted. "No jury's going to believe an unarmed, hundred-ten-pound woman is capable of making an able-bodied, hundred-eighty-pound man go anywhere against his will. If Mr. Noon's fool enough to press charges, he'll be laughed out of court."

As usual, Margaret's analysis made eminent good sense, but Elizabeth's conscience insisted that the end did not justify the means.

No matter what the provocation, shanghaiing Joshua Noon was wrong. She couldn't rationalize DEEPC's skulduggery; not legally, not ethically, not morally. Nor could she sit idly by while Noon turned Half-Moon Island into some sort of yuppie la-la-land.

"Well, Miss Libby? You in or out?"

Elizabeth stiffened her spine, mustering the courage of her convictions. "In," she replied.

Trask's dour expression did not brighten. He reached into the pocket of his sweater-vest and removed an old-fashioned timepiece. "Mr. Noon'll be along any minute now. I'd best get back to his boat."

"Have you put it out of commission?"

"Ayuh. Motor won't start without spark plugs." Homer stepped from the gently heaving side deck to the pier, then turned to scan the sky to the east, streaked pink and gold by the sunrise. "If I was you, I'd get into my foul-weather gear."

"But the rain's stopped."

"For the time bein'. In an hour or so, it's gonna rain like a son of a gun." Homer's gaze shifted from the cloud formations to her. "DEEPC's dependin' on you, Miss Libby."

"I'll deliver Mr. Noon to Half-Moon. That's a promise."

Elizabeth hoped Homer Trask would attribute the tremor in her voice to the early-morning chill rather than lack of commitment to the Coalition's goals, but the truth was, she hadn't much faith in the outcome of this venture.

According to the dossier Margaret Ogilvie had assembled, Joshua Noon was a hyperactive huckster who kept his own counsel and irregular hours.

"It's not uncommon for him to work his people round the clock, with hardly a coffee break," Margaret had reported.

"His employees must find him intolerable," said Elizabeth.

"One would think so, but they're loyal. Our informant's never heard any of his people say anything bad about him."

"He'd probably fire them if they did."

"Could be. To be fair, though, he pays them well, and he's as demanding of himself as he is with them. When his crew calls it a night, he goes on working. Brainstorming, he calls it. These sessions might go on two or three days at a stretch. Once in a while he'll party or play tennis or get in a round of golf, but even when he's playing, he's working. He has one of those minirecorders, and he takes it with him everywhere he goes. If inspiration strikes, he'll whip out that tape recorder and dictate a memo, wherever he happens to be."

Elizabeth marveled at the man's nonstop pace. "When does he sleep?"

"He doesn't. Not much, anyway. But the point is, his movements are unpredictable. He doesn't stick to a schedule, except for Friday mornings."

"What happens on Fridays?"

"At seven-thirty exactly he leaves the inn and takes his dory down to Southwest Harbor, where he catches the commuter plane for Bangor. He arrives in Bangor in time to board a flight to Chicago. Sometimes he's gone the whole weekend. Sometimes he's back by Saturday night. Then again, he might not return till Tuesday or Wednesday. Obviously, if we're going to get to him, it'll have to be on his way west."

"Where?" asked Elizabeth. "At Bangor?"

"No, not Bangor," Margaret answered. "We're going to waylay him before then. As soon as he leaves the Windlass. And Libby, that's where you come in. . . ."

Raindrops spattered the surface of the water. The sun had been vanquished by clouds. Elizabeth fastened the heavy canvas canopy over the fly bridge, and went below to find some rain gear. She was searching the forward hanging locker when she heard voices from the direction of the Inn.

"If Lansford calls, what should I tell him?"

"*When*, Sally. When he calls."

"Gotcha, boss. What should I tell him?"

"That's up to you. You want this account?"

"Do you think I'm ready for it?"

"You're ready."

"Then I want it. Only I'm not sure—"

The rest of Sally's response was swallowed up by the wake from a passing trawler. Wavelets slapped against the cabin cruiser's hull, and Elizabeth looked through the window, hoping to catch a glimpse of Sally's boss.

Was he the infamous Joshua Noon?

The rain had settled into a fine, soaking drizzle that misted the window and blurred her view. Unable to see the couple walking on the quay, she pulled on a hunter's orange poncho and hurried back to the cockpit.

"So what can I bring you from Chicago?" the man was asking.

"How about Kevin?"

"Are you that homesick?"

"Yeah, I miss him," Sally replied with a shaky little laugh. "What about you, Josh? Don't you miss Blair?"

If Noon answered this question, Elizabeth couldn't hear him. She scrambled up the ladder to the bridge, and from that vantage point she spotted Homer Trask, hunched against a lamppost at the edge of the Windlass's dock. She saw the white-painted dory that tugged at its moorings nearby, and after an interval of silence, Noon and his companion came into sight.

They descended the stairs from the jetty and strolled along the dock, absorbed in conversation, speaking in lowered tones, so that Elizabeth caught only snatches of what they said. But as they drew nearer, she realized that Joshua Noon's appearance did not conform to her image of him.

She had imagined him as a predator, with dark hair, hawkish features, and eyes as hard as obsidian. Instead his features were clean-cut, and his hair was only a few shades darker than her own sun-streaked brown.

Dressed in jeans and Topsiders, his sport coat unbuttoned over a crewneck sweater, he was leaner, fitter, *younger* than she had expected. He couldn't be more than two or three years past thirty, and judging by his "aw-shucks" grin, a boyish thirty at that.

He seemed good-natured and engaging, but that might make the threat he posed more dangerous than she had anticipated.

Elizabeth shivered, suddenly aware of the bone-chilling cold, and listened to Joshua Noon and Sally saying their goodbyes.

"Where's your raincoat?" Sally inquired.

"In here." Noon hoisted the nylon duffel he carried, then swung the bag into the dory and climbed in after it.

"The coat won't keep you dry in your suitcase. You ought to put it on."

"I will, Sal. Soon as I'm underway."

Elizabeth sat at the helm, her hands poised above the controls. Timing was everything now. In the same instant Noon pulled the starter cord on the dory's outboard, she hit the ignition.

The cabin cruiser's diesel roared to life, then subsided to a well-turned idle.

The dory's motor coughed, sputtered and died.

Noon tried the cord twice more in rapid succession, with the same unsatisfactory result. He scowled at the motor, jiggled the throttle lever, and yanked the cord again, again and again.

After a hasty look at the lowering sky, Elizabeth switched on the running lights. She removed a plastic-laminated Water Taxi sign from a cubbyhole in the chart rack, positioned it in the windscreen, and checked the sign's visibility as she moved forward to cast off.

Forty yards away, Joshua Noon was bent over the outboard, peering into the fuel tank.

"It's full," he said. "What the devil's wrong with it?"

Homer pushed away from the lamppost. "Take a whiff of them fumes, young feller. She's flooded. Let 'er sit a few minutes, and give 'er another crank."

"That tears it," Noon muttered. "I'm going to miss my flight."

Sally started toward the Inn. "I'll see if I can arrange a charter."

"No need," said Homer. He shone his flashlight toward Elizabeth, cueing her to gun the engine. "There's a water taxi yonder, just gettin' set to take off."

Noon hooked the straps of the duffel over one shoulder and sprinted along the dock. "Hey, wait up!" he shouted.

Elizabeth waved to show she'd heard him, but he didn't slow his pace until he reached the floating pier.

"Can you take a passenger?"

"That depends. Where you bound?"

"Southwest Harbor. The seaplane dock. There's an extra twenty in it for you if you get me there by nine."

Elizabeth wanted to tell Joshua Noon there were some things he couldn't buy. She wanted to tell him that she was one of them. But all she allowed herself was a grudging, "Cast off then, and get aboard."

Noon hesitated for a moment, gazing up at her, one hand shielding his eyes from the icy autumn rain, and then he cast off the stern line and jumped aboard the cruiser. He remained in the cockpit, sending a thumbs-up signal to Sally, while the vessel pulled away from the landing.

"There's a thermos of coffee in the galley," Elizabeth informed him. "You're welcome to help yourself."

"Thanks, I will. And thanks for the lift, Miss—"

"Pilgrim. Elizabeth Pilgrim."

"Josh Noon."

He extended one hand toward the bridge, but she pretended not to see it. She spun the wheel hard to starboard, steering the boat through a wide, banking turn that took it toward the breakwater beacon, and wondered what Joshua Noon would say when he discovered how sorely misplaced his gratitude was. He had to lower his arm and hang onto the ladder as the hull skipped across its own wake, but even while he strove to maintain his balance, she sensed his scrutiny.

"I really appreciate this, Elizabeth. If you hadn't happened along, I'd have been in for one long hassle."

She relinquished her death grip on the helm to flex her fingers and tie the hood of her poncho under her chin, smiling at him with more irony than amusement.

"Well, Mr. Noon, this must be your lucky day."

"Memo from Josh Noon to Sally Gillette regarding the Lansford account: Sally, now that you're Gordie Lansford's account executive, you should be the first to know that I've found the perfect mermaid for Lans-

ford's clam chowder commercials. Her name's Elizabeth Pilgrim, and she's skipper of a water taxi,
Pilgrim's Progress out of Day's Harbor."

JOSH PAUSED for a sip of coffee, his first of the morning.
Even black, with no sugar, it was surprisingly good.

Out of habit he reached for his cigarettes. He had fished
one of the Marlboros out of the box before he remembered
he was trying to cut back. Sighing, he returned his lighter to
his pocket and dropped the package of Marlboros onto the
table, next to the cassette recorder.

After another swallow of coffee, he picked up the recorder and spoke directly into the microphone, raising his
voice to make himself heard above the throb of the engine.

"If you've done your homework, you're aware that
Lansford's seen our library of videotapes. We've trotted a
dozen candidates by him. He took exception to all of
them—said they were too slick for this campaign. In retrospect, I have to admit he has a point. Mermaids should not
wear false eyelashes. So maybe it's time to break with tradition and go with an unknown. Which brings me back to
Elizabeth—"

Josh propped his chin on one hand and stared into space,
absently tracing his thumbnail over the nautical logo on his
coffee mug while he made a silent inventory of Elizabeth's
charms.

With her luminous brown eyes, tawny skin and stubborn
chin softened by a dimple, she was fresh and natural, the girl
next door, as wholesome as whole wheat toast. Yet her
mouth could only be described as sexy and her figure was
lovely, leggy and elegant. If what she did for dungarees was
a fair example, she could probably make a gunnysack look
like a designer original, and if, please God, she was photo-
genic, she'd be a knockout in the underwater sequences.

She was attractive, all right. No doubt about it. But what impressed him most was her candor, her lack of guile. She looked as if she was incapable of lying, and if that quality came across to the viewing audience, Lansford would have to keep his canneries running full tilt to meet the rising demand for his chowder.

Josh drank the last of his coffee and pressed the Record button. "This is a young lady with integrity," he said. "Take a look at her, Sally. If you agree she'd make the most sensational mermaid since Daryl Hannah, go ahead and contact her. See if you can get her to come in for an audition."

By EIGHT-FIFTEEN they were nearing the halfway mark. The sheer granite spires of Otter Cliffs loomed out of the mist, fortresslike and impregnable.

If Elizabeth had intended to taxi Josh Noon to Southwest Harbor, she would have steered south-southwest, keeping East Bunker's Ledge to port. But instead of rounding Ingraham Point, she set a course due south, on a heading that would carry them through the Cranberry Isles to the navigable cove at Half-Moon, where they would rendezvous with DEEPC's executive committee.

Once she had delivered her passenger to Margaret Ogilvie, Elizabeth would be free to leave. Her mission would be accomplished.

Until then, she prayed the rain would continue. She prayed that Noon would stay in the cabin, that he would not notice she had taken the wrong heading, and that Margaret and the rest of the committee would be on time.

A quarter of an hour later, less than seven miles from their destination, they were plowing along at a steady fifteen knots when something scraped the bottom of the boat and dragged against the stern. The cruiser shuddered and listed to port, then broke free of the obstacle, veering off at a slight angle to the east.

The mishap was over so quickly, it seemed unreal. Elizabeth's first thought was that her troubled conscience must be playing tricks on her. But she had felt the deck vibrate beneath her feet, and when she tried to bring the boat back on course there was an odd slackness in the wheel.

Her heart hammered against her ribs as she spun the wheel this way and that, with no response.

She shook her head, as if she could deny the incident. "I'm imagining things," she murmured.

Although the engine was running smoothly, she surveyed the control console. Fuel gauge, pressure gauges, voltmeter, tachometer—all the displays were normal. Only the compass was off. Instead of 185 degrees, the needle wavered between 165 and 170.

She tapped her fingers against the compass, and tried the wheel again. Again there was no response. The compass continued to register fifteen degrees off course.

Fifteen degrees! But that meant—

A shiver of foreboding scudded down her spine. She looked up, focusing on the distance.

Off the starboard bow lay the rain-drenched mound of Baker Island. Some miles beyond that, the great piny folds of Bass Harbor Head floated like a shadow on the horizon. The ghostly wail of the Schoodic Point whistle drifted over the port quarter. And directly ahead—

Nothing.

Chapter Two

"Something wrong?"

Joshua Noon's voice came from just behind her, so close that she started. She cut the engine, and in the comparative silence that followed, watched him ease into the copilot's seat.

Stay calm, she told herself. *You don't want to frighten him.* "We hit something, Mr. Noon. Maybe a deadhead."

"A what?"

"A submerged log."

"And?"

"I believe it damaged the rudder. We seem to have lost our steering."

Josh rocked back in his chair. "That means we won't make Southwest Harbor by nine."

"Yes," said Elizabeth. "I'm afraid it does."

She held her breath, waiting for the fireworks to begin, but after a terse, disgruntled, "Damn!" he reached for the binoculars on the console.

"May I?"

"Please do." Anything to keep him occupied while she figured out what she ought to do next.

While Joshua took stock of their surroundings, she found a pencil and spread the appropriate charts on the console.

Her thoughts were racing, trying to encompass the many factors she had to consider. The time, the tides, the currents, the weather; the rocks and reefs and shoals. But first she had better rule out the possibility that they could simply put out an anchor—

"What's that you're doing?" Moon inquired.

"Calculating our position."

He leaned closer, reading the map over her shoulder. "How long will it take?"

"Not long. A few minutes." If only he'd stop quizzing her.

"I see," he said soberly. "And once you've radioed for help, how long do you estimate we'll be stuck here?"

Elizabeth forced herself to meet his eyes. They were deep-set, intensely blue, penetrating. They seemed to see right through her, yet she couldn't look away. She distracted him with an awkward motion of her hand, calling his attention to the portion of the console that housed the electronic gear.

"Forgive me, Mr. Moon, I assumed you'd noticed—We don't have a radio."

His harsh intake of breath told her he was beginning to understand the gravity of their dilemma. "What kind of taxi doesn't have a radio?" he demanded.

A taxi that's not a taxi, she thought. *A boat that hauls bluefin rather than passengers.*

She debated telling Joshua about DEEPC's plan for him. It would be a relief to tell him the truth. Confession, so the saying went, was good for the soul, and an honest answer would help appease her conscience.

But a confession wouldn't fix the rudder. It wouldn't provide a radio. And it wouldn't help Joshua Noon.

Her lies and deceit were reprehensible. They had put him in jeopardy. To burden him with the truth now would be like rubbing salt into a wound. It would add to the outrage.

I'll tell him the whole story when we're safely ashore, she resolved. *This is not the time to confess.*

But deception did not come easily, and she permitted herself a half truth. "Funny you should ask," she said. "I've often wondered the same thing myself."

"Then the boat's not yours?"

"No, Mr. Noon. It belongs to my brother. But I've been sailing as long as I can remember, and I'm thoroughly acquainted with these waters."

Her response seemed to satisfy him. He lighted a cigarette and studied her through a stream of smoke.

"I'm not questioning your seamanship, Elizabeth, but this is a new experience for me. I'd appreciate it if you wouldn't pull any punches. Just tell me how desperate our situation is."

"I wouldn't call it desperate. Both of us will be missed. Sooner or later there'll be a search. But even before that, another boat could spot us. We're not far from the sea lanes. The Yarmouth ferry passes less than five miles from here, and there's a fair amount of traffic hereabouts."

"Not much now though."

There was no denying that. "It's this weather," she said.

Joshua took another drag on his cigarette, scowling at the rain. "That's one thing that bothers me. From the yarns you natives spin, the weather might not improve till spring. And according to that chart of yours, if we drift out of the bay there's nothing between us and France but a few offshore islands and a whole lot of ocean."

That bothered Elizabeth too, but for his benefit she replied optimistically. "Let's not borrow trouble. I have every confidence we'll be rescued. It's just that it may take a while."

"What do we do in the meantime?"

"We wait, Mr. Noon. We wait."

Joshua rose and flipped the cigarette overboard, then leaned against the safety rail and watched it disappear to stern.

"There's a lighthouse on that island," he observed.

Elizabeth nodded. "Baker Light."

"How far would you say it is? About two or three miles?"

"I'd say double that, so if you're thinking of trying to swim to the island, forget it. Between the undertow and the water temperature, you'd never make it."

Josh leaned farther out and watched the bow slice through the foamy gray water. "How cold is it?"

"Forty-eight degrees, Mr. Noon. Or less. You wouldn't last thirty minutes."

He squared his shoulders and turned to her. "I'm a strong swimmer."

"I'm sure you are, but you're not superhuman."

"I'm not overly patient, either."

"Then perhaps a bit of practice would not be amiss."

He shrugged and planted one foot on the railing. "You may be right, but I'm used to keeping busy. If there's any way I can help out, all you have to do is ask."

Elizabeth got to her feet, rolling the charts into a neat cylinder. "As long as you mention it, there are a couple of things I need to take care of below—"

Joshua held up one hand. "Say no more. I'll keep watch up here."

Before she left the fly bridge, Elizabeth rummaged through the bench seat locker and found the flare gun. "In case you spot another boat, do you know how to use this?"

"I think I can figure it out."

She handed him the gun and a box of cartridges carefully, so that their fingers didn't touch.

"You know, Elizabeth, given the circumstances, it'd be nice if you'd call me Josh."

She agreed, of course. There was no reason not to. None she wanted to share with him, at any rate. But calling him Josh complicated matters. It made him seem more distinct, less distant, less the generic villain.

It cast new uncertainties over DEEPC's tactics—

She wondered which of them was the good guy and which the bad as she tucked the charts beneath her elbow and clambered down the ladder, and since she could no longer think of Joshua as the enemy, she chose not to think of him at all.

FROM NINE TILL TEN the rain came down in torrents. Josh chain-smoked, paced the perimeter of the foredeck and peered through the binoculars till his eyes burned, scanning the horizon for other craft on the bay. But all he saw were passing seabirds and the unrelenting rain. And as if they didn't have enough trouble, the breeze freshened and pushed them farther toward the ocean.

By the time the rain subsided, they were abeam of Baker Island, close enough that he could hear waves breaking on the island's seaward shore.

He fired one of the flares, hoping to attract someone's attention. The only response came from Elizabeth, who dashed out of the cabin and up the ladder without stopping to put on her poncho.

"Is there another boat? Where is it?" she cried, scrambling onto the bridge.

Her eagerness faded as he apologized for the false alarm. "I should have explained, the light's automated," she told him.

"You mean nobody's there?"

"Probably not, but it was worth a try."

He felt like a fool, another new experience; one he did not relish.

You could strip him naked and set him down in any big city, without a guidebook or friends or a penny to his name, and he would prosper. Within twenty-four hours he'd know where the action was. He would establish contacts, a line of credit, and he'd capitalize on them.

He knew his way around a boardroom. Given a balance sheet and some marketing data, he could blaze a trail through red tape and blind alleys to the places where opportunity lay.

He had an instinct for survival in the corporate jungle. But his instincts weren't much help in this briny wilderness, where the skyscrapers were granite headlands rather than high rises. He was out of his element and he knew it; now Elizabeth knew it too, and it seemed vital that he redeem himself.

Somehow, Josh promised himself, before this misadventure was over, he would earn her respect. His pride demanded it, and because he sensed that she was not easily impressed, her good opinion mattered to him.

Or maybe it was just that he was bored and wet and miserable, and she provided a welcome change of scenery.

He admired the graceful economy of her movements as she attached a pennant to the flagpole on the transom. But she went about her work so seriously that he could not resist teasing her.

"What's with the flag? Are we heading for a parade?"

"It's the international distress signal."

Her answer was matter-of-fact, as practical as her deck boots and baggy sweater and sensibly braided hair. Without a wasted word, without a wasted gesture, she returned to her charts in the cabin, leaving Josh to draw his own conclusions.

The red and white pennant fluttered in the breeze, striking a dissonant cheerful note.

Elizabeth Pilgrim, he decided, was that rarity of rarities: a woman devoid of feminine wiles. She was 99 and 44/100 percent pure. Only her smile seemed fake.

BY MIDAFTERNOON Josh was down to his last cigarette. When he went into the cabin to get another pack, Elizabeth was putting lunch on the table.

"It's not much," she told him. "Just crackers and cheese and some cocoa."

"If the cocoa's hot, let me at it." His face was ruddy from the raw northwest wind, and he wrapped his hands around his mug to warm them.

She sat across from him, keeping a watchful eye on the porthole as she said, "There are one or two things we need to discuss."

"Fire away."

"Well, the first thing is, I expected the incoming tide to carry us back the way we came. Maybe as far as Seal Harbor."

"But it hasn't."

"It's this wind," she said, bending over her cup. "It's counterbalancing the current. For now we're holding steady, but I have to tell you, I'm a little worried."

Josh raised an eyebrow. "Only a little?"

"Well, the tide only turned an hour ago. With any luck, the breeze'll die down or shift to the south."

"Do you honestly think it will?"

"I couldn't say, Mr.—Joshua."

"What if it doesn't?"

"That depends on how soon a search gets underway. If we drift beyond Baker Island, it'll make it harder for the coast guard to find us. As you said earlier, there's a whole lot of ocean out there."

"In other words, we might be eating cheese and crackers for supper, too."

This was one prospect she would rather not contemplate. She munched on a Wheat Thin, stalling while her thoughts turned toward the committee.

How long had they waited at Half-Moon Cove before they realized Noon would not be joining them? And once they'd left the island, had they notified the authorities or checked with Homer Trask?

If they talked to Trask, he would tell them she had picked up Noon on schedule. He would also tell Margaret about the pep talk he'd given her. And once he confided in Margaret, would she assume Elizabeth had changed her mind?

She would, Elizabeth thought. Which left her brother.

But Caleb had gone to Boston for the weekend. He wasn't due home till Sunday evening, and chances were he wouldn't notice the boat was gone till Monday.

Her spirits fell as she confronted the possibility that she might not be reported missing for another seventy-two hours, and that the best hope for rescue lay with Joshua Noon.

"What time were you supposed to get into O'Hare?" she asked.

Joshua frowned at her over the rim of his cup. "How'd you know I was going to Chicago?"

She stared at him, shaken by her blunder. "You must've mentioned it."

"No," he said. "I didn't."

"Then your friend must have."

Josh shook his head, trying to reconstruct those last harried minutes before their departure. "Sally didn't say anything about Chicago." His frown deepened. "At least, I don't think she did."

"One of you must have. How else would I know where you were going?"

"Beats me. Unless—" He grinned suddenly, recalling the gist of his conversation with Sally before they reached the dock. "Why, Elizabeth, you little dickens. I do believe you have a secret vice."

"Beg pardon?"

"Come on, admit you were eavesdropping. You heard me ask Sally what she'd like from Chicago."

Elizabeth drew herself taller. "I'll admit no such thing. I don't even know why we're talking about this. I assure you, all I'm interested in is whether anyone's meeting your plane."

Her eyes were wide and solemn; ingenuous, he thought. "Give me some credit," he said. "I know what you're asking, and the answer's yes and no. Yes, someone's meeting the plane, and no, she's not likely to send out a search party."

"You seem very sure of that."

"Yes," he said. "I am."

"Based on what?"

"Past experience. Blair Healey is not known for her resourcefulness. She's sweet and funny and something of a flake. She's also chronically late. If the flight's on time, she'll think I left without her. She'll invent some excuse and leave messages at the agency and my apartment and hurry home to wait for me to return her call. When she doesn't hear from me, she'll think I'm angry. She'll probably console herself with a shopping spree and have dinner with friends, and if, by some miracle, she realizes I'm not in Chicago, she'll take it as a personal slight. She might see her therapist. She'll most certainly see her hairdresser. But she won't phone Sally, and it won't occur to her to call out the marines. Not in a million years."

"What about the other people in your office? Won't they miss you?"

"Sure they will, eventually. But the office is closed Saturdays. If any of the staff happen to be putting in overtime, they won't be looking for me. And since I haven't confirmed any appointments with clients this weekend, I doubt anyone will figure out what's happened till I don't show up at the Windlass on Sunday." Josh set his cup down with enough force that cocoa sloshed onto the table. "So, Elizabeth, what's the verdict?"

Elizabeth caught her breath and let it out in a sigh. "It looks as though we'd better prepare ourselves to spend the night."

"Cheese and crackers for breakfast, right?" Josh speared a sliver of cheddar with the tip of his knife. He smiled. Elizabeth didn't.

"Things aren't that bad," she said. "We have enough canned goods to last a few days. Soup, beef stew, applesauce—that type of thing. And the freshwater tank's full."

"How're we fixed for blankets?"

"We have a sleeping bag and a couple of survival blankets."

"And each other," Josh added.

His lazy drawl brought a rush of color to her cheeks. This was another possibility she preferred not to contemplate.

She rose and moved toward the companionway slowly, so that it wouldn't seem like a retreat. Once she had put some distance between them, she stopped to look at him.

"It'll be dark soon," she said. "There's a portable lantern by the sink and one in the head. We'll keep the running lights on all night, but I'd appreciate it if you didn't use the overhead lights. I'm afraid they might drain the battery."

"Okay," said Josh. "No problem."

"All right then. I'll take the next watch topside. You can relieve me at eight."

Josh responded with a smart salute and a jaunty, "Aye-aye, Cap'n." But the moment Elizabeth was gone, his grin vanished.

Something about the lady did not compute.

While he finished the cocoa, he remembered the way she'd dodged his question about the radio. He rinsed the cup and poked through the cupboards, wondering how she'd known he was going to Chicago.

Why had she gotten so defensive when he'd accused her of eavesdropping? It was a human failing, after all.

Was it an accident that she'd been at the public landing this morning? In the weeks he'd been headquartered at the Windlass, he'd never seen a water taxi on duty so early in the morning. And, come to think of it, his dory had always started before.

Josh smoked a cigarette while he grappled with these questions, trying to put two and two together. By five-thirty he was tired of his own company. He had exhausted the supply of magazines in the salon and dealt himself three losing hands of solitaire. He had also dictated an addendum to his memo.

He sprawled on the sofa, with the cassette recorder on his chest and his feet propped higher than his head, while he rewound the tape and listened to it play back.

"Sally," he began, "you'll be pleased to know there's a can of Lansford's chowder aboard, but I haven't said anything about an audition to Ms. Pilgrim. For reasons I won't go into here, I'm leaving the negotiations to you.

"I have an idea for the print ads, though. Picture this: In the background there's a beach, a clambake, a crowd of college kids sitting around a driftwood fire. In the foreground there's a cast-iron pot—no, make that a soup tureen—big enough to accommodate our mermaid. She's holding a can of chowder. And the caption reads, 'Isn't This a Pretty Kettle of Fish?' ''

There was a pause for dramatic effect, and then he continued. ''Think it over, Sal. If you like the concept, send up a trial balloon and see who shoots and who salutes. If Lansford approves, we can adapt the idea for TV. It might be interesting to make spots reminiscent of those old beach-party movies. Who knows? If we mix some sixties music into the sound track—maybe one of the Beach Boys' numbers—we might tap into the nostalgia craze.''

The cassette trailed into silence and finally wound to a stop, but Joshua's enthusiasm had soured. He considered the toes of his sneakers and asked himself who the hell he was kidding.

He prided himself on being a good judge of character, and just now his better judgment was screaming that Elizabeth Pilgrim would never involve herself in anything as frivolous as playing a mermaid on TV.

He rewound the tape and listened to it again, more critically. Without Elizabeth as the focal point, his ideas seemed uninspired.

Besides, Lansford's was Sally's account. She was a talented copywriter, and the most efficient administrative assistant he'd ever had. It wasn't fair to offer her a promotion, then deny her creative control of the campaign. If she needed his help, she would ask for it—provided he ever got off this boat.

Until then, he'd be well advised to keep his suggestions to himself. And, incidentally, save the cassette for something more important. Much as he loved his work, he didn't want his last recorded message to be about clam chowder.

Josh swung his feet to the floor and punched Rewind and Erase. As he watched the ribbon of tape spin from reel to reel, his thoughts wound back to his unanswered questions, and it occurred to him that someone must have tampered with the dory.

Elizabeth, for instance.

She'd had the time. She'd had the opportunity. And she herself had told him she'd been sailing for as long as she could remember, so she certainly had the expertise.

The more Josh thought about it, the more positive he became that Elizabeth had dismantled the outboard. The only question that remained was why.

And although he hated to admit she'd put one over on him, now that he was wise to her, he'd be damned if he'd let her get away with it.

"Don't get mad, get even," he muttered. That would be his motto.

Chapter Three

The wind fell to a whisper toward evening; too late to do them much good. For an hour or so they floated toward Seal Harbor. Elizabeth saw the lights along the shore draw closer, winking like fireflies through the trees, but she was not deceived. She knew the next turn of the tide would carry them out to sea.

At about six-thirty Josh brought a thermos of coffee to the bridge. "Thought maybe you could use some of this," he said.

"Thanks," she said, taking a sip. "This is really nice of you."

"Hey, what's a first mate for?"

They sat side by side on the cushioned bench and watched gauzy plumes of sea smoke creep across the surface of the water.

"Fog's rising," she remarked.

"Figures," said Josh.

Elizabeth hugged her arms to her sides to keep from shivering. The coffee cup trembled in her hand. "Do you suppose we should send up some flares?"

"Might as well," he replied. "Seems like we ought to do something."

She held his cup while he loaded the gun and fired. Over the next five minutes he launched several rounds. The flares exploded against the sky in a burst of sizzling phosphorescence and arced, still white-hot, into the bay. But the light they shed was fleeting. In moments it was gone, and the night seemed darker than before, and colder. Lonelier. The distant clang of a bell buoy made their isolation seem complete.

"Do you think anyone saw?" Elizabeth asked.

"I don't know."

She tucked her hands beneath the cuffs of her sweater sleeves, wishing Josh had answered with a simple yes or no. Either was preferable to uncertainty.

"That's the hardest part," she said. "Not knowing."

"But look at the bright side. If you'd run into that log half an hour later, I'd be in Chicago and you'd be out here alone."

She shivered again. "This might sound selfish, Josh, but I'm glad you're not in Chicago."

Josh leaned back and spread his arms along the railing. "We're making progress, Elizabeth. You actually said my name without choking on it."

She stole a wary look at him and realized he was teasing. "My friends call me Libby," she said.

He grinned and tweaked her braid. "So, Libby, now that you've decided I won't bite, why don't you tell me how the hell you sabotaged my boat?"

He knows, she thought. Dear God, he knows! The question was, how much? "What makes you think—?"

"Too much coincidence," Josh broke in. "The motor goes on the fritz, and there you are, Libby on the spot, ready to take a fare."

"Coincidences happen," said Elizabeth. "They happen all the time."

"Granted, but this one's too convenient to be true. I may be gullible, but I'm not a total idiot, so I asked myself who had access to the dory. And the answer is you."

"Why would I sabotage your boat?"

"You might be a spy for one of my competitors—"

"I'm not," she protested.

"Then perhaps your reasons for wanting to meet me are more personal."

His audacity was astonishing. "Of all the colossal egos—!"

"I notice you're not denying it."

Elizabeth wanted to deny it, but even more compelling was the need to protect the Coalition. And her brother. It was bad enough that she'd taken Caleb's boat; if she dragged him into this mess, he'd never forgive her. She would never forgive herself.

Her only option was to brazen it out and try not to say anything Josh could use against her.

"Believe what you want," she said. "I don't have to justify myself to you."

That took the wind out of Josh's sails. But only temporarily. After a moment's silence, he replied, "Very well, Libby. If that's the way you feel."

"It is," she declared as firmly as she could.

"Then we'll drop the subject for now. But since you're not in the mood to confide in me, what would you like to talk about?"

She managed a wan smile. "I'd rather you'd talk and I'll listen."

Josh gave her an assessing glance. "Shall I tell you a story then?"

"What kind of story?"

"I guess you could call it a morality tale. It's about two boys who grew up in a small town in northern Illinois. They lived next door to each other and shared the same baby carriage, the same teething ring, the same sand pile. They swapped baseball cards and bubble gum. They roughhoused with each other, watched Saturday morning cartoons together. They had the same heroes and soloed on their bikes the same day. By the time they started kindergarten they were inseparable—more like brothers than friends.''

Josh paused to light a cigarette. He stretched his legs and crossed one ankle over the other, and the more relaxed he looked, the more uncomfortable Elizabeth became. She felt cornered, like a bird in a snare, and wished he would lose his temper and get it over with instead of keeping her on tenterhooks, waiting for him to pounce.

She wrapped her arms about her waist, making herself as small as possible as he continued.

''Things went on pretty much the way they started through grade school and junior high. If the boys were assigned to the same classroom, they tended to get into trouble, so from the first grade on they had different teachers, but once they hit the playground they made up for lost time. Not that they were bad kids. Just high-spirited. Always bombing people with water balloons and letting the air out of bicycle tires.''

Josh shot another look her way, this one probing and cynical. ''I'll bet you were a model child. You probably had too much *integrity* to do anything like that.''

''I've dropped my share of water balloons,'' Libby replied, inching away from him.

His hand settled on her shoulder, pinning her to the bench. ''Am I crowding you?''

Not physically, but his presence was overwhelming. He seemed to fill all the available space on the bridge. She felt as if she were suffocating, but she was not about to admit it.

"N-no, I have plenty of room."

"Good," said Josh, releasing her. "Now, where was I?"

"On the playground—"

"Oh, yes. Well, the summer before high school, a cute little redhead named Linda moved into the neighborhood, and by the Fourth of July the boys had developed what their mothers called 'social graces.' They were changing their socks every day and carrying pocket combs and snitching their fathers' after-shave."

"What happened then?" Libby prompted, hoping to speed things along.

"The inevitable." Josh studied the tip of his cigarette, eyes narrowed against the smoke. "Linda was the kind of girl who's born with an awareness of her own attractions. She knew these kids had a crush on her. They were a little young, but she was eager for experience, and she decided to give them a whirl."

"Both of them?"

"Both of them," said Josh. "Simultaneously. And the next thing you know, two-thirds of the trio was going steady, and when the boys found out Linda was two-timing them, they didn't blame her. They blamed each other. They even came to blows. But what neither of them had foreseen was that Linda would mature faster than both of them combined. After a week or ten days of cutting her teeth on freshmen, she moved on to a sophomore who had a driver's license *and* his own car."

Josh took a last drag of his cigarette and threw it over the railing, and Libby seized this opportunity to make her escape. But the moment she got to her feet, Josh caught hold of her wrist.

"I'm not finished yet," he said.

She tugged at the rolled collar of her sweater. "Can't this wait till tomorrow? I'd like to get some sleep before the midnight watch."

"This won't take long if you stop interrupting."

Josh tightened his hold on her wrist until his fingers overlapped, and Libby offered no resistance as he pulled her down beside him.

"Even with gallons of Old Spice, there was no way a pair of gawky fourteen-year-olds could compete with a fifty-five Chevy—although God knows they tried. But by the end of September, the boys set aside their rivalry. It dawned on them they missed their friendship more than they missed Linda, and they made a pact. Nothing would ever come between them again. And for quite a while nothing did. Sometimes they romanced the same girl, but they didn't forget the lesson Linda taught them. A friend, they agreed, was what you have left when you've lost everything else."

Libby cleared her throat, fascinated in spite of herself. "Is that the moral of the story?"

"One of them. Another is, never trust a female whose name begins with *L*."

The taunt found its mark, and she lifted her chin proudly, torn between curiosity and resentment. "Whatever became of the boys?" she asked.

"They graduated from high school and went their separate ways. One went to college on the East Coast, one stayed in the Midwest. Both of them had visions of being the big campus stud. Neither was sure how to go about it, but they swore they'd get together over Christmas vacation and compare notes."

"And did they?"

"Uh-huh, and both of them lied like hell. But after that Christmas, they lost track of each other. They said they'd keep in touch, but you know how it goes. Neither of them did.''

"Did they ever see each other again?"

"Yes. But that's a different story. Let's save it for another night."

She intercepted his gaze as he boosted her to her feet. "You'll call me for the next watch?"

Josh nodded. "I'll let you know if there's any change."

At the top of the ladder, she hesitated. "I enjoyed the story about your friend, Josh, but one thing puzzles me."

"Oh? What's that?"

"Well, I wondered why you tell it in the third person."

A stillness came over Josh. Although they were separated by the width of the bridge, she sensed his reticence and knew that she had overstepped some invisible boundary of privacy.

"Get some rest, Libby. I'll wake you at midnight."

His voice was gruff with annoyance. Chilled by his dismissal, she made her way below decks and through the galley to the salon.

Her fingers were stiff with cold as she turned on the portable lantern and folded out the sofa bed. She took off her boots, her dungarees and sweater, then switched off the light and crawled into bed, flinching at the clammy touch of the sleeping bag liner.

She curled up on her side, shielding as much bare skin as possible with her flannel shirt and woolen socks. When she closed her eyes she imagined she could feel the fog oozing into the cabin, thick as marsh mud.

It took a long time before she began to feel any warmth, still longer for her to fall asleep. Her nerves were as tightly wound as her body, her senses attuned to the slightest motion, the smallest sound, the least variation in the tempo of the sea.

She heard Josh moving back and forth on deck, pacing like a tiger in a cage.

He has a right to be upset, she thought, *but if he's angry now, how will be react when he finds out about DEEPC's plot?*

Sometime after the tide turned, she fell into a fitful doze, but when Josh came into the salon at a quarter past twelve, she was instantly alert.

"What's happening?" she inquired.

"The fog's heavier. For the last two hours our compass heading's been one-ninety. That's about it."

Cocooned in the now-warm sleeping bag, she dreaded leaving the lantern-lit cabin for the long, cold vigil on the bridge.

Her sweater and dungarees were icy to touch. Josh turned his back for the few seconds it took her to put them on, and while she was in the head, he got out of his clothes. He was zipping himself into the sleeping bag when she returned for her boots.

"Better bundle up," he said. "Wear my jacket if you like."

Elizabeth might have taken Josh up on his offer if he had sounded less remote. As it was, however, she scooped up the plastic envelope that held one of the survival blankets. "Thanks just the same. I think I'll try one of these."

She took the charts and the spare lantern with her to the bridge, preparing to update the ship's log. She recorded the day, the time, the wind speed and weather. She entered their change of course, but she could only guess the speed at which they were drifting.

"Under these conditions," she wrote, "I believe we are three miles southeast of Baker Island."

She doublechecked her math and wrote in the longitude and latitude, but she didn't look at the charts again.

Considering the less than accurate data and the dense curtain of fog, she was navigating blind—by guess and by God. Her estimate of their position could be off by a mile or more. They might be farther south or west or east. But precision seemed redundant. The smooth rise and fall of the swells told her all she cared to know and confirmed her worst fear—they were adrift in the open Atlantic.

Elizabeth spent the rest of the watch wondering how on earth she was going to break the news to Josh, but as it turned out, she didn't have to. Nor did she have to wake him for his shift.

At four-fifteen, when she went below to rouse him, she found him in the galley, filling the teakettle, already dressed and brimming with energy.

She, on the other hand, felt totally drained. She barely made it to the dinette before her legs gave way beneath her.

"Morning, Libby. You look as if you had a rough night."

"You don't," she answered crossly. "I gather you slept well."

"Like a top. Must be the sea air. Or maybe it's just that my conscience is clear." Josh set the kettle on the grate and began priming the burner. "How about some soup and a cup of cocoa before you turn in?"

"Make mine coffee," she said. "I'm not going back to bed till we've had a talk."

Josh spooned coffee into one mug, cocoa into another. "If you're looking for a tactful way to tell me we're heading for Nova Scotia, you might as well save your breath."

"You've already figured it out?"

He slanted a grin her way. "I have."

She slumped over the table, holding her head in her hands. "Do you have to be so happy about it?"

"Well, the thing is, I've been thinking. Maybe I can fix the steering."

"Fix it? How?"

"The first step, obviously, is to take a look at the rudder and find out how bad the damage is, and since we're a long way from the nearest boat yard, I'll have to make a dive under the boat."

"We went over this yesterday, Josh. Nothing's changed since then. The water's too cold."

"For swimming, yes, but I'm talking about a single dive. I'll be in and out in a jiffy. Five or ten minutes, maybe less. Then we'll know what the trouble is, and whether we can repair it. Maybe the rudder's jammed. Maybe something's fouling it—a length of cable—a branch from that deadhead. If that's all that's wrong, I should be able to handle it."

"What if it's not so simple?"

"Then I'd have to make a series of dives, but I'll take time between them to warm up. And if the damage is more extensive, at least we'll have given it our best shot."

Elizabeth shook her head. "Forget it, Josh. It's too risky."

"I don't see how it's any more risky than sitting on our duffs, waiting for someone to spot us. Hell, Libby! I've seen the charts. Sure, there are some islands out there, but there's no guarantee we'll come anywhere near them. I've also looked in the cupboards, so I know what kind of provisions we have. If we ration the food, there's enough to last us a week—"

The whistle of the teakettle interrupted Josh's argument. He dumped water into the mugs and passed one to Elizabeth with barely concealed impatience.

"We can do some fishing," she said.

"That'll be great! If we're lucky, we might even catch something. But supposing we do. The freshwater supply won't last forever."

"We can stretch it out with rainwater," she countered.
"No, Josh. I still say it's safest to wait."

"And *I* say we can't afford to go on drifting around like flotsam. Not indefinitely. For now the weather's calm, but that could change any minute. If a nor'easter blows in, it'll be goodnight, Irene. If the ocean doesn't get us, starvation will—or dehydration, or exposure. I don't know about you, Libby, but I don't happen to like those choices. As long as there's any possibility we can fix the steering and be on our way, I'd rather take my chances in the water."

"Well, I'd rather you didn't. I'm sorry, Josh. I realize you've given this a great deal of thought, but I just can't let you do it."

"How're you going to stop me? You may have the rank, Cap'n Pilgrim, but I've got the muscle. And may I remind you, if it weren't for you, I'd be in Chicago."

Libby winced. The skin across her cheekbones prickled with embarrassment. "That's a cheap shot, Josh. It's just not fair."

"If it's fairness you want, you shouldn't have tampered with my boat."

"You have no proof!"

"Why would I need proof when we both know you're guilty? Fact is, I'm not a hundred percent certain you're not lying about the steering."

"You can't believe I'd lie about a thing like that."

"Maybe you wouldn't, but I only have your word for it." Joshua leaned one shoulder against the bulkhead and folded his arms across his chest. "With your approval or without it, Libby, I intend to get a look at that rudder. But if it'll ease your mind, I'll wear some sort of safety harness. At the first sign of trouble you can haul me out."

Elizabeth inclined her head, grateful for this concession. "When do you plan on making this dive?"

"Soon as it's daylight. And, Libby, if you're telling the truth, I honestly don't see any need to worry about it."

She rapped her knuckles against the oaken brightwork that edged the dinette table. "Say that again when you're in the water, and I might believe you."

She remained unconvinced four hours later, in the midst of preparations for the dive. She told herself there was no cause for panic. Josh claimed he was a strong swimmer, and she had taken every precaution.

She had slung a rope ladder over the stern and strung ring buoys from the transom, life vests from the port side, flotation cushions from starboard.

Josh accused her of being overzealous. "If it floats and it's not nailed down, you've thrown it into the drink."

"Wherever you come up, I want you to have some sort of lifesaver to hang onto," she explained.

"But look at all that stuff! Don't you think you're going overboard?"

"No, but you are, Josh. Literally. If I'm being thorough in the safeguards I take, it's for your benefit. I have a healthy respect for the ocean, even if you don't."

At her insistence, Joshua had given his word that he would stay within arm's length of the hull, but even while he stripped to his briefs, she couldn't shake the premonition that his effort to make repairs was doomed to failure.

"I wish we had something to grease you down with," she said.

"Stop fussing, Libby. I'll be fine."

He sat on the railing, covered in goose bumps, and allowed her to slip the harness she had fashioned over his head. She distributed the nylon rope webbing evenly and tied on the safety line in back.

"How does that feel?"

Josh hunched his shoulders and windmilled his arms to test the fit. "It's a bit snug."

Her gaze wandered over his shoulders and chest, measuring the tautness and buik of well-defined muscles. A furrow appeared between her brows as she loosened several knots.

"You're bigger than I thought," she fretted.

"You're the first woman who's ever complained about *that*," said Josh.

"I'll bet," she grumbled, more to herself than to him.

She made minor adjustments to the harness, coiled up the excess tether, looped the free end around a cleat, and stepped back to survey her handiwork.

"All set?" said Josh.

"All set."

He hopped onto the transom, directly above the engine well. "Give me plenty of slack."

She arranged the tether on the deck and draped the line loosely across one palm, so that the coils would play out naturally. "Two tugs means you want me to pull you out," she said.

Josh circled this thumb and forefinger, indicating his agreement. He balanced on the transom, looking down at the opaque pewter-gray water, his rib cage heaving like a bellows as he sucked in drafts of air.

Elizabeth unconsciously mimicked him. When his lungs expanded, so did hers. When the muscles in his thighs bunched, her own legs tensed. And when he bent his knees and pushed off, she felt as if she were suspended in space.

He plunged into the water headfirst, and surfaced almost immediately.

"Sure you won't reconsider?" she called.

"What, and listen to you say I told you so?"

"I wouldn't," she said.

"That was a joke, Libby." He skimmed one hand over the water, sending a geyser her way, then rolled onto his face and swam the length of the boat and back.

She followed him on deck, making sure the safety line stayed clear.

"It's not so bad once you get used to it," he said. "Long as I'm in, I may as well finish the job."

Elizabeth nodded, resigned to the inevitable. "Take care of yourself down there," she whispered, but she had no idea whether Josh heard her.

He flipped into a dive that carried him deep into the water, and as the ocean swallowed him up, she felt the sting of its coldness, felt it chill her skin and seep into the marrow of her bones.

She stared at the ripples that marked his passing until they, too, were gone, and then she focused on her wristwatch, timing his descent.

Fifteen seconds...sixteen...seventeen.... The safety line trailed limp and unmoving across her palm.

Thirty-three...thirty-four.... Her fingers were numb. She felt utterly useless.

Forty-one...forty-two.... A cat's-paw breeze stole through the mist and fanned across the water. Otherwise, nothing.

Sixty seconds! Her mouth was dry, her heart racing. She was unaware she had been holding her breath until the numbers on the watch face blurred. She gulped in air, and the dizziness receded.

Where was Josh? Why didn't he surface?

She studied the rope, praying it would offer a clue.

What if his harness had snagged on something? He might be trapped under the boat, struggling to free himself.

In another five seconds I'll reel him in, she decided.

She gripped the tether with both hands. Her nails dug into her palms, and in the millisecond before she hauled on the rope, Joshua shot to the surface of the water.

"Hang on!" she cried. "I'm pulling you out."

"Not yet," he shouted, and before she could object, he gasped for breath and submerged once again.

IT WAS LIKE DIVING into an icy whirlpool.

Damn, it was cold! And dark! The only comparison Josh could make was to Dante's description of Satan, icebound in the blackest pit of Hades.

If this glacial oblivion was not Hell, it was only one torment removed.

He could not see a thing. He had to rely on his sense of touch to guide him to the rudder, and what made a difficult task next to impossible was that the boat continued drifting. He had to keep his head down and his legs scissoring to keep pace.

On his last dive he had scarcely located the propeller before he ran out of air. This time he found the drive shaft more quickly, but the constantly shifting hull buffeted him about and finally knocked him away.

By the time he found the drive shaft again, the cold was getting to him. Either that or the lack of oxygen had dulled his thinking. If his mind had been clear, he would have taken more care in the way he approached the blades. In the instant he fumbled for a handhold, the hull slammed into his skull.

He felt himself sinking, felt something sharp graze his forearm and glance off his shoulder. There was a buzzing in his ears. Stunned and winded, barely conscious, it was all he could do to level off.

It dawned on him that he needed help. He groped for the tether, and his fingers closed around a frayed stub end of rope. It took precious moments to realize that the knife-sharp metal had cut his safety line.

An adrenaline rush spurred him upward. *Move!* he commanded his feet. *Kick, damn you!*

His throat ached. His lungs were on fire. The urge to inhale was strong, but the will to survive was stronger. Inch by painful inch he battled his way toward the surface, and when it seemed he could battle no more, he broke free of his watery prison into foggy light and blessed, glorious air and saw Elizabeth's face, ashen with concern as she hauled in the life vest he'd grabbed.

He tried to smile. He wanted to reassure her, but all he could do was cling to the vest as she pulled it in hand over hand.

Somehow, between the two of them, he made it up the ladder.

"Your arm's bleeding," she said. "Are you all right?"

"It's nothing. Just a scrape."

She gave him a quick rubdown with a towel and wrapped the sleeping bag around him. His skin was dusky, his nailbeds blue. He was shaking so violently, it seemed to him she was the one source of warmth and steadiness left in the world.

"The rudder—" he croaked as she helped him into the cabin.

"Blast the rudder! You are not going in the water again, Joshua Noon."

His knees buckled. Elizabeth staggered beneath his weight, but her tone was spirited and her resolve remained unbowed. Her feistiness restored a portion of his bravado. He produced a grin, but didn't try to say anything more.

Sometime he might confess that she was right, that she had been right all along. He should have listened to her in the first place. He should have *trusted* her.

And he definitely had to tell her about the damage wrought by their collision. But that could wait till this afternoon, or even till tomorrow. Later there would be ample time to tell her that the rudder had sheared off; that it was simply, irrevocably gone.

Chapter Four

The skies cleared later that morning. The air was almost balmy. Joshua stretched out in the cockpit, one arm shading his eyes, and let the sun bake the last residue of coldness from his body.

"Under other circumstances, this wouldn't be half bad," he allowed in a drowsy murmur.

Speak for yourself, thought Elizabeth.

Although he'd stopped badgering her since he'd seen for himself that she hadn't lied about the steering, the potential for unpleasantness remained. It kept her on edge, waiting for round two to begin.

Her hands shook a bit as she clamped a lead sinker near the end of her fishing line and began rummaging through the tackle box for a lure. "I wish we had some minnows," she said.

Joshua peered at her beneath the crook of his elbow. "As long as you're wishing, why settle for minnows? Why not wish for a halibut or a lobster or the whole seafood platter?"

She shook her head. "I don't mind fishing. It'll help pass the time. If I had a rod and reel, I guarantee we'd have fish for supper, but since I have to make do with hand lines, it'd be nice to have some minnows to use as bait to catch a bigger fish.''

One corner of Joshua's mouth twitched into a smile. ''That's a pretty good definition of the advertising business.''

''What is?''

''Big fish gobbling up little ones.''

Libby mulled this over while she tied on a lure and cast it over the railing. She let the line spin off the spool as the boat drifted away from it, then anchored the spool with one foot and began rigging another line.

''I guess that means, in rising to the bait, a big fish risks getting hooked himself.''

''Absolutely,'' said Josh. ''Say a man outmaneuvers the competition and becomes a huge success. He discovers there are strings attached. When he was one of the small fry, all he had to worry about was himself, but now that he's the big fish in the pond, he's got responsibilities. Not only does he have to contend with budgets and trends and keeping the sharks at bay, but he also has a reputation to maintain. He knows he's only as good as his last campaign, and dozens of people are counting on him to make the right moves. So all at once, without his knowing how it happened, he's under tremendous pressure. And no matter how slippery he is, there's no escape. In the end, all he can do is get out or get caught.''

Libby wondered if Josh was speaking from personal experience, but after a surreptitious look at him, she decided he couldn't be. If he were inclined to cave in under pressure, she would have expected him to show signs of anxiety by now. But instead of losing his cool, he was basking in the sun as if he hadn't a care in the world.

As she cast the second line it occurred to her that his air of nonchalance might be a front. It wouldn't surprise her to find out that he adhered to the stiff-upper-lip code of masculine behavior. Most men did, her brothers included.

She remembered an occasion years ago when Adam had dislocated his shoulder playing football. He'd been stoic, courageous, a tower of strength. He'd made light of his injury and insisted on walking off the field, and while the team doctor was examining him on the sidelines, he'd pleaded with the coach to send him in for the final downs.

Torn ligaments and strained muscles couldn't keep a veteran running back like Adam Pilgrim out of the lineup. No, sirree! Not for long.

But in the privacy of his own room, with no one but his mother and kid sister to impress, Saturday's hero had groused and moaned and kept Marian Pilgrim hopping, giving him back rubs, fluffing his pillows, fetching him juice, soothing his ego.

At the time Libby had been stunned by the transformation, but in retrospect she realized the incident illustrated one of the basic differences between the sexes. Men exhibited toughness to hide their vulnerability, while women displayed their vulnerabilities to hide their toughness—

A breeze fluttered the distress flag and ruffled the wisps of hair at Libby's temples. Jarred from her musings, she watched a line of whitecaps streaming toward the boat.

"Would you listen to that," said Josh.

Libby tipped her head to one side, frowning. "I don't hear anything. Just the wind and water."

"That's what I mean. It's so quiet, I can hear myself *think*."

She tugged at one of the fishing lines, testing the drag on the lure. "This must be quite a change from Chicago."

"Sure is," said Josh. "The thing about cities is, something's always happening. There's traffic noise, sirens, phones ringing, radios blaring, some kind of action twenty-four hours a day.''

"Sounds hectic."

"Yeah, but it's also stimulating." The pool of sunlight had shifted, and Josh shifted with it. "If I were home right now, I'd be ordering sauerbraten at Berghoff's and talking shop. Since basketball season's just around the corner, before long one of the guys would mention the Bulls. One thing would lead to another and we'd wind up shooting some buckets, and after the game I'd stop by the office to pick up my messages and dictate a few letters and check out the most recent market surveys. And then, toward evening, I'd grab a shower and meet Blair for dinner—''

Josh lapsed into silence. He didn't say how the evening would end, but from the affectionate note that crept into his voice whenever he talked about Blair Healey, Libby assumed they were more than friends.

She tested the other line, then sank back against the transom and closed her eyes, turning her face toward the sun. "If I were home right now I'd be antiquing my kitchen cabinets. I put on the second coat of enamel last Sunday. It's kind of bright—almost magenta—but the stain should tone the color down to a nice dusky rose."

"What else?" Josh sounded amused, as if he were entertained by the thought of her broiling a steak surrounded by the decadence of a lush pink kitchen.

"When the cabinets are finished, I'm going to put up wallpaper—''

He chuckled and she scowled at him. "I meant what else would you do today," he explained.

"Oh. Well, the usual Saturday chores. Laundry, housework, grocery shopping. That type of thing. And this evening I'd probably do some reading."

"Fiction or nonfiction?"

"Just now I'm in the middle of Rachel Carson's *Silent Spring*."

"No date?"

Josh looked smug, even arrogant; sure of himself, and so blasted sure that her social life was less than exciting that Libby considered inventing a hot romance. But inventions seemed too complicated. After a moment's hesitation she stuck to the truth.

"I'm due to became an aunt any day," she said, "and my sister-in-law hasn't had an easy pregnancy. The last time she saw her obstetrician, he warned her he might have to deliver the baby by cesarean, so I'd planned to stay close to the phone."

"Will this by your first niece or nephew?"

"Yes, it will." With a bemused smile, Libby added, "Dan's such a clown, I can't imagine him being a father."

"Is Dan the brother who owns this boat?"

"No, that's Caleb."

Josh propped himself on one elbow. "How many brothers do you have?"

"Four. Adam, Benjamin, Caleb and Daniel."

"Solid biblical names," said Josh.

"Like yours," she replied. "But the fact is, my mother named them after characters in her favorite movie."

"Which is?"

"*Seven Brides for Seven Brothers.* Mom had this huge crush on Howard Keel. I think that's why she fell in love with my father."

"He resembles Howard?"

"No, not physically. But Dad has a wonderful singing voice."

"So they got married and produced five children."

Libby nodded. "If I'd been a boy, my name would be Ephraim."

"And your father would've had his own basketball team."

"Actually, our game was hockey."

"I'll bet you played goalie."

"How did you guess?"

"You said you're the youngest, and you've got the tenacity for it." Josh sighed and stretched out again, hands clasped behind his head. "I used to wish I had a brother. What was it like growing up with four of them?"

"Kind of like what you said about living in the city. There were always traffic jams. Phones ringing, radios blaring, nonstop action. And I could never get into the bathroom without waiting in line."

Josh gave her a sharp-eyed glance. "Do I detect a certain ambivalence?"

She lifted one shoulder in a shrug that was both understated and eloquent. "Probably."

"I suppose your brothers bullied you."

"Unmercifully—when they weren't being overprotective." With another shrug she turned away from Josh, recalling her own adolescent crushes, the teenage boyfriends her brothers had scared off, and the would-be suitors of her college days who had suffered by comparison with her brothers.

How could she help making comparisons? Adam was athletic. Ben was brilliant. Caleb was adventurous, the most fearless man she had ever known. Dan could charm the feathers off birds. And she was her parents' afterthought, the exception that proved the rule.

The rest of the Pilgrims were big, blond, gregarious. She was an introvert lost in the noisy crowd. As a little girl she had idolized her brothers, even though she found them somewhat daunting. She'd laughed at their jokes, put up with their teasing, applauded their accomplishments, and for the most of her life she had tried very hard to fit in. But the harder she tried, the more she felt like Avis in a family of Hertzes.

Only recently had she begun to recognize that she had strengths of her own. She might not talk as freely or smile as readily as her brothers, but she was focused, industrious, feet-on-the-ground.

And Josh's assessment was right. In her own quiet way she was tenacious. Once she had made up her mind to do something, she was not easily dissuaded.

Stubborn, she thought. *That's me. And that's what got me into this fix.* Which brought her full circle. Back to DEEPC's conspiracy. Back to trolling with useless hand lines from Cal's disabled cruiser. Back to the wide blue emptiness of sea and sky, and back to Joshua Noon.

Libby glanced at Josh, and discovered that she could study him at her leisure. He had dozed off, but even in sleep he exuded a restless energy.

He lay on his side, one leg jackknifed, one arm outflung, as if he were running a foot race, and to her fanciful gaze he seemed more athletic than Adam, more clever than Ben, bolder than Caleb, and infinitely more intriguing than Daniel.

Of their own accord her fingers reached out to brush back the shock of hair that had fallen over his forehead, but at the last moment she caught herself, arrested by the notion that if she touched Josh, he might emit sparks.

She stared at him for what could have been another minute—or two, or five, or ten—and when he stirred, she made herself look away.

In the last half hour the stiffening breeze had launched a flotilla of whitecaps. They sprang from the crests of the swells like miniature galleons, unfurling topsails of foam.

Clouds were massing to the east; another unfavorable sign.

She reeled in the lines and removed the lures and sinkers. She stowed the fishing gear in the tackle box, and then, because the gusting wind was chilly, she covered Josh with the sleeping bag.

A climb to the bridge revealed that the mainland had vanished. No other boats were in sight. She picked up the binoculars and scanned the horizon, but saw only blue water blending into an endless sky.

The glass was falling, but she didn't need a barometer to tell her a storm was brewing. It occurred to her she ought to have a catnap while she could. Since Thursday morning she'd had a total of five hours sleep, and once the squall blew in, she would have to remain alert. Heaven only knew when she'd get another chance to rest.

Libby went below to lie down on the sofa bed. She fell asleep the instant her head touched the cushion, and while she slept she traveled backward in time, to a day when she was six years old, racing along in her Uncle Toby's souped-up jalopy.

At first the road wound up hills and dipped into gullies, following the coastline. But after a mile or so it turned inland, through forests of spruce and pine, climbing, always climbing toward some distant unseen summit.

The car twisted and turned and doubled back on itself, and every time it hit a bump, all four wheels left the ground and they went flying.

She wasn't afraid, though. Not with Toby Pilgrim in command. Her father called him a speed demon, and her mother prophesied, "That hot rod'll be the death of him." But Libby trusted her uncle implicitly, with a child's unquestioning faith.

Uncle Toby could do handstands. He could play the harmonica. He could pull quarters out of her ears. She believed he could do *anything*, and so whenever they approached a dip in the roadway, she giggled and clapped her hands.

"Faster, faster!" she cried.

Her uncle obliged, and they rounded one last curve. Hurtling over the brink of a ridge, they landed on a straightaway that dropped abruptly toward the sea. But still she was not afraid.

"Faster, faster!" she cried, and the car accelerated.

Boulders and trees flashed by in a surreal wash of color. Her pigtails streamed out behind her and the wind snatched one of her hair bows. She tried to capture the ribbon as it spiraled away, but it eluded her. She craned her neck and watched the ribbon perform aerobatics, tracing red velvet loop-the-loops against the sky.

And then, without her knowing how it happened, the car was airborne and they were soaring, gliding and swooping, chasing the ribbon through space. They flew so high that she felt weightless and clung to the edge of her seat. Otherwise she might fly away.

Suddenly the engine stalled and they were tumbling, falling.

"Hang on!" her uncle told her. "We're out of gas."

She saw ocean and treetops rushing closer... closer. She felt a twinge of fear, but Uncle Toby grinned and untied her other hair bow. He handed one end to her, and in the fantastic way of dreams, as soon as the ribbon stretched between them, it became a parachute.

For a few seconds they hung suspended; then the fabric filled with air, and as it billowed overhead, they floated gently back to earth.

Gorry, what an escapade! She could hardly wait to tell her brothers about it. They would be green with envy. Especially Cal.

Libby laughed with the sheer joy of being alive, and in the midst of rejoicing she awoke to a keening wind, the sickening lurch of the sofa bed, and the groaning protests the cruiser made under the assault of pounding seas.

An early dusk filled the salon, only partially relieved by a swath of light from the galley.

Josh must be in there, she thought.

She turned onto her side and poked one stockinged foot from beneath the survival blanket, testing the temperature in the cabin. It was colder than she had expected it would be, and she lay immobile, recreating bits and pieces of her dream.

She touched one hand to her braid, remembering her Uncle Toby. He had given her piggyback rides and called her Betsy Browneyes and brought her peppermints and licorice whips. She recalled one memorable day when he had given her a rainbow of ribbons for her hair, and gradually a plan took shape in her sleep-befuddled mind.

She stood up, eager to share the idea with Josh.

Moving carefully, struggling to keep her footing on the swaying slant of the deck, Libby followed the light to the galley and found him bending over a chart, smoking a cigarette.

"Sorry if I woke you," he said.

"You didn't," she replied. "I think it was the storm."

As if on cue, a blast of wind hit the boat. It shuddered and nosed downward, skidding into a trough. The portable lantern slid across the table, and Libby staggered the few steps to the dinette. Josh threw out a steadying hand, and as she subsided onto the bench the boat wallowed from side to side, savaged by the gale.

She clutched at Josh's hand. "It's worse than I thought. Looks like we're in for it."

"That's the bad news," said Josh. "The good news is, there's an island out there, about five degrees off the port bow."

Five degrees? Dear God! If the idea suggested by the ribbon parachute was feasible, the most she had hoped for was surviving the night. Was it possible she could effect a change of course that would take them to a landfall?

"I was thinking of making a sea anchor," she said.

Josh nodded. "That might do it."

She inhaled deeply and loosened her grip on his hand. "How far is this island?"

"Not far. A couple of miles." He angled the chart toward her and jabbed a finger at the southernmost islands of the Cinnabar group. "I figure it's one of these."

"Probably Sagamore," said Libby.

On the state maps, Sagamore Island was little more than a speck, but the more detailed chart enabled her to see that the island was shaped like a moccasin, measuring half a mile at the ball of the foot and three times that distance from toe to heel. On first glance it appeared innocuous enough, but a closer look revealed that Sagamore sat on a rocky shelf, surrounded by a moat of reefs.

She indicated a narrow channel through the moat. "There's only one navigable inlet. No wonder this area's known as a graveyard for ships."

"So it won't be easy, but what choice do we have?"

"If we use the sea anchor to turn the bow into the wind, there's a possibility we can ride out the storm."

"How big a possibility?"

"A slim one. We're taking our chances either way."

"In that case, I'd rather make for the island." The wind had risen to a furious crescendo, and shouting to make himself heard, Josh added, "How long can the boat take this kind of punishment?"

Libby lifted her gaze to his. "It can't," she admitted. "It's a miracle we're still afloat."

"Then what are we waiting for? Instead of sitting here talking, we ought to be making that sea anchor."

She shook her head. "I can take care of the anchor. You'll have to buy us some time by manning the bilge pumps."

Josh stubbed out his cigarette and pushed decisively to his feet. "All right. Let's do it."

Under the best conditions, jury-rigging a sea anchor would have been difficult, but the conditions that night were terrifying.

The wind howled. The sea raged. The turbulent chop of the waves rained spray upon the decks, leaving them slippery and treacherous. Just getting about, assembling the materials she needed to make a frame for the anchor required the utmost care. One false step would be her last. She would not have the chance to make another one.

She and Josh wore life vests, and even when they were in the cockpit they attached their safety lines to the handrails. But both of them realized their precautions would not be much help if their luck ran out and they were swept overboard. And although neither of them spoke of the dangers they faced, they were acutely aware that disaster could happen.

At any moment a wave could take them. They could broach, or capsize, or founder. Tons of water could come crashing down on them—

Libby tried not to think about the ways disaster could strike. To think of them would lead to panic, and so she worked frantically, desperately, fashioning a frame from aluminum landing nets and metal coat hangers, then covering the frame with the canvas awning from the fly bridge, stitched to shape with fishing line.

While she worked, to take her mind off the storm she thought about Sagamore Island. She had read about it but had never been there. Nor had anyone else she knew. Its location discouraged visitors.

Situated thirty miles east of Matinicus, twenty-five miles south of the Cranberries, and more than fifty miles from the mainland, Sagamore was removed from the shipping lanes. The lighthouse on the seaward shore had been decommissioned long ago, and since the coast guard's departure the island had been uninhabited. The ferries didn't call there, and because fierce currents guarded its headlands, even the hardiest lobstermen gave it a wide berth.

Some, who were superstitious, said Sagamore was haunted.

One faction claimed the spirits of the island's earliest settlers, a band of Indians known only as the Red Paint People, patrolled the heights above the coast, ready to repel invaders. Others said the ghost was a pirate, keeping watch over his ill-gotten treasure. Still others claimed the spirit was that of a woman, falsely accused of witchcraft and sentenced to exile on the island.

There was widespread dissension about the identity of Sagamore's ghost, but the various factions agreed that the spirit was malevolent.

Of course, Libby was too enlightened and much too rational to believe in evil spirits.

But she didn't walk under ladders. She went out of her way to avoid black cats. She didn't take unnecessary chances on Friday the thirteenth, and try as she might, she could not convince herself that ghosts did not exist.

And whether or not Sagamore was haunted, it remained steeped in mystery, shrouded by myth; a place so remote, so desolate, the gulls would not nest there.

Libby knew that if their luck held, if the sea anchor worked and she and Josh made it to the island, no one would look for them there.

And that, she decided, *is another thing I don't want to think about.*

In the last two days, she realized, she had accumulated a long list of subjects she would rather not dwell upon, and she worked even faster, reinforcing the canvas with lengths of rope laced through the grommets.

She weighted the frame with chunks of lead from the tackle box, stuffing them into the hollow tubing on the landing nets, and when the anchor was finished, Josh said it looked like a kite crossed with a wind sock, "only bigger."

Libby thought it looked fragile.

The swells had built to mountainous proportions. Beneath the surface the water would be relatively calm, but it seemed unlikely that the anchor could withstand the battering of the waves.

Josh had the solution to this problem, however. He jettisoned a canister of diesel fuel, and in the brief respite the slick provided, they deployed the anchor, lowering it off the starboard quarter into the dark, oily water. It submerged immediately, torn from their grasp by the sea, its ropy umbilicus, lashed to the railing, whipped through their hands and stretched taut.

"It's working," Josh shouted. "I can feel it."

Libby felt it, too. A hint of stability, a slowing, as if someone had applied the brakes.

She dropped to her knees, brought the rope to eye level and sighted along it, estimating the angle of correction.

Then, as the cruiser hovered on the crest of a wave, she turned to look toward Sagamore.

She couldn't see the island. The night was too dark, the ocean too wild, the air so dense with spindrift that she could barely pick out the port light on the bow. But she envisioned rocky ledges and barren cliffs jutting from the sea, and her stomach did a slow rollover.

Josh clapped her on the back, laughing. "You did it, Libby. By God, you did it! The anchor's holding."

"So far," she qualified.

Intuition warned it was too soon to celebrate, that the worst was yet to come. She tried to imagine what would happen when they got into the surf, when they finally ran aground, and horror welled up inside her, a dread too frightening to contemplate.

All at once she became aware of physical discomforts; of the dozen razor-fine cuts the fishing line had inflicted, of the rope burns on her palms. Her shoulders ached from wrestling the anchor overboard. Somehow she had sprained her wrist, and there were other injuries she had no recollection of acquiring.

She was a mass of scrapes and bruises. She was thirsty, hungry, cold. The wind funneled into her poncho and cut through her soggy clothing, penetrating to the bone. And most of all she was exhausted. She wished she could sit down for a few minutes—just long enough to catch her breath.

But the cockpit was filling with water, and when Josh suggested one of them ought to round up some supplies, "just in case," she elected to man the pumps.

"You can do the packing," she told him. "I'd rather brave the elements than go back inside the cabin."

Josh didn't argue. He had started to leave the cockpit when a rumbling cannonade of sound echoed through the night.

He stood motionless, intent, his head cocked to one side. "What's that? Breakers?"

Libby worked the pump handle faster. "Hurry, Josh. We don't have much time."

THE SALON WAS ANKLE-DEEP in water. Josh paused to get his bearings, one hand braced against the bulkhead, the other holding the lantern.

No wonder Libby doesn't want to come in here, he thought. He'd never been bothered by claustrophobia, yet he felt as if he were sealing himself in a coffin as he secured the hatch cover.

He spotted his duffel bag and waded toward the galley, aware that if he and Elizabeth made it ashore they would need certain basics to survive. They'd need water, food, shelter. They would need to keep warm, and chances were, they'd need the first aid kit.

Eventually—soon, he hoped—they would need some means of signaling would-be rescuers. And they would have to transport their provisions from the boat to the island under perilous conditions, in a limited time.

One trip would have to do it, he figured, and with that in mind he dumped his belongings out of the duffel and replaced them with canned goods, crackers and cheese, a jar of instant coffee, the tin of cocoa, salt and sugar, and a box of matches that he wrapped in aluminum foil.

When he had emptied the cupboards, he filled the thermos from the freshwater tank and stuffed it into the duffel, hoping that small amount would last until they found another source.

He threw in the can opener, a saucepan, plates and cups, some flatware and a couple of kitchen knives. At last he tossed in the carton of foil and zipped the duffel. He was strapping one of the spare life vests around it when the bow pitched forward, buried by a wave.

The boat quaked, straining to resurface, then canted to port, and Josh heard the splintering noise of stone punching through wood. The cruiser teetered to and fro as seawater gushed into the cabin, and with the flood lapping about his calves, he dragged himself toward the head.

It didn't take long to clear the medicine cabinet. He simply wadded everything into a towel, but by the time he returned to the salon the water was up to his knees.

Every second counted now, and moving as quickly as he could, he rolled the towel, the sleeping bag and the spare lantern into the survival blankets. He tied the bundle tight, fastened a life vest around it, and hooked the vest over his shoulder. He filled his pockets with odds and ends—extra socks, his fleece-lined gloves, the flashlight and cassette recorder, the last pack of Marlboros and his cigarette lighter—then backtracked to the galley to collect the duffel bag.

The boom of the surf deafened him when he opened the aft hatch cover. He didn't bother sealing the hatch. It wouldn't serve any purpose. He knew there must be a hole in the hull beneath the waterline.

Libby must have known it too, yet she was still working the pump, cranking the handle as if she would defy the storm.

She called out to him, but the wind stole her words away before they could reach his ears. He cupped his hands to his mouth and yelled, "It's hopeless. We're on the reef."

The pace of her pumping quickened. "The flare gun," she cried. "Get the flare gun. And the ship's log."

The cruiser had settled on its side, with the superstructure tilted at a sixty-degree angle. Getting to the bridge was going to be tricky. Too tricky to attempt loaded down with the supply packs.

Josh tied the packs to the taffrail before he began the climb. He negotiated the ladder easily enough, but the bridge lay on a diagonal that made standing up an invitation to disaster. Crouched on all fours, he scrambled crablike toward the helm, and once he reached it, hitched an elbow through the wheel while he searched the chart rack.

He found the logbook and tucked it inside his life vest, then turned his attention to the flare gun. It was where he'd left it, in the bench seat locker. He notched the gun through his belt, and put the box of flares in his coat pocket for safekeeping while he dug through the locker, hunting for anything that might prove useful to castaways, but when Libby called out to him, urging him to hurry, he gave up the search, aimed his feet toward the ladder, and dropped back to the cockpit in one fast slide.

Libby abandoned the pump and launched a flare while he retrieved the packs, and when the light burst overhead he was stunned by the violence of the gale.

The nor'easter had whipped the ocean to a frenzy. Josh watched a wave break over rocks as sharp as shark's teeth, shooting great gouts of spray into the air, and as the light from the flare dwindled, he saw a windswept promontory etched against the sky, stark and forbidding as a moonscape.

Brief as it was, that glimpse left an impression of pitiless grandeur.

He turned to Libby, but before he could ask whether she had seen the island, a towering breaker lifted the boat off the reef and rammed it against the next rocky barrier with enough force that its timbers split.

Josh half staggered, half fell against the railing. With one hand he made a reflexive grab for the anchor rope, with the other, he grabbed Libby.

"This is it," he shouted. "End of the line."

A wall of water sluiced over the foredeck and swamped the cockpit. As the wave swept past she clung to his arm, holding onto his coat sleeve as if it were a lifeline.

"I won't make it to the island, Josh. I can't—"

"You have to Libby. It's the only way."

"Don't you understand? I can't swim."

"You what?"

"I can't swim."

Josh's jaw dropped. This was one complication he had overlooked, but it didn't change anything. The cruiser had had it. If they stayed with the boat, they'd be fish food. Sagamore was their only chance.

"You'll be okay," he said. "The life vest'll keep you from sinking, and I'll be with you all the way."

Libby did not respond. She was rigid, stupefied, ashen with fear. He wanted to offer encouragement, but he couldn't take the time. And so, in lieu of reassurance, he wrenched the flare gun from her grasp and gave her a shake to rouse her.

"I'll fire one more round. Then we'll go ashore."

She drew in a sobbing breath and held it while he loaded a cartridge into the cylinder. She exhaled, and he felt her resistance drain away.

"Take my hand," he instructed, and she laced her fingers through his.

"Promise you won't let go."

"I promise, Libby." He squeezed her hand, touched by her confidence in him. "Whenever you're ready, say the word and I'll fire. We'll jump on the count of three."

She closed her eyes. He felt her trembling.

"Ready," she said weakly, resigned.

Josh launched the flare the instant she spoke. He counted, they jumped, and seconds after they hit the water, a breaker tore them apart. Even while Josh floundered to the surface, he reached for Libby, striving to recapture her hand, but his fingers closed around frigid water.

He thrashed about, scanning the darkness. *God, this can't be happening. Libby trusts me. I can't let her down.*

With all his strength he fought the current that carried him toward shore. He *had* to find her. He'd given his word he would hold onto her, stay with her—"

"Libby!" he howled. "*Liiibbeee!*"

He called her name again and again, until his throat was raw. But his only answer was the banshee wind and the incessant roar of the sea.

Chapter Five

The breaker sent Libby tumbling head over heels through a vast tumultuous darkness. Her flailing arms encountered stone. Barnacles scraped her palms. Seaweed twined about her legs and anchored her to the ocean bed. She was twisting, writhing, fighting to escape its slimy tentacles, when a second wave freed her and spun her on.

God, help me, she petitioned. *I don't want to die. Especially this way. Alone. With Josh on my conscience.*

She was despairing when, as if in answer to her prayer, the wave deposited her in the shallows near the shore. Her toes barely touched bottom, but bit by dogged bit she worked her way closer to the island.

After what seemed an eternity she discovered, by craning her neck and standing as tall as she could, her nose was clear of the water. But before she could catch her breath, the surf slammed into her and knocked her off balance.

Her fingers curved into talons, clawing furrows through beach pebbles as she struggled to right herself.

The life vest was sodden and useless. Worse than useless, it was an impediment, a burden that dragged her under, but she would not lose ground, dammit! Not when safety was mere yards away.

She could feel the shoreline sloping toward the beach, and a resurgence of hope gave her the strength to shove herself to her feet. She plunged forward a step or two, then fell again, and when she rose, the surf foamed about her chin.

Another two steps, another fall, and her chest was clear of the water.

She planted her heels in the gravelly bottom, husbanding her energy while she gulped in air. She managed a cry for help before the surf retreated and her gravel foothold crumbled. She lurched forward, and another wave pounded into her back, throwing her to her knees.

Seawater clogged her throat and seared her nostrils. Her head was reeling. She was dizzy, disoriented, but she fought the undertow. She was trying to regain her footing when strong hands seized her near the scruff of her neck and hauled her, coughing and struggling, clear of the surf.

"It's all right, Libby. Everything's all right. I've got you."

"Josh?" she choked. "Is it really you?"

Her legs were rubbery. After a few wobbly steps she stumbled. She would have fallen if Josh hadn't caught her and swept her up into his arms. She felt giddy with relief, almost euphoric as he carried her onto the beach.

"You made it, Libby! Thank God, you made it!"

Josh's voice was hoarse but exultant. She touched his cheek, brushed questing fingertips over the stubble on his jaw, marveling that he was alive.

"I'm not imagining this? You're really here?"

He threw his head back and laughed. "We're both here, Libby, on solid ground. We're safe, and I intend to keep it that way."

Safe.

The way Josh said it made her forget the numbing cold and the inhospitable darkness. When she rested her head against his shoulder, the drumming of his heart drowned out the shriek of the wind.

They had survived the storm. They had survived the ocean. Surely Sagamore could not defeat them.

NEITHER OF THEM SLEPT that night.

They took shelter in a narrow grotto, huddled together for warmth. The supply packs were soaked, but the sleeping bag provided a makeshift roof. A survival blanket, slung between the rocks, gave them protection from the wind.

By daybreak the storm had abated, but only wreckage was left of the cabin cruiser.

"Caleb'll never forgive me," she said.

"Sure he will," said Josh. "Boats are replaceable. Sisters aren't."

Libby might have debated the point, but she wasn't ready to admit she had taken the boat without her brother's knowledge. Besides, her teeth were chattering so much that she could hardly talk.

Just when she thought she would never be warm again, Josh got a fire going. He left her to sort through the duffel bag while he roamed among the tide pools, salvaging the detritus that had washed ashore. He didn't find much, just a hank of rope, an empty fuel can and one of the flotation cushions. His face was grim as he added these items to the meager store of provisions Elizabeth was spreading on the rocks to dry.

"We'd better get out of our wet clothes," he said. "I'll put up a line so we can dry them."

Elizabeth ducked behind a boulder to undress. Her dungarees had dried to sticky dampness, and she grimaced as she peeled salt-crusted folds of denim away from her legs. When she pulled off her sweater, sand sifted into her eyes.

She unbuttoned her shirt, then hesitated, gripped by the certainty that she was being observed.

The almost palpable sensation made her flesh crawl. The fine hairs at the nape of her neck stood on end. Her first thought was of Josh, but a quick glance over her shoulder assured her that he was nowhere in sight and soft, rustling sounds from the far side of the boulder confirmed that Josh was some distance away, getting out of his own clothes. He couldn't possibly be spying on her.

But someone was watching. She could *feel* it.

She whirled about, hugging her shirt to her bosom, her gaze searching the cliffs that walled in the narrow crescent of beach.

No one was there. At least, no one *human*.

The ghost! she thought. The legend's true!

Nonsense, the voice of reason replied. *Stop being fanciful.* But instinct told her that she and Josh were not alone.

She turned in a half circle, searching the cliffs again. With the exception of a transient seagull, they appeared to be deserted.

Let's be practical about this, said the inner voice. *Even if the ghost is up there, you can't afford to be modest. You'll catch your death of pneumonia.*

Instinctively Libby agreed.

She turned her back on the cliffs and took off the rest of her things, then hastily got into the poncho and gathered up her sweater and jeans, eager to get back to the fire.

She found Josh wearing his raincoat, appraising the damage to his belongings. She draped her clothing next to his over the line he had strung and leaned against the rock while she dumped the sand from her boots.

"This is it," Josh said, holding up a single intact Marlboro. "Once it's gone, I'll have to quit cold turkey."

"Then this won't have been a total loss."

Josh gave her a sour look. "My watch is shot, too, and the saltwater played hob with my tape recorder."

"Funny, the things we can't do without."

His scowl darkened. "You mean like you and your log-book."

"No, not exactly. A ship's log is an official document. It's—history."

"And history's important to you."

"Not just to me. To everyone. If we want to avoid making the same mistakes we made in the past, we can't do without it."

"Horsefeathers."

Libby was taken aback. "You don't agree that we learn from our mistakes?"

"If we do, it doesn't necessarily mean we won't repeat them. Some people are governed by their hearts as much as their heads, Libby. Not everyone's as sensible as you."

Sensible! Was that how he saw her? As if she were one-dimensional, pure logic, without tenderness or passion?

She was hurt, insulted. She wanted to protest, but Josh seemed to have lost interest in the conversation. She sat on a driftwood log with her bare legs tucked under the poncho, and maintained an offended silence while he removed the battery from his cassette player and carefully wiped away the sand that had filtered into the case.

"You know, Libby, this little gizmo is as important to me as the ship's log is to you, and I won't apologize to you or anyone else for not wanting to get along without it."

Her hands curled into fists. She was determined to prove that he had misjudged her. "I wasn't suggesting you should apologize."

"Weren't you?"

"No! I just thought—that is, I wondered how long you've had the recorder."

"I bought it the day Walt Healey and I filed to incorporate the agency."

"Healey?" she murmured pensively. "Is he any relation to Blair?"

Josh set the battery aside and began inspecting the wiring. "Walt was her husband. He died about six months ago."

Libby stared at Josh, contrite. "I had no idea. I'm sorry."

"You're not alone. Everyone who ever knew Walt is sorry."

She cleared her throat. "He must've been very special."

"He was," said Josh. "And since his death this cassette recorder's been my best friend. I've confided in it the way I used to confide in Walt, which hasn't made for lively discussions, but it's helped me over some rough spots. It's let me get a grip on certain problems. Talk them out. Think them through. And it's never once betrayed my trust."

"You're saying it has a sentimental value."

"Yes, I guess it does at that." Josh slipped the battery back into its socket and pressed the On switch. Nothing happened.

"Do you suppose it needs a new battery?"

"Could be," Josh replied. His morose expression prompted Libby to change the subject.

"How about some breakfast?"

"Don't you think we should wait a while?"

She bent down to pull on her boots. "I think, after what we've been through, and with all we have to do today, we need to keep up our strength—and our spirits."

"That's a tall order, considering we don't have much food."

"We'll find more. Maybe not a lot, and it certainly won't be fancy, but somewhere on this island there has to be something edible.

"Such as?"

"Mussels, periwinkles, rock crab—"

"I'm no naturalist, Libby, but even I know you need some kind of trap to catch rock crab."

"So we'll make one."

"You know how?"

"I could manage. It shouldn't be too difficult." She dusted the sand off her hands and extended them toward the fire. "What'll you have for breakfast? Crackers and cheese or cheese and crackers?"

"The crackers are soggy."

"Then we'll take potluck." Libby contemplated their cache of canned goods. The tins were dented and the labels had washed off. She tried to recall what they'd had in stock, and finally made a selection. "This one's either peaches or applesauce."

Josh shrugged. "Suit yourself. Makes no difference to me."

As it turned out, the can contained stewed tomatoes—not Libby's favorite. Under ordinary circumstances she would have turned up her nose at them, but she hadn't eaten since noon the day before. Even then all she'd had was some chicken noodle soup, and she was famished.

The sky brightened while they ate; Josh's disposition did not, even though he finished the meal by lighting his last cigarette. He sat staring out to sea, brooding and distant, and Libby chose not to intrude upon his thoughts.

She crisscrossed their rocky outpost, moving between the water's edge and the base of the cliffs, collecting armloads of driftwood. Now and again she glanced toward the cliffs, but aside from a colony of seabirds there was not a hint of movement.

When the cold drove her back to the fire, Josh emerged from his reflective mood.

"Where do we go from here?" he asked.

"I'd suggest the lighthouse."

Josh leaned forward, elbows on his thighs. "There are buildings on this island? That's a break in our favor."

"It's not the only break." She dropped to her knees and fed a chunk of wood to the flames. "There aren't many places on Sagamore where we'd have made it ashore."

"In other words, we're lucky to be alive."

"Trite but true."

Josh did a mock double take. "Was that a pun? My God, I don't believe it! You actually have a sense of humor."

"Of course I do. Did you honestly think I didn't?"

"I was beginning to wonder. You don't often smile, and I've never seen you laugh."

Libby flushed. Her fingers tightened around the piece of kindling she was holding. "You'll have to forgive me if I haven't been good company. Being shipwrecked is not my idea of fun. And I don't like being teased."

"Are you sure it's not me you don't like?"

Libby faltered. Her eyes shied away from his. "Why wouldn't I like you?"

"Darned if I know, but I get the impression you don't approve of me."

"That's ridiculous. I don't know you well enough to disapprove of you."

Hoping to put an end to the argument, she began rearranging the clothing on the line, and when she moved her shirt closer to the fire, a distinctive brass lapel pin fell out of the pocket. Josh scooped it up before she could retrieve it.

"What's this?"

Libby didn't answer. She couldn't find her voice. She bit her lip while Josh scraped away a layer of sand with his thumbnail, and the DEEPC trident appeared, forest green against the dull metallic surface.

Josh eyed the insignia then looked at her, his mouth turned down at the corners. "Don't tell me you're involved with this bunch of weirdos."

"You call them weirdos because you don't sympathize with their cause—"

"Wrong," said Josh. "It's not their cause I object to. It's their tactics."

"T-tactics?"

"You heard me. I'm as concerned about the environment as they are, but there are limits to what I'll do to demonstrate my concern. I won't cave in to threats. I won't trample on someone else's rights any more than I'll let DEEPC ride roughshod over mine, and I sure as hell won't put up with the way they've harassed Sally Gillette."

"Wh-why would they harass Sally?"

"Because she's my representative. DEEPC's opposed to my plans for developing Half-Moon Island. So okay. I can handle that, and I can't fault them for wanting to protect Half-Moon. But would they listen to reason? No! Sally spoke to their representatives. She met with the executive council and delivered copies of the environmental impact studies to their head hatchet woman, Margaret Ogilvie— studies that *prove* a retreat of the type I've proposed would have no negative effect. But Ogilvie doesn't give a damn about the truth. All she cares about is slinging mud and grabbing headlines. The woman's a petty tyrant. She'll stoop to anything to consolidate her power base—and that includes kidnapping, doesn't it?"

The force of Josh's indictment struck Libby like a blow. She wished she could refute his charges, yet how could she deny the truth? She wanted to defend the Coalition, but guilt kept her mute.

"Answer me, dammit!"

Her thoughts were in a turmoil. She tried to turn away, but Josh clamped his hand about her braid, compelling her to face him.

"Wha—what is it you want from me?"

"Names, Libby. I want the names of everyone involved."

"What makes you think there are others?"

Josh growled an epithet. His eyes were coldly furious. "Don't insult my intelligence by pretending you're in this alone. You can begin with your brother."

"Not Caleb! He has nothing to do with this."

"You expect me to buy that when he provided the boat?"

"It's true, Josh. I swear it. Caleb has no idea I took his boat. He's in Boston this weekend, and he was getting ready to put the boat in dry dock. That's why the radio wasn't aboard."

"So you're a thief as well as a kidnapper." Josh's gaze wandered over her, wintry with contempt. His hold on her braid threatened reprisals if she did not make a full confession. "Names, Libby. Give me names."

"I can't," she replied in a cracked whisper. "Not unless you give me your word you won't press charges."

His hand slid to the base of her throat with deceptive gentleness, but the hard set of his jaw offered no quarter. "You're in no position to bargain. If you're half as clever as I think you are, you'll give up trying to protect your accomplices at DEEPC and worry about protecting yourself."

"I can't, Josh. Without some sort of assurance, I can't implicate anyone else. All I can tell you is no one meant you any harm. If things had gone the way they were supposed to, you wouldn't have been detained more than a few hours— long enough to meet with the executive committee—"

"Then they *are* in on it."

"They're not! As far as they knew, you'd agreed to the meeting. And if it had come off, it might have worked to everyone's benefit. You might have reached a compromise—"

Josh silenced her with a bark of laughter. "Why should I compromise? I'm not the one who's been spreading rumors, using the press to increase membership and fatten my bank account with contributions. I own Half-Moon. It's in my interest to protect my investment. I only want the best for the island."

"So does DEEPC. And regardless of what you think, the Coalition isn't responsible for the bad press you've been getting."

"Are you suggesting I am?"

"No, Josh. All I'm suggesting is that the executive committee's at the mercy of the media, too. And the sad thing is, if you'd gone through channels and accepted the invitation to meet with them, they might've recognized that your goals don't conflict with theirs."

"That won't wash, Libby. I did go through channels. Sally represented me at the public hearings."

"But you didn't attend them yourself."

"I'm a busy man. I have to delegate authority. And in any case, my actions aren't the issue here."

"Neither are DEEPC's."

"That leaves you."

Josh studied her features with a kind of tender regret, drawing his forefinger along the curve of her mouth. Her lips tingled. Her heart skipped a beat. For a moment she had the insane notion that he was going to kiss her. But then he pulled away from her and hurled the lapel pin into the surf as if he found the slightest contact with DEEPC repugnant.

With a sad shake of his head he said, "It's a shame, really. You're a pretty thing, and the last I heard, kidnapping was a federal offense."

The threat he implied was unmistakable, but somehow she found the strength to defy him. "I won't name any names," she said. "I can't betray my friends."

"Then you're either incredibly loyal or incredibly foolish." Josh swung around to look at her. His expression hardened. "My vote goes to foolish."

Libby returned his frown. "If I'm foolish, that's my prerogative."

"Well, mine is seeing that someone makes reparations, and since you insist on stonewalling, that someone will have to be you."

She drew in a ragged breath. "I understand why you want your pound of flesh, Josh. I'd feel the same way if I were you. But the punishment will have to wait till we're rescued. If we're going to get off this island, we'll have to work together. We need to be able to rely on each other."

"I'll tell you what you can rely on, Libby. I always collect what's owed me. So don't be misled if I defer payment for now. You won't get off scot-free. Someday, if it's the last thing I ever do, I'm going to see that the books are balanced."

Chapter Six

By midmorning their gear was dry. They got dressed, and working quietly, not saying a word that might disturb the fragile truce they had established, reassembled the packs and set off for the seaward side of the island.

As the gulls fly, they were less than two miles from their objective, but with the terrain broken by great crags and deep gorges, they had to hike twice that distance.

Even then it was rough going.

They scaled rocky outcroppings slick with lichen, and cut through woods so dense that the breeze couldn't penetrate the thicket of branches. More than once the trail they had chosen became impassable, requiring them to take a more circuitous route.

The first time they had to backtrack, Libby mumbled a protest.

Every muscle in her body ached. Her deck boots were rubbing blisters on her heels and each step was torture. And because she couldn't shake the feeling that someone was following them, she was jumpy, on guard, constantly looking over her shoulder.

She'd have given her lunch rations to share her concerns with Josh, but he was still seething with anger, albeit silently. And coming on top of this tension, having to double back seemed the last straw, the ultimate indignity.

The second time the trail petered out, she hadn't enough energy to object, and by the third time she was past caring about the detour. She'd stopped worrying about the ghost, and she didn't give a damn if Josh was angry.

She was numb with lack of sleep. A strange floating sensation filled her head. Her movements were cramped and uncoordinated, and even with Josh's assistance, it was all she could do to put one foot in front of the other.

The sun was directly overhead before the trees began to thin. Minutes later they made their way to a knoll overlooking the sea, and from that vantage point they saw the lighthouse.

"It's gray," Josh declared flatly. "I thought it would be white."

"It used to be. I've seen pictures—"

But the years of neglect and abandonment had exacted their toll. Surrounded by the weathered remains of the keeper's bungalow and a scattering of ruined outbuildings, the gaunt stone tower clung to a precarious perch on the very edge of the bluff.

Dazzled by the sunlight, Libby tilted her head to one side, resting it against Josh's shoulder. "Am I imagining things, or is the lighthouse leaning?"

"It's leaning," he said. "It looks as if a good wind would blow it over."

She closed her eyes. "It's making me dizzy."

"Maybe it's not as bad as it seems."

With a supporting arm about her waist, Josh guided her across the clearing, past mounds of corrugated siding and twisted beams that had once been supply huts and storage sheds, toward the tumbledown house that crouched at the foot of Sagamore Light as if it were seeking protection from the elements.

On closer inspection, the condition of both structures was appalling.

The beacon tower was little more than a shell. There were chinks in the walls where the mortar had crumbled and loose stones had fallen away, and the spiral staircase had rusted. When Josh attempted to climb it, the metal struts snapped before he reached the first landing, denying him access to the lantern deck.

But dilapidated as the lighthouse was, the keeper's residence was worse. Broken windows gave it a sullen look, and its foundation had eroded so that the house was sinking into its cellar.

Once inside, they found that the floor joists were warped and partitions had collapsed. There were great gaping holes in the roof.

"Skylights," Josh called them.

His caustic tone of voice was more than Elizabeth could bear. She sat in a pool of sunlight in a sheltered corner of the parlor while he continued exploring, trailing sarcasm in his wake.

He prowled from the basement to the attic, and when he returned to the parlor, he stood at a shattered window and admired the view of the Atlantic. He extolled the virtues of cross-ventilation and the coziness of southern exposures until, fed up with his euphemisms, Libby pointed out that the window faced east.

"And it's drafty," she said.

Josh spread his arm wide. "Be it ever so humble, this is it, Libby. Our home away from home. We may as well make the best of it."

"Why here?" she demanded. "Why not the lighthouse?"

"No way to heat it, and no way to shore it up. This room has a fireplace, and there's enough scrap lumber lying around to provide plenty of firewood, even after we make some repairs."

Libby propped the bedding pack behind her and used it as a back rest. She could not stop yawning. "Do you think the fireplace works?"

"The chimney seems solid, and the flue checks out. I don't see why it shouldn't. What I'm worried about is water."

"Don't be," she answered sleepily. "There must've been a well to supply the house."

"If there was a well, why aren't there any water pipes?"

She rubbed her eyes, fighting to keep them open. "Maybe this place predates indoor plumbing."

Josh had resumed his restless pacing. He did not seem reassured. "I read somewhere that on some of these offshore islands drinking water has to be shipped in."

"That's true, but as a rule they're smaller than Sagamore."

He stopped in front of the fireplace, and swung around to face her. "Did you notice any standing water this morning?"

"No, I didn't."

"Neither did I." Josh brought his fist down on the mantel, driving home this point. "No streams, no bogs, no marshes."

"So?"

"So doesn't it strike you as odd that after all the rain we had Friday, not so much as a puddle is left?"

Odd was putting it mildly.

Suddenly more thirsty than tired, Libby dragged herself to her feet and headed for the door.

"Where are you going?" Josh asked.

"We have several hours of daylight left. Why don't we look for that well?"

They spent the rest of the afternoon searching, Libby on the southern and western sides of the house, Josh to the north and east, along the bluffs that sloped precipitously to the ocean.

He roved here and there with no discernible pattern, pausing now and again to study the underbrush or prod the turf with a stick. But in this, as in other things, Elizabeth kept to a system.

After dividing her share of the compound into three pie-shaped wedges, she went over each section foot by foot, inch by inch. Always thorough. Always conscientious. Giving it her all, even though digging through the rubble was tedious, dusty work, and her exertions yielded nothing more valuable than shards of crockery, broken hand tools and a field mouse's nest.

By late afternoon her mouth felt as if it were lined with cotton batting. All she could think about was water.

She thought about walking through a summer shower, catching raindrops in her mouth, letting the rain soothe her parched lips and trickle down her throat.

She thought about a pitcher of ice water, complete with beads of moisture on the glass. And then she imagined how delicious it would be to drain the pitcher in one long gulp.

She thought about bathing her face in warm perfumed water, rinsing her hands in it, soaking in a hot relaxing tub.

At sunset, while she poked about the skeleton of a supply hut, visions of waterfalls danced in her head. She was only vaguely aware that Josh was nearby, whistling tunelessly while he applied the business end of a crowbar he'd found to a particularly stubborn slab of stone.

Her imaginary waterfall plunged into a mountain stream, and she was about to do the same when the stone shifted.

"Got it!" Josh shouted.

Libby glared at him. She did not appreciate his interrupting her fantasy. But as he levered aside smaller stones, she saw a concrete standpipe and realized that the soil about the pipe was wet.

She was at his side in an instant, heaving bits of masonry out of the way. Between the two of them, the excavation quickly widened, and by the time the last glimmer of sunlight faded, they had uncovered a spring that bubbled out of the ground, frosty and clear.

The joy of discovery made them forget the hostilities of the morning. Neither of them stopped to worry whether the water might be contaminated, and they didn't bother with such niceties as cups. They simply captured the water in cupped hands and drank it, and when they could drink no more they splashed water over their heads, into the air, onto each other.

As a finale to their celebration, Josh expelled a mouthful of water in twin jets, in a remarkable imitation of a fountain.

"I'll give you ten points for distance, three for technique," Libby applauded, tongue-in-cheek.

He cocked an eyebrow at her. "What's wrong with my technique?"

"No style. No finesse."

"I'd like to see you do better."

"No kidding?"

With that exit line and a disdainful toss of her head she would have walked away, but Josh took hold of her elbow and ushered her toward the spring.

"Come on, sport. Put up or shut up."

Libby rose to the challenge. She managed a fair approximation of Josh's performance until she heard him chuckling. His laughter was infectious. She couldn't help giggling, which triggered a paroxysm of coughing when some of the water went down the wrong way.

"Nice try," said Josh, pounding her on the back, "but all I can give you is five points for distance."

"What about style?"

"With your style, you're lucky I didn't deduct points."

"That's not fair, Josh. You cheated."

"Me cheat? Tell me how."

"You made me laugh."

"That's not cheating. It's what's known as finesse."

"Hah!" Libby grumbled, unimpressed. She bent down to dry her face on her shirttail, and when she straightened, Josh offered her a roguish grin.

"Those are the breaks, Libby. You can't win the game if you don't know the rules."

He winked at her then and gave her a hug, and it seemed the most natural thing in the world to hug him back.

After the dangers and disappointments of the last few days, after all the anguish and fear, finding the spring had left her in a rare reckless mood, feeling giddy and playful.

Besides, when she considered the hardships she and Josh had been through, she felt a kind of affinity for him—a bond as deep and enduring as the kinship she felt for her brothers.

But Josh's embrace was not remotely fraternal, and there was nothing sisterly about her response to him.

The touch of his hands made her pulses leap, and when he hauled her close, an alien heat and languor pervaded her limbs. His lips grazed her forehead, her temple, her cheek, and something inside her stirred. Her own lips parted, anticipating his kiss, and the rush of physical sensations reached flood tide when he claimed her mouth.

She was exquisitely aware of the rough abrasion of his beard, the possessive glide of his tongue, the hardness of muscle and bone and sinew, the supple warmth of his skin. His arms were strong and confident, his mouth seeking and persuasive, and when she felt the surge of his arousal, her flesh grew pliant and yielding, shaping itself to his.

Yet even while her body invited greater intimacies— yearned for them—a small, insistent inner voice urged caution.

Careful, it warned. *You hardly know this man.*

And everything feminine in her countered, I do know him. I've always known him.

That's nonsense, the voice whispered. *Silly, romantic nonsense.*

What if it is? Libby wondered. Aren't I entitled to have a little romance in my life?

She tried to ignore the inner voice, but it would not be still.

Think of the consequences, it said. *Think of the risks. If you won't listen to me, remember Josh's advice. Don't play the game if you don't know the rules.*

This recollection was enough to make her pull away from Josh, but once he had released her, she was uncertain what to do next.

Should she make light of her emotions and compliment him on his expertise? Should she give him a perfect score for technique? Should she pretend indifference, and act as if nothing had changed?

Thanks to her deception, Josh already had cause to doubt her honesty. If she admitted she was not accustomed to dealing with situations like this, would he assume it was a line? Would he make fun of her shyness, tell her naiveté was no excuse?

Would he think she was a tease? Would he be upset or irate or turned on or turned off? Or—what if he didn't react at all? Kissing her might've been a passing fancy. It might've been an act of vengeance. He might be totally un-moved.

Swamped by confusion, Libby folded her arms about her middle and studied the toes of her boots, too self-conscious to look at Josh, much less think of anything clever to say.

It was he who broke the silence.

"It's been fun, Libby, but I guess it's time to get back to work."

He sounded businesslike and faintly amused. Was he smiling?

She stole a glance at him but couldn't be sure. She couldn't see his face in the gathering dusk.

"It'll be dark soon," he said in the same brusque tone. "I'm going to build a couple of signal fires out on the bluffs. I figure one on either side ought to do it."

She nodded, chilled by his reserve. "While you're taking care of that, I'll rustle up some supper."

"That reminds me—here's something you can throw in the pot." Josh removed what looked like a giant-size wal-nut from his hip pocket and handed it to Libby. "I dug this up by the back porch."

"A potato," she marveled. "This is wonderful, Josh! I'll bet you found the vegetable patch. I'll check it out tomor-row."

"Let's hope it's not necessary, Libby. If there are any boats nearby, we could be out of here by morning."

On that optimistic note, Josh turned on his heel and strode toward the bluffs, leaving Libby to stare after him, wishing that he would look back, or wave, or say some-thing personal.

He didn't though, and still she watched until the twilight closed around him and he blended into the shadows.

It was as if he had never held her in his arms. Never kissed her. As if the interlude they'd shared was as insubstantial as a dream.

Chapter Seven

At seven-fifteen the following morning, while Joshua and Elizabeth were catching up on some much-needed sleep, Cal Pilgrim was studying the bill of fare in Kate Blackledge's Pie Shop.

The name of the place was misleading. Although Kate's was famous for pastries, in the off-season the café did a brisk business catering to the breakfast and supper trade.

Caleb was one of the regulars. When he walked into the Pie Shop, a chorus of greetings welcomed him, and if the atmosphere was friendly, the food was the greatest.

For supper he was partial to the Yankee pot roast, but the boiled lobster was just as good. For breakfast he alternated between a combination platter called the Stevedore and his personal favorite, a specialty of the house known as the Lumberjack.

In his opinion, the majority of the world's problems would dry up and blow away if everyone started the day with a tall glass of orange juice, hearty portions of steak and eggs, a helping of baked beans, and a basket of blueberry muffins hot from the oven.

Just reading the menu made his mouth water.

"Mornin', Cal. How be ya?" Josie the counter girl inquired with a smile.

"Hungry enough to eat a boiled owl," Caleb answered.

He ordered the Lumberjack, and to save Josie the trip, helped himself to a mug of coffee and carried it to a table by the windows where he could watch the town pass by.

Tourists called Day's Harbor "quaint." Caleb called it home, but he still enjoyed the view.

From those leaded glass windows he could see the length of Main Street, from the dry goods store to the library, and beyond the commercial district, where Main Street intersected Eggemont, he saw houses nestled into hillsides that descended like stair steps to the bay. He could see the cannery and the public wharf, piled high with lobster pots, and since the morning was clear, he could see across the harbor to the private pier where *Pilgrim's Progress* was docked—

Should've been docked.

Caleb narrowed his eyes against the glitter of sunlight on the water. When he left for Boston Thursday evening, the cruiser had been tied up to the pier, snug as a baby in its cradle. Today it was gone.

So was his appetite.

"Damn," he muttered. "Double damn."

The crowd cleared a pathway before him as he stalked the length of the counter. He marched past Josie without breaking stride.

"Somethin' wrong, Cal?" she asked.

"Some dirty pirate's swiped my boat!"

Outrage propelled him through the entryway to the sidewalk, and across the street to the police station.

"Is my brother in?" he demanded of a bleary-eyed clerk.

"Sure, Cal. Have a seat. I'll buzz Chief Pilgrim and tell him you're here."

"Never mind," said Caleb. "I'll tell 'im myself."

He was not in the habit of throwing his weight around, but this, he figured, was an emergency.

Daniel didn't see it that way. "Let's not assume the worst," he advised when Caleb had told his story. "We had quite a blow this weekend. The boat might've slipped its moorings."

"That boat was secure, Dan. I checked those lines myself, and I'm tellin' you, they couldn't have given way without some low-life whale dung helpin' 'em along."

"Do you want to file an official complaint?"

"Bet your badge I do. I'm prepared to offer a reward— Yeah, that's it! I'll put an ad in this afternoon's paper—"

"Simmer down Cal, and think this through. A reward's apt to be counterproductive. You'll get calls from every kook in the county."

"It'll be worth it if it turns up even one lead."

"It won't," said Dan. "Believe me. You're certain the boat's been stolen. So okay. I'll take care of it. But before I put out an APB I'd like to take a look at the dock, maybe talk to some of your neighbors."

"You think they might've seen something?"

"It's possible." With a calming hand on Caleb's shoulder, Dan steered him toward the hall.

"Will you let me know what the neighbors say?"

"I'll call you soon as I have anything to report," said Dan. "But you gotta let me handle the investigation my way."

DAN DIDN'T CALL THAT MORNING. Caleb interpreted this to mean his brother hadn't turned up any witnesses.

He sat in his office at Wilderness Guides Unlimited, waiting for the phone to ring. It was the longest morning of his life.

He read his mail and went over some invoices, but all he could think about was the missing cruiser. It was a link to his seagoing forebears, his prize possession, a dream attained—and as the hours dragged by, the conviction grew that he would never see it again.

At noon he phoned his insurance carrier. "You're covered," the agent told him. "Don't worry about a thing."

He was at his desk, leafing through a boating magazine, pricing comparable boats, when Daniel paid him a visit.

"What'd you find out?"

Dan shoved a stack of brochures to one side and sat on the edge of the windowsill. "Enough to know this case is more complicated then either of us thought."

"How so?"

"It's beginning to look as if Libby took the boat."

Caleb slapped his magazine down on the desktop. "Of all the cockamamie— You expect me to believe that?"

"It's true, Cal. I didn't believe it any more than you do at first, but all the evidence points to her."

"What evidence?"

"Her car's in the visitors' lot at your condo."

"I didn't see it."

"That's not surprising. It's parked behind some bushes, clear to heck and gone away from the building. It's like she didn't want anyone to see it."

"But lots of folks drive Toyotas, Dan. Are you sure this one's Libby's?"

"We have a make on the license number. And it looks as if the car's been there a while. We found a receipt for gasoline, dated the thirtieth, from an Amoco station in Rockport, and the gas tank's almost full. Near as we can tell, she drove from Rockport direct to your place late Thursday night or early Friday morning."

"How'd you pin down the time?"

"The station's close to her apartment, so the attendant recognized her."

"Okay, but if Libby took the boat, where is it? And where the hell is she?"

"I don't know, Cal. That's one we're still working on. She didn't show up for work today, and none of the family's heard from her."

"How about her friends?"

"We're checking with them. So far, nothing."

Caleb shook his head. "People don't just disappear, Dan. Somebody must've seen her."

"Somebody did. At least, that's the assumption I'm going on. A woman named Sally Gillette."

"Never heard of her."

"No reason you should have, but she contacted the Bar Harbor police this morning and reported her boss missing. According to Mrs. Gillette, he left the Windlass Inn Friday morning for the seaplane landing at Southwest Harbor, only he never got there. Far as we've been able to determine, nobody's seen him since."

"What's that got to do with Libby?"

"Well, it seems this feller, Joshua Noon, took a water taxi from the Windlass, and Gillette's description of the taxi matches *Pilgrim's Progress*."

"I still don't see a connection, Dan. I don't recall Libby ever mentioning anyone named Noon."

Daniel shrugged. "She's twenty-six. I imagine there are quite a few things she doesn't tell you."

"But this whole thing with the water taxi could be coincidence."

"I hope so, Caleb. I sincerely hope so, 'cause we're talking about something a lot more serious than a stolen powerboat."

Caleb slumped forward, head in his hands. "When'll you know?"

"Soon. One of my men's gone out to Mount Desert Island to talk with Gillette, see if she can identify Libby's photograph."

"And if she does?"

"He'll notify us here, either way."

Chapter Eight

If Josh lived to be a hundred, he would never understand women. Especially a woman like Libby.

To outward appearances she was a product of her time, ready to accept any challenge, even if it meant stepping outside the law.

But beneath the liberated exterior, she was a bundle of contradictions that puzzled and disturbed him, and occasionally drove him wild.

Last night at the spring, for instance, he had discovered that although she might look starchy, she was delightful to hold. Soft. Warm. Feminine. And although her kiss was not terribly practiced, he'd found it surprisingly erotic. Her shyness excited him, and the trusting way she melted into his arms made him feel protective.

If she had been any other woman, he would have interpreted her response as a come-on and made the most of it. With Libby, however, he wasn't sure what to make of it.

She was a kidnapper, after all. God only knew what ulterior motives guided her behavior. She could be trying to seduce him for the same reason she had lured him aboard her boat. But if she thought making love to him would convert him to DEEPC's party line, she was sadly mistaken.

I'd rather be frustrated than a fool, Josh thought. But what if he was both?

He frowned as another example of Libby's inconsistencies occurred to him.

Under his interrogation she had confessed that she didn't operate a water taxi. A question or two later she'd admitted that she was an archivist at a college near Rockport.

"What does an archivist do?" he'd asked.

"My primary responsibility is cataloging the diaries and letters and other collections of private papers bequeathed to the school by some of its more illustrious alumni."

"Sounds interesting," he'd said.

The truth was, it sounded boring, but who was he to criticize? Libby said she enjoyed her work, and on this issue he'd been willing to take her at face value—until this morning, when the levelheaded archivist, who professed a fondness for musty historical fact, had wakened him with some tall tale about pirates and witches and ghosts.

"You've been dreaming," he told her, and with that observation he'd rolled over and closed his eyes. But she wouldn't let him go back to sleep.

"I'm wide-awake," she insisted, shaking his shoulder. "I've been awake for hours, and since I didn't want to disturb you, I decided to find the vegetable garden. So I went outside, and I started looking near the back porch, and I heard this noise—like a floorboard creaking. At first I thought it was you. So I said good morning, but you didn't answer—"

He'd opened one eye and glared at her. "How could I? I wasn't there."

"I know you weren't, Josh. That's the point. But I definitely heard that floorboard creak, and when I realized it wasn't you, I looked up. And that's when I saw her...him...."

He'd opened the other eye and sat up, resigned to going along with the gag. "Make up your mind, Libby. Which was it?"

"I'm not sure. It was over so fast. All I got was a glimpse of this—this *figure* disappearing around the corner of the house."

"Are you sure you don't mean fig*ment*?"

Libby shook her head. "I saw something, Josh. I didn't imagine it."

"Then it must've been an animal."

"It wasn't," she said.

"If you only got a glimpse, how can you be certain?"

"I saw enough to know it was human."

"But not enough to distinguish its gender?"

"N-no," she answered hesitantly. "All I can tell you is, whoever it was—*whatever* it was—is dressed in black and very thin and sexless."

"You've just described Michael Jackson." He'd stared at Libby, registering her dark tragic eyes, her tremulous lips, her pallor, and then, to prove that he hadn't bought a single word of the fable, he had congratulated her on her performance.

But he had to hand it to Libby. She had stayed in character, playing her role to the hilt. She'd even contrived to look offended.

"I don't like what you're implying," she'd said.

"Well, I don't like being lied to."

His coolness rivaled hers, and the temperature in the parlor seemed to acquire an arctic chill. Libby had withdrawn into reproachful silence, as if *she* were the injured party.

Josh sighed and looked at Libby. Even now, twelve hours after the dawn of the new ice age, he saw no signs of a thaw.

Women! he thought, à la Henry Higgins. Why do they have to complicate everything? What makes them so touchy and perverse?

He sighed again and glanced about the parlor. He'd spent most of the day patching the roof and boarding up broken windows, and had Libby thanked him for the repairs he had made? No! All he had to show for his efforts was splinters and calluses and more of the cold shoulder from her.

But two could play that game, which was why he had purposely withheld comment about the improvements she'd added, even though her contributions gave the parlor some measure of comfort.

While he had reshingled the bald spots on the roof, she'd made mattresses of pine boughs and plugged the holes in the siding with old newspapers she'd found in a crawl space. While he'd made the shutters and hung them, she had recycled nails and pounded them into the studs to use as clothes pegs. And while he'd installed brick-and-board shelves near the hearth for a pantry, she'd used a survival blanket to screen one corner of the room.

"For privacy," she'd said, and the frost in her voice made it clear to Josh that those few square feet of floor space were off limits to him.

In the late afternoon Libby went foraging for supper, and when she returned she boasted about her resourcefulness.

That was okay with Josh. He was too hungry to give a damn where the meal came from, but for the sake of courtesy he pretended to pay attention while she explained that the potatoes and turnips had survived the growth of weeds in the kitchen garden, and that she'd found the dandelion greens and wild mushrooms in the woods beyond the clearing.

"It's good," he said, when he finished the last morsel of food on his plate. After the day's hard labor, he just wished there was more.

With her version of a flourish, Libby produced two wizened windfall apples. "Your dessert," she said, offering one to Josh.

He took it, astonished. "Where'd you find these?"

"There's a tree, just barely alive, north of the lighthouse."

Libby bit into her apple. It tasted as bad as it looked; mealy and bitter on the outside, tart and woody at the core. On the mainland, she realized, farmers fed such apples to their livestock, but on Sagamore it was a treat.

And Josh, she noted, seemed properly appreciative. While she was still chewing her first ladylike bite, he had already wolfed down most of his apple.

He paused for breath and caught her watching him. "I don't suppose you happened to find any tobacco growing in the woods?"

She detected a serious note beneath his banter and gave him a tentative smile. "It must be hard to quit smoking."

"T'ain't easy." Josh started to ask Libby if she'd seen any more of the ghost, but at the last moment decided he'd had enough of the silent treatment. He tossed his apple core onto the coals and reached for his coat.

"Are you going to start more signal fires?"

"Yes," he said, "and this time I'm going to tend them all night."

Barring miracles, Libby had no hope the fires would accomplish anything. Unless Josh came up with a practical way of duplicating the elevation of the lighthouse tower, chances were the beacons wouldn't be visible many miles out to sea. But she kept her doubts to herself.

Josh's forceful stride and squared shoulders, the determined set of his jaw, told her that he had made his plans and nothing she could say would change them. Eventually he might listen to reason. Till then she might as well save her breath.

Besides, she thought, *I've had all the ridicule I can take for one day.*

Josh's lack of confidence in her was painful, and the knowledge that his mistrust was not entirely unwarranted compounded her discomfort. Why should he believe she had seen the phantom of Sagamore Island, when she scarcely believed the evidence of her own eyes?

After he left she cleared away the supper things. Then, feeling uneasy, she rinsed out her undies and washed the ocean salt from her hair. It was very late before her hair was dry, but she was much too jumpy to sleep.

She couldn't stop thinking about the ghost, and as she wandered aimlessly about the room—keyed up, starting at shadows—Joshua began to seem like the lesser of two evils. Certainly his company was preferable to her own.

She made coffee and filled the thermos. "If you can't beat 'im, join 'im," she muttered as she got into her sweater.

The night was cold and utterly still, as if nature were holding its breath. She stood on the porch, fastening the snaps on her poncho and looking up at the sky, counting stars that seemed close enough to touch. Frost had settled on the beach grasses, leaving them stiff and spiky. They crunched beneath her feet as she trudged across the bluff.

The twin signal fires gave her a destination, but Josh had stationed himself midway between them. Until he hailed her, she didn't see him sprawled on the ground, using a moss-covered stone as a headrest.

"How's it going?" she inquired, veering in his direction.

"Not bad," he answered, yawning. "The hardest part about this job is staying awake."

That makes one of us, thought Libby. She held up the thermos. "Would you like some coffee?"

"Sure would."

He levered himself to a sitting position and she sat beside him, Indian-style, and uncapped the flask.

"It's sugared," she cautioned.

"That's okay. I can use the calories."

Much to Libby's relief, he seemed happy to see her. Or perhaps it was the coffee that mellowed his response. He drained his cup in one long swallow, and she gave him a refill before she poured her own.

"Know what gets me about this place?" he said.

"No. What?"

"There's no white noise—no distractions." He glanced at Libby, and her intent expression encouraged him to go on. "It reminds me of something that happened to me in college, when I was a guinea pig in one of the psych department's experiments—"

"Shh. What was that?"

Josh frowned at the interruption. "What was what?"

"I thought I heard something." Libby tensed, listening for all she was worth, but aside from the hiss and crackle of burning driftwood and the rhythmic wash of the surf, the night was shrouded in silence.

"I don't hear anything."

"Neither do I. At least, not now." She gave a shaky little laugh. "I'm sorry, Josh. You were telling me about the psych experiment—"

"Yes, well, as part of this experiment, I was put into the sensory deprivation tank. The water was skin temperature, I was blindfolded and my ears were plugged. At first I could hear my heartbeat, but after a while I couldn't even hear that, and that's when I began to lose my equilibrium. Everything seemed distorted. I couldn't tell where my arms were, or my legs, or whether I was floating faceup or facedown. It was like my body had been disconnected from my head."

"That sounds horrible," said Libby.

"It was," said Josh. "I felt like a shutdown computer, except that my mind was racing. And the slower the sensory inputs, the faster the thoughts came."

"What kind of thoughts?"

"I don't remember. But what I thought about doesn't matter. What's important is, I fixated on this idea that if I stopped thinking, even for a split second, I wouldn't exist anymore."

Libby glanced at Josh from beneath her lashes, wondering if he knew how revealing this anecdote was. "Do you still feel that way?"

"Not often. It's just lately—since Walt died. We'd been through an awful lot together, and—I don't know, Libby. It's like his life validated mine."

"Is Walt the friend you told me about? The one you grew up with?"

"Yeah, that was Walt." Josh sighed and shoved his fingers through his hair. "God, I miss him."

She sipped her coffee, trying to dislodge the lump in her throat. "How did the two of you happen to meet again?"

"I was working for Sherman and Dunne—maybe you've heard of them."

"Not that I recall. Are they an advertising agency?"

"The best in Chicago before Walt and I came along. Now they're just the biggest."

"You sound as if that gives you a great deal of satisfaction."

"It does, and I'll tell you why. I started writing copy at S and D fresh out of college, and for three or four years I was happy there. My first month on the job, I came up with a concept for the Norwich account—"

"Norwich?"

"The people who make the rain boots. You probably had a pair when you were a kid. You know the kind I mean. Plain black rubber, practical but dull. Anyway, I persuaded them to manufacture their basic boot in a variety of colors, slap on a designer label for snob appeal, and market them with the slogan, 'Norwich—When You Want to Make a Splash.'"

"And the boots you suggested made a splash?"

Josh nodded. "That particular line gave Norwich a hefty share of the teenage market and a new lease on life. And the campaign brought me to Burton Dunne's attention. He took a personal interest in me, and I moved up in the agency. I got promotions, raises, the toughest assignments, and I made the most of the opportunities that came my way. I was on my way to the top; the fair-haired boy at S and D—until Burt Senior retired and Junior took command."

"I take it the son was not like his father?"

"They were different as day and night. Burton Senior was a man of principle. I might even say to a fault. He was too honorable to recognize that Junior was mean-spirited, small-minded, corrupt—everything that gives advertising a bad name. But I didn't recognize it, either. Not immediately. A couple of prize accounts went to Junior's buddies. 'So okay,' I told myself. 'He's entitled.' A couple of clients severed their association with the firm. 'These things happen,' I told myself. 'We'll replace them.' A couple of vice-presidents resigned, and I accepted the explanation that they'd left because of personality differences. There were rumors to the contrary, but I didn't pay any attention to them. All I saw was that there were no major reversals of policy—at least, none that affected me. The name on the letterhead stayed the same, so I assumed nothing had changed.''

"When did you realize they had?"

"Not till Junior's knife was in my back." Josh patted his pockets, automatically searching for cigarettes as he went on. "In my own defense, I have to tell you that I was involved in a promotion for a chain of fast-food places. I was out of the office most of the time. Even so, I should've seen it coming—"

"What, Josh? What happened?"

"The old double cross. Junior took my presentation and sold it to a competing fast-food chain. And the way he handled the deal made me look like the bad guy."

"But that's—it's piracy!"

"Maybe so, but it was business as usual for Junior."

"What did you do about it?"

"Not what he expected. He figured I'd punch him out, run to the client, publicly accuse him of fraud—give him some excuse to fire me."

"And you didn't?"

Josh shook his head. "Blowing the whistle wouldn't have served any purpose except to discredit me. I was green, Libby, but I wasn't stupid enough to play into Junior's hands. I knew the only way to salvage my reputation was to come up with a new promotion for my client."

"So that's what you did?"

"Uh-huh. With a lot of help from my friends. Luckily for me, I was working with a terrific team—most of them are still with me. We were a weekend away from the deadline, but we had one advantage. We knew the commercials the competition would be running made a big deal of the 'secret ingredient' in the sauce they put on their burgers, so we were able to capitalize on inside information. The thrust of our campaign was, if you've got the best burger in town, you don't keep it a secret. You share it with your customers."

"And your client went for the idea?"

"Hook, line and sinker. And that's when I informed Junior I was leaving S and D."

With that brusque statement, Josh got up to put more wood onto the signal fires. Libby hurried after him.

"What about Walt?" she asked.

"What about him?"

"You were going to tell me how you got together."

Josh glanced at her over the stack of driftwood in his arms. "Once I'd given notice, I had to find another job. But things were slow. The country was in the middle of a recession, and there wasn't much available. So after a month of pounding the pavement, I wound up at an employment agency that specialized in placing junior executives. And guess who my career counselor turned out to be."

"Walt."

"Right." Josh replied in a careful, neutral tone, but his sudden smile was nostalgic, affectionate, profoundly sad— and gone so swiftly, Libby might have imagined it. He added several pieces of wood to the nearest fire, then continued along the bluff. "You know how embarrassing it can be when you run into an old friend you haven't seen for a long time, and it's like meeting a stranger?"

Libby nodded.

"Well, it was just the opposite with Walt and me." With gestures as tightly controlled as his emotions, Josh sat on his haunches and began refueling the second fire. "It was like old home week, Libby. We talked—God, how we talked! Filling in the gaps, bringing each other up to date. When my hour was up, we'd barely scratched the surface, so Walt canceled his next appointment and we went to lunch, and by the time lunch was over, we'd decided to go into partnership.''

"So quickly?"

Josh shrugged his shoulders, staring into the flames. "If we'd stopped to think of the consequences, it wouldn't have made any difference. Walt was as miserable in personnel work as I'd been the last few weeks at S and D, and we were young, Libby. Not much older than you. We thought we were invincible. And you have to keep in mind, we weren't totally without assets. Both of us had some savings, and a couple of my clients had asked me to keep in touch. I figured it'd be fairly easy to persuade them to switch their accounts to our agency. On the strength of my experience and some real estate holdings of Walt's, we managed to scrape up some financing. It wasn't a huge amount—about enough to cover start-up costs—but at the time we had no idea what we were letting ourselves in for.''

Libby fed a handful of twigs to the fire and watched the blaze consume them. "It must've been difficult getting established.''

"I suppose it was, but looking back what I remember is the excitement. I liked the planning, the strategy sessions, the challenge of wining and dining prospective clients on a beer and pretzel budget. I even liked the long hours and the whirlwind pace—there were times when I was supposed to be three different places at once, till I learned how to budget my time. But what gave me the biggest kick was the way Walt and I complemented each other.''

Josh smiled, remembering his partner's exploits. "I'm telling you, Libby, it was a pleasure to see Walt in action. He had a talent for organization. He was a stickler for detail, yet he never lost sight of the big picture. And I've always been at my best in a crisis—''

"I've noticed," she said.

Josh looked at her and sobered, his face tinted copper by the firelight. He settled back on the ground, and she sank down next to him. His voice dropped an octave, so that she had to lean close to hear him as he picked up the thread of his narrative.

"Walt used to say, 'When the going gets rough, you can rely on Josh to have an escape hatch.' At the risk of sounding immodest, I have to admit it's true. Whenever I'm negotiating a deal, I try to keep one eye on the loopholes. It's a trick I learned as a kid, a way of keeping my cool. When trouble threatens, I ask myself, 'What's the worst possible outcome?'"

"Isn't that a bit morbid?"

"Could be—although I wouldn't call myself a pessimist. It's more that defining the worst helps me keep things in perspective. It lets me clarify which variables are within my control and which aren't."

"And that gives you an edge?"

"Yes it does, because after that, instead of worrying about the uncontrollable, I concentrate on restacking the deck in my favor."

Libby doubled over, chin on her knees, and tried to envision Josh worrying about *anything*.

"You're a survivor, Josh."

"So are you, Libby. You're also a damned good listener. Since Walt's death I've avoided talking about him—talking, hell! I've avoided *thinking* about him."

"Then maybe it's time to revive some memories."

"Maybe it is. Only it hurts, Libby. Know what I mean? I still can't believe he's gone."

Josh held out his hand and she took it. His fingers seemed to swallow hers up. His palm was broad, his grip powerful, almost punishing. But she made no attempt to pull away.

She tipped back her head and watched a galaxy of sparks spiral toward the sky. They twinkled briefly and faded; miniature stars extinguished by their own brilliance.

"A cinder in God's eye," she murmured.

"Come again?"

"That's something my mother used to say to my Uncle Toby. He was kind of wild, and Mom used to nag him about settling down. She'd say, 'You mark my words, Tobias Pilgrim. If you keep burning the candle at both ends, you'll wind up a cinder in God's eye.'"

"What did your uncle say to that?"

"He'd laugh. Sometimes he'd humor her and promise to reform. But mostly he ignored her."

Josh's hold on her hand gentled. "He never settled down?"

"Not so you'd notice." After a brief hesitation Libby added, "Uncle Toby was a lobsterman. His boat went down in a storm when I was ten."

"With Walt it was a heart attack."

"But he can't have been very old."

"He was my age. Thirty-three. He jogged and watched his diet and exercised like a fiend, and Blair saw to it that he stayed off caffeine and cigarettes. He'd just had his annual physical, and his doctor had given him a clean bill of health, but less than a week later he was gone."

Libby twined her fingers through Josh's, wanting to comfort him. "It's hard when it's unexpected."

"Everyone claims time helps."

"It does, Josh. It isn't that Uncle Toby's death makes any more sense now than it did when it happened, but after a while I learned to accept it. Other things began to fill the emptiness."

"I wish I could believe that, Libby. Just now all I know is, I'll never have another friend like Walt. There was nothing I couldn't tell him, and I'd have sworn he felt the same way. I thought he was happy with our partnership—"

"Wasn't he?"

"No, he wasn't." Josh let go of her hand and, on the pretext of stoking the fire, turned away from her. "A few weeks before Walt died, I ran into Junior Dunne at a banquet. That was unusual in itself. Not that we went out of our way to avoid each other, but we moved in different circles. Anyway, that night Junior and I found ourselves at opposite sides of the same table, and that was enough to make me wonder if he'd juggled the seating arrangements. We were polite to each other, though. He asked me to pass the salt, and I didn't throw it at him or anything like that. Then, after dinner, he invited me to have a drink with him in the lounge."

"That must've been a surprise."

"I was stunned," Josh replied in a lazy drawl, poking at the fire with a stick. "My first inclination was to tell him to get lost, but my instincts said the smart move would be to find out why he was cozying up to me."

"So you accepted?"

"Naturally I did. How could I pass up the chance to spy on the little creep?"

"Well, what happened?"

"We had our drinks, Junior poured on the charm, and I was on my best behavior. It was all very civilized until we were outside the restaurant, waiting for the parking valet to bring our cars around. At the last minute, Junior gives me an oily smile and says, 'By the way, old chap, when can I expect a response to my offer?'"

"What offer?" asked Libby.

"That's just what I said. 'What offer?' And Junior says, 'Why, my offer to purchase your agency, of course. Surely your partner told you about it.'" Josh gave the embers an irate prod, then tossed the stick onto the fire. "Dammit, Libby! If Walt wanted out, why didn't he tell me? Why'd I have to hear about it from a third party?"

"You mean Junior was telling the truth?"

"Oh, yeah. It was true, all right. He'd made a bid to buy out Healey and Noon, and my good buddy Walt planned on selling. Only he hadn't got round to informing me."

"Had you suspected—?"

"I didn't suspect a thing. A far as I knew, Walt was content with the status quo. He'd married Blair that winter and taken six weeks off for a honeymoon. I'd assumed some of his responsibilities while he was gone, and when he got back he didn't seem eager to relieve me of those duties. That seemed kind of strange, but I didn't press him about it. In fact, to show you what a dope I was, the morning after my run-in with Junior, when I stopped by Walt's office to tell him about it, I thought he'd be amused. I thought we'd have a laugh at Junior's expense. But, as it turned out, the laugh was on me—"

Josh broke off abruptly, leaving the end of the story dangling. Even after all this time and all that had happened in the interim, he couldn't recall that meeting with Walt without being overcome by dismay.

"Advertising is your life," Walt had said. "You've never regretted the sacrifices the agency requires, but I do. And that's why I've decided to divest myself of my interest in the corporation."

While Josh was still reeling from the shock of that announcement, Walt had reminded him that he'd never intended to stay in advertising permanently.

"I used to dream of becoming a serious writer," he'd said, "but I'd forgotten how much writing meant to me till Blair came across a one-act play I wrote when I was in college. It was a rough draft, Josh, not my best work by any yardstick, but Blair liked it. She raved about it. And that started me thinking that I ought to give my dream another chance. Before, when I was trying to write, it was catch-as-catch-can. I was working a forty-hour week to pay the rent. But now, with the proceeds from the sale of my half of Healey and Noon, I wouldn't have to worry about money. I could write full-time.''

Josh had to steel himself before he could tell Libby about this revelation. Even then, the best he could manage was an expurgated account of his reply.

''I told Walt, if it was time he wanted, he could take as much as he liked. There was no need to sell, and he could still have his income from the agency.''

''What did Walt say to that?''

''He apologized. He told me he realized he should have confronted me with Junior's offer as soon as he received it. He said he hadn't meant to keep me in the dark, that he'd been waiting for the right moment to tell me he was leaving the firm. In the interest of fairness, he did agree to one concession. He gave me a month to raise the capital to buy him out, but aside from that, he refused to reconsider. The bottom line was, his decision was final. He said he hoped I'd understand.''

Josh had tried to understand. He had tried to look at the situation objectively, from Walt's point of view. But no matter how he tried, he couldn't overcome his resentment. Not completely.

Before Walt's death he'd felt betrayed. Since then he'd felt guilty—

''Is that how it ended?''

Josh heard a note of compassion in Libby's voice and found he couldn't look at her. How could he acknowledge her sympathy when he didn't deserve it? And how could he answer her question, except to say, ''It's not over yet.''

The legacies of friendship didn't end when one friend died, and neither did the obligations. And Josh's conscience would not be appeased until he had honored his debt to Walt.

Chapter Nine

A squall blew in toward morning. At the first sprinkling of rain, Libby suggested they run for cover, but Joshua refused to leave his post. He was determined to tend the signal fires as long as he could.

"You'll get drenched," she told him.

"It won't be the first time," he said.

"But what's the point? It'll be daylight soon."

"Precisely. That's why every minute counts."

Josh resumed his hunt for firewood, and realizing it was futile to argue with him she demanded, "Are you always so perverse?

"Not at all. If necessary, I can be a lot more perverse than this. But how about you? Must you always have your own way?"

"Only when I'm right."

Josh subjected her to a probing glance. "How often is that? Once in a blue moon?"

Libby gritted her teeth and peeled off the poncho. "Since you're too pigheaded to come in out of the rain, you'd better wear this."

She didn't wait for Josh's reply. She simply dropped the poncho, turned on her heel and marched away from him, fuming.

If he wanted to risk life and limb, let him. As for her, she had had it! Trying to reason with him was like talking to a brick wall. For all she cared, he could strip to the buff and sit on a rock in the wind and the cold till the cows came home. He was a grown man, supposedly of sound mind and unquestionably of sound body—

A rush of images came to mind; images of Josh's body. He was lean without being bony, strong, compact and ruggedly proportioned—in a word, gorgeous! And thanks to his dive, Libby found she could remember him in intimate detail, some of which she was surprised she had noticed.

Not that she didn't appreciate an attractive man. She was a woman, after all, with a healthy curiosity about the opposite sex. Still, considering the circumstances, she was dismayed by the nature of her interest in Josh.

Her face felt hot. Her chest had constricted so that she could hardly draw a breath. Her footsteps lagged, and when she arrived at the house, second thoughts made her stop to see if Josh had put on the poncho.

When she saw that he had, her relief was overwhelming.

Wondering if she had judged him too harshly, she lingered on the porch to watch him sprint from one dying beacon to the other. For a while it seemed his persistence might be rewarded. Only gradually, as the sprinkling of rain became a downpour, did the fires smolder and drown.

But even when the last flame had flickered out, Josh remained undefeated.

He stood at the end of the bluff, etched in proud silhouette against the sky, looking at the sea as if he had every expectation that a ship would sail out of the blue at any moment, with the express purpose of rescuing them.

His obstinacy was maddening. It was also endearing. He was like a young boy, a romantic in cynic's clothing, believing in the impossible, dreaming impossible dreams—and sometimes making those dreams a reality.

He'd done that with the agency. He and Walt.

And now that Walt was dead, Josh was determined to repeat the accomplishment by establishing a retreat on Half-Moon Island.

"I want to get back to basics," he had confided in the anonymous predawn darkness. "No telephones. No TV. In fact, the fewer frills the better. Just a camp where men like Walt can live in harmony with nature, and learn firsthand that there is life after retirement."

"But according to the newspapers, your assistant referred to the project as an executive theme park," she replied.

"Which just goes to show you, you can't believe everything you read in the paper," said Josh.

"Are you saying she was misquoted?"

"No, but the quote was taken out of context, and it grossly misrepresents my plans. So far, the only thing the media's gotten right is that I'm targeting a specific market—burned-out M.B.A.'s. We'll have a lodge with a kitchen and dining hall, and rooms where groups can meet for bull sessions, but the guest cabins will be small, scattered through the woods for privacy, and fairly rustic."

"If what you say is true, why would the reporter write something so misleading?"

"Controversy sells paper," said Josh. "Believe me, Libby, I have no intention of building an elaborate resort. I don't want to turn Half-Moon into another Atlantic City, and I'm sure as hell not going to develop some macho Disneyland. Why would I want to exploit the island? I want it to be a refuge!"

"I believe you," she'd said, and Josh had smiled mockingly, not at all appeased.

"Better late than never, I suppose."

His response made her feel about two inches tall and more than a little defensive, but she hadn't let herself succumb to exasperation.

"I don't blame you for being bitter," she'd said. "I made a mistake and I'm sorry. When we get back, I'll talk to Margaret Ogilvie. I'll intercede in your behalf. Somehow, I'll make it up to you."

"Damned right you will, and it's going to take something more substantial than talk."

"Name your price. Tell me what you want from me."

The insolent way Josh looked her over, the way he seemed to sum her up, made her feel naked and exposed, aware of her inadequacies and intensely aware of him.

"I don't know," he answered slowly. "I haven't decided yet. But I can tell you this much. Whatever my price is, it's going to make being shipwrecked look like a Sunday school picnic."

She had turned the other cheek and Josh had slapped it. The battle lines were drawn. His camaraderie of the night had led her into hazardous territory. Only the need to preserve her dignity had kept her from making a hasty retreat to the keeper's house.

Dignity and fear of the ghost.

There, thought Libby. *I've admitted it.*

And having confessed her apprehension, she realized how senseless it was.

It's one thing to speculate about whether ghosts exist, she told herself. But when you begin to think you've seen one, when you start acting as if they're *real,* when you're so sleepy you can't think straight but your imagination gets the better of you and you seek the company of a man who treats you like the enemy instead of spending a peaceful night alone, that's crazy.

Crazy or not, however, she had seen *something* yesterday morning—a nightmare figure almost like a scarecrow. Perhaps it was only an animal or the shadow of a low-hanging cloud, but it took all the courage she could muster to open the door and walk into the house.

She did it because she had to; because she needed to prove that her fears were groundless. But once inside, she could not make herself close the door.

"There's nothing to be afraid of," she murmured. "You're safer in here than you would be with Josh."

The quaver in her voice was hardly reassuring. Her footsteps echoed along the murky length of the hall. A cobweb brushed her cheek, and her heart leaped into her throat. She hesitated, not entirely convinced there was no need to panic.

"Come into my parlor, said the spider to the fly."

The instant the words were out, Libby wished them unspoken, and the instant she entered the parlor, she wished she had waited for Josh.

The fire had gone out, and the room was like an icebox. But otherwise nothing seemed to have changed.

Their belongings were where they had left them. The pine-bough pallets were undisturbed. But despite benign appearances, Libby sensed something was wrong.

She inhaled, scenting the air. Beneath the blend of wood smoke and pine she detected another, more pungent odor.

She sniffed again and identified the smell.

Menthol! The place fairly reeked of it.

Someone had been there during the night.

ALTHOUGH HE KEPT his back to the house, Josh knew to the minute when Libby went inside. He stared at the ocean, counting off seconds until another five minutes had elapsed.

The rain was turning to sleet, and his mood was bleak as the weather when he finally left the bluff. The poncho leaked like a sieve, and he'd lost all sensation in his fingers and toes, but he guessed he had shown Libby a thing or two.

After he'd spent the night freezing his backside gathering driftwood, doing his damnedest to get them off this rock, she had the nerve to call him perverse.

Him! Josh Noon! The best-natured, most compatible, most reasonable of men.

Well, he wouldn't let her get away with it. If she thought he was perverse, he'd give her grounds for comparison.

"Might as well have the game as the name," he muttered.

Head down, fists jammed into his pockets, he traversed the bluff in long, indignant strides, kicking at any unfortunate tufts of grass that happened to cross his path.

He wasn't aware that Libby had left the house until she ran into him full tilt.

The force of the impact caught him unprepared. Her head bumped his chin and he staggered backward, off balance. His arms closed about her automatically, and hers found a stranglehold around his neck. She burrowed into his chest as if she were seeking a hiding place and clung to him, gasping and incoherent, while he tried to wrestle free of her grasp.

"Watch it!" he growled. "You're choking me."

She sobbed his name. A shudder passed through her, and when he got a look at her face, his irritation vanished. He drew her close again.

Her heart was racing like a wild thing. He could feel it fluttering against his ribs.

"Easy, Libby. Take it easy."

He ran his hands along her spine and stroked the nape of her neck, calming her with his touch, and just when he thought he had the situation under control, she started babbling about the ghost.

"Slow down," he said. "You're talking nonsense."

"I'm not!" she cried. "I'm telling you, Josh, we're not alone here. If you won't take my word for it, I've got evidence."

"What evidence?"

"Come with me and I'll show you."

Libby tugged at his arm, dragging him toward the house. He followed, unsure what to expect.

Either she was mentally incompetent or the consummate actress. If he was swayed by her performance, if he believed she'd come unhinged, she would avoid prosecution for kidnapping. How could he press charges if she didn't have all her marbles?

Although his guess was that she was faking, to be on the safe side he had to consider the alternative, and if her fear was genuine, she might have imagined any number of ghostly manifestations. Maybe she'd heard the rain on the roof and thought it was the rattling of chains, or she could think she'd seen a winding sheet or globs of ectoplasm.

One thing was certain. If she was hysterical, he'd have a devil of a time talking her out of her delusions.

The possibility that Libby might be telling the truth never occurred to Josh until she towed him into the parlor. He noticed the odor immediately and hauled her to a stop.

"What's that smell? It reminds me of the stuff my mom used to rub on my chest—"

"Vick's Vap-o-rub," said Libby. "*Now* do you believe me?"

Josh's expression brightened as he looked about the room. This was beginning to get interesting! "We've had a visitor, all right, but it wasn't any ghost."

"You're forgetting I saw it!"

"You saw a person, Libby. Ghosts don't get head colds."

Libby paled. Her nails dug into his forearm. "But that means—"

Josh nodded. "It means our intruder's very much alive."

CALEB SPENT MOST of Monday night on a long-distance phone call to Boston, reporting the sequence of the day's events to his brother Adam, whose reaction was similar to his own.

"Libby did *what*?" he bellowed.

Caleb had to repeat the whole story before it began to sink in, but he certainly couldn't blame Adam for finding it hard to accept that Libby could be involved in anything shady. He could scarcely believe it himself.

Libby played by the rules. She had never given their parents a minute's worry. Even as a preschooler, coloring in her coloring book, she'd stayed within the lines. She revered order and hated dissension. In family squabbles she was the peacemaker, the referee.

So even though the Gillette woman had identified Libby's photograph, Caleb couldn't imagine his conscientious kid sister doing anything that was not strictly on the up-and-up.

If Libby had taken his boat and picked up a total stranger—and as he reluctantly told Adam, it was beginning to look as if she had—she must have had a reason.

Caleb wished he could figure it out, especially with Adam bombarding him with questions. He replied as well as he could, but more often than not he didn't have the answers, and after a long, grueling conversation, he attempted to put an end to the third degree.

"Listen, Adam," he said, "I know you're worried, and I give you my word, you'll be the first to know when we learn anything definite, but you've gotta understand, we just discovered Libby's missin' this morning."

"And you have to understand that I don't like cooling my heels, waiting for information to surface."

"Can't say I blame you," Caleb replied quietly. "All I can tell you is Dan's got his men workin' overtime, checkin' out leads, and Commander MacAuley of the coast guard's handlin' the search—"

"Dammit, Cal! Libby's my *sister*. I can't just sit around and do nothing. Can you think of one good reason why I shouldn't get on a plane and come up there?"

Caleb had to admit he couldn't; not off the top of his head. "What time will you be gettin' in?"

"Don't bother meeting me at the airport," said Adam. "We've already wasted too much time."

Caleb sensed a set of instructions coming on and reached for a pencil and notepad. There had been a time, not so very long ago, when he would have resented Adam's take-charge attitude, but in the heat of crisis, his older brother's habit of playing quarterback gave him consolation.

"What do you have in mind?" he asked.

"We'll organize our own search, Cal. You and me and whoever else we can round up."

We meaning me, thought Caleb. "I was about to call Ben. He'll want in on this."

Adam agreed and rattled off the names of uncles and cousins and more distant relatives who might volunteer to join the search. "How about that friend of yours? The one with all the lobster boats?"

"Jacques Dubois," said Caleb, scrawling the name on his list. "Anyone else?"

"No, that ought to give us a start." Adam heaved a sigh, then added, "There's one more thing I'd like you to do, though."

"Yes, what is it?"

"Find out everything you can about Libby's passenger."

"Josh Noon?"

"Right," said Adam. "It'd be helpful to know what Libby was up to—why she did this. And if the answer doesn't lie with her, it must have something to do with him."

THE STORY of Libby's disappearance made the front page of Tuesday's paper, sandwiched between features on the high school debating team and Dexter Thurmond's prize-winning squash. Caleb read the article over breakfast, scowling at its emphasis on Josh Noon. His scowl solidified as he studied the file photo that accompanied the article.

Noon looked like a world-class charmer. The kind women fell for. The kind who boasted about his conquests in the locker room. The kind Caleb might pal around with, whose way with the ladies he might secretly envy, but not the sort he'd introduce to his kid sister. And, generally speaking, not the sort who appealed to Libby.

She usually went out with eggheads; guys who read Homer and wrote scholarly essays and used lots of syllables when one would do.

Rightly or wrongly, in recent years Caleb had dismissed the men she dated as wimps. He couldn't fathom what Libby saw in them, but so long as they posed no threat to her virtue, he didn't lose any sleep over her association with them.

But an operator like Noon was a different matter. The thought of the liberties he might take, stranded with Libby on the open Atlantic, took away Cal's appetite.

Poking his forefinger at Noon's picture, he growled, "You better not lay a finger on my sister, hotshot. Not if you know what's good for you. If I ever find out you touched her, so help me, I'll tear you limb from limb."

AFTER THE NIGHT on the bluffs and her discovery of the trespasser, Libby was sleeping.

Josh was tired, too. He slumped against the mantel, chin in hand, trying to slow the racing thoughts that buzzed through his head.

His gaze wandered over the graceful line of Libby's body from thigh to waist to shoulder, and she stirred, lifting one hand to her face in unconscious defiance, as if even in slumber she were shielding herself from his scrutiny.

He saw that she was shivering, and bent down to tuck the sleeping bag around her. She whimpered and, without opening her eyes, tried to sit up.

"There, there now. You're safe, Libby. Everything's all right. It's just a bad dream."

The sound of his voice seemed to soothe her, and he wrapped his arms around her and rocked gently from side to side, whispering assurances that they were alone in the house, that he'd made a thorough search and the intruder was gone, cradling her close until she stopped struggling and relaxed against his chest.

Her response made him feel possessive, but much as he wanted to go on holding her, something made him release her.

She murmured a protest, reaching out for him, then subsided onto the pine boughs, and as she nestled into the tunnel of warmth beneath the sleeping bag, he leaned over her, taut with awareness.

He studied her face—the winging brows and long silky lashes, the vulnerable mouth and fine cheekbones—surprised that she seemed so fragile.

Awake she was spirited and scrappy. When the going got tough, she got tougher. Instead of complaining, she pitched in and worked all the harder. But at no small cost to herself.

She's lost weight, he thought. *She's living on her re-serves. Both of us are. If we don't get help, how much longer can we last on short rations, with winter coming, with no possibility of rescue? Two weeks? Three? A month?*

"Stop it!" Josh told himself. "You're not beaten yet."

Time was the enemy, and hunger and cold, but the great-est enemy of all was a defeatist attitude. If either he or Libby gave up hope, they might as well throw in their chips and be done with it.

A blast of wind savaged the house, sending billows of smoke down the chimney. A loose shingle flapped against the roof, and a sudden sense of desperation propelled Josh to his feet and along the hall to the front porch.

By now it was obvious, even to him, that unless a ship was directly offshore, the signal fires were about as effective as a message in a bottle. He had to find another escape hatch. But in the meantime, others had survived on Sagamore. The Indians Libby had told him about. The lighthouse keepers. And, of course, their mysterious visitor.

At first he hadn't understood why Libby was less horri-fied by the legendary ghost than she was by the knowledge that another human being was on the island. He'd been in favor of tracking down the intruder, even if they had to search the entire island, but Libby had argued against it.

"Don't do anything rash," she'd pleaded. "If you have to conduct a manhunt, take some time to think it through."

"What's to think about?" he'd demanded. "We find our visitor and tell him, next time he brings the welcome wagon around, he ought to call first, to make sure we'll be home."

"Be serious, Josh. What kind of person could see what we're going through and not offer help? What kind of per-son would stay out of sight, keep us under surveillance, snoop through our things?"

"Five to one it's not Michael Jackson, but he could be a hermit or maybe a survivalist."

"But what if he's hiding out here? What if he sees us as a threat?"

He'd grinned indulgently. "C'mon, Libby. A person would have to be paranoid to see us as a threat."

"Exactly," she'd said. "And that's what scares me."

Josh had to concede she had a point. He had agreed to restrict his search to the house, at least until the weather cleared.

And now, as he stood sentry duty on the porch, he admitted that anyone who'd choose to live on Sagamore must be off his rocker. But while Libby found that frightening, he found it heartening.

If some poor lunatic can survive on the island, so can we, he thought.

What was more, this lunatic had a head cold, which he couldn't have caught without fairly recent contact with the outside world—

"Good Lord! How could I have overlooked that? Either our visitor's been entertaining company, or he's been off the island."

Josh bounded off the porch. A few long strides carried him to the center of the dooryard. "Are you out there?" he shouted toward the woods. Then, cupping his hands to his mouth, he angled toward the bluffs. "Can you hear me?"

He turned again, surveying the granite ridge that divided the clearing from the southern end of the island.

"Wherever you are—*whoever* you are—we don't mean you any harm." Almost as an afterthought he added, "We sure could use your help."

He lowered his hands, glancing warily from ridge to bluff to woods, but even while he waited for a reply, part of him prayed no one had seen him.

He felt like an idiot hailing the trees, negotiating with the overcast sky.

"That's all I wanted to say," Josh mumbled. And pivoting on his heel, he hurried back to the porch.

IT WAS ALMOST TEN O'CLOCK before Caleb finished contacting everyone on his list, but even though he'd gotten a late start, he stopped by the police station on his way to work that morning. He wanted to talk to Dan, find out how the investigation was going, and report his own progress.

When he walked into the squad room, Dan was feeding coins to one of the vending machines.

"Any news?" he inquired.

"Some." Dan pocketed his change and collected the two cups of coffee he'd purchased. "Come on back, Cal. There's some folks in my office I'd like you to meet."

The folks turned out to be female. One, a brunette in her late twenties, would have been attractive had she been less uptight. She was perched on the edge of her chair, and when she accepted the cup Dan offered, her hand was shaking so badly that she spilled coffee onto her skirt.

She stared at the spreading stain, at a loss, until Dan removed the cup from her hand and replaced it with his handkerchief.

"There you are, ma'am. That must be hot."

She answered with a nervous bob of her head, dabbing at the stain, while Daniel hovered over her solicitously.

"There's a ladies' room just down the corridor, if you'd like to sponge that," he said.

"No, thank you. This'll be fine."

"Well then, Mrs. Gillette, I'd like to introduce you to my brother Caleb."

After an absent smile at Cal, Sally Gillette continued scrubbing at the coffee stain and Caleb's attention shifted to his brother's other guest.

This aristocratic matron occupied her chair as if it were a throne and extended her hand to Caleb as if she were conferring knighthood on him.

He bowed from the waist and kissed the air above her fingertips, then spoiled the effect by winking at her. "Nice to see you again, Maggie."

"Indeed," Margaret Ogilvie answered in a cool contralto. "But I must say I'm sorry the circumstances aren't more pleasant."

"As I recall, the circumstances weren't much better the last time we met."

Daniel cleared his throat. "You two know each other?"

"In a manner of speaking." Margaret fumbled with the strand of pearls that was draped across her impressive bosom, and Caleb sat on the corner of his brother's desk, relishing the spectacle of her discomfiture.

"Maggie and some of her activist friends picketed Wilderness Guides when we had the scrimshaw exhibit. They damn near put us out of business."

A tide of color washed over Margaret's face. The pearls went clickety-clack. "I have nothing against you personally, Mr. Pilgrim. I was merely doing my bit to save the whales."

"A worthy cause," said Daniel.

Sally stopped dabbing at the coffee stain. "It would appear Ms. Ogilvie is full of worthy causes."

Caleb grinned. "Whatever she's savin' this time, I'll bet it's not oysters."

Margaret let go of the pearls; her hands fluttered to her lap. "You'd win," she declared, meeting Caleb's gaze.

"This time I was trying to save DEEPC. We've had a decline in membership, and I—"

"Hold on a minute, ma'am," Daniel broke in. "Do you object to Caleb's bein' here?"

"Of course I object! I wish none of us had to be here. I regret this whole thing. But if you're asking if I want your brother to leave, the answer's no. He has a right to hear my statement. So, Chief Pilgrim, whenever you'd care to call in a stenographer—"

"All in good time, ma'am. Let's not get ahead of ourselves. I get the impression you intend to repeat the story you told Mrs. Gillette, so before you say anything more, there's a little formality I've got to attend to."

Margaret folded her hands, then unfolded them. She smoothed her skirt across her knees while Daniel fished a dog-eared card from his wallet.

"Now then, Ms. Ogilvie," he continued, reading from the card, "You have the right to remain silent—"

Caleb's jaw dropped. "Holy Miranda!"

Dan glared at him, annoyed by the interruption, but Margaret Ogilvie seemed unoffended. She inclined her head, her bearing more regal than ever, and said, "Right again, Mr. Pilgrim."

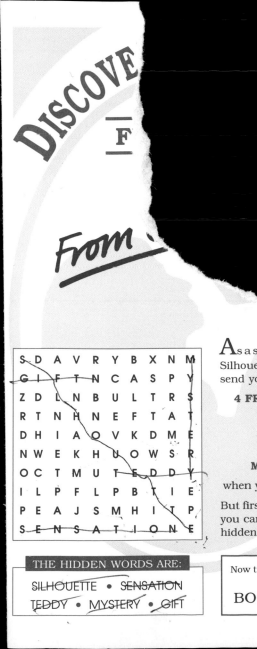

DISCOVE

F

From

As a s

Silhoue

send yo

4 FR

M

when y

But firs

you can

hidden

S	D	A	V	R	Y	B	X	N	M
G	I	F	T	N	C	A	S	P	Y
Z	D	L	N	B	U	L	T	R	S
R	T	N	H	N	E	F	T	A	T
D	H	I	A	O	V	K	D	M	E
N	W	E	K	H	U	O	W	S	R
O	C	T	M	U	T	E	D	D	Y
I	L	P	F	L	P	B	T	I	E
P	E	A	J	S	M	H	I	T	P
S	E	N	S	A	T	I	O	N	E

Now t

BO

THE HIDDEN WORDS ARE:

SILHOUETTE • SENSATION
TEDDY • MYSTERY • GIFT

superb Sensations every month for just £6.00, post and packing FREE. If I decide not to subscribe I shall write to you within 10 days. The FREE books and gifts will be mine to keep in any case. I understand that I am under no obligation whatsoever - I can cancel or suspend my subscription at any time simply by writing to you.

FREE TEDDY

MYSTERY GIFT

Mr/Mrs/Miss _____ 6SOSS
(Please write in block capitals)

Address _____

_____ Postcode _____

Signature _____
I am over the age of 18.

MAILING
PREFERENCE
SERVICE

Chapter Ten

During a lull in the storm that afternoon, Josh hiked down the bluff to the shore. The descent was hazardous, the trail steep and icy underfoot, but he welcomed the challenge.

It was better than doing nothing, he thought. Better than prowling about the house, craving a cigarette, listening to Libby's even breathing and wishing he could fall asleep. Better then counting the seconds, waiting for the weather to clear. Better than boredom—

"Hell, yes! Anything's better than that."

His gruff exclamation startled a gull into flight. It sprang from the underbrush mere inches away from his feet in a rush of feathers and fury, and only his quick grab for a nearby sapling prevented a nasty fall.

He proceeded more cautiously after that, picking his way along the face of the bluff with newfound respect for the terrain. As he was crossing the jumble of boulders that marked the high-water line, he came upon a hollow in the stone and stopped to look at a colony of starfish that was trapped in the tidal basin.

The surf washed in, and when it retreated, a dozen tiny saltwater snails were scattered among the starfish. He dodged another wave, and when it withdrew he saw that one indigo periwinkle had been added to the population of the pool.

He waited for a third wave, and a fourth, and a fifth, fascinated by the microcosm of marine life he had discovered. With each advance, the ocean left another deposit in the pool. A jellyfish. A clam shell. A smooth white pebble. An oval of polished driftwood, lustrous as topaz.

Josh watched, aware that he was witnessing the creation of something unique. Something no one had ever seen before. Something no one else would ever see. And although the experience was exhilarating, he knew that he would savor it more if Libby were there to share it with him.

Despite the loneliness, however, he stayed by the pool until the tide ebbed and the sediment in the basin settled, and when the water became tranquil and clear, he felt as if he were peering through a window into a shining undersea world.

Impulse made him push back his sleeve and plunge his hand into the pool. He wanted to touch one of the anemones that blossomed at the bottom, lavender and white and pink, but at the approach of his fingers, its fronds folded shut.

He dropped to his knees, filled with a sense of wonder that such a simple organism could be showy as a dahlia one moment and masquerade as a mushroom the next.

That evening after supper he told Libby about the tide pool. They sat on the hearth with the fire warming their backs, tearing the Classified section from one of the old newspapers into rectangles the size of playing cards, while he summed up his reaction.

"People could learn a lot from anemones," he said. "If I were that adaptable, being stranded on Sagamore would seem relatively minor. The sky would be the limit. There'd be nothing I couldn't accomplish, no hardship I couldn't overcome."

"Don't underestimate yourself, Josh. You're more adaptable than the anemone. In fact, you're probably much more adaptable than you realize."

Libby's reply sounded flippant, as if she were trying not to laugh, and keeping a wary eye on her, Josh uncapped his pen and began marking a stack of rectangles as clubs and spades.

"You could be right," he allowed. "I know, when I was a kid, I took change in stride."

Libby gave him the last of the diamonds and hearts and, after shuffling these suits into the pack, he began dealing out the cards. She picked hers up one by one and made a neat fan of them in her hand.

"If you could adjust to change then, you can do it now," she said. "It's not an ability you lose."

"You might not lose it, but you sure can forget how to use it."

He put the undealt cards on the hearth between them and turned the topmost one faceup. After a glance at it, Libby drew from the stack.

"I don't see how a person can forget an ability," she said.

"It happens. Take it from me. That's one of the prices we pay for progress. We get so accustomed to changing our environment to fit our needs, we begin to think life's not worth living without ConEd and AT&T and IBM and CBS—"

"Not in Maine, we don't."

Libby punctuated her comment by dropping the ace of spades onto the discard pile, and after an extravagant double take, Josh picked it up and made his own discard.

"Don't tell me you don't miss certain conveniences, Libby. For example, if you had the chance to take a nice hot shower, would you turn it down?"

"Naturally I wouldn't, but I've never felt as excited about a shower as I was the other night when we found the spring. I can indulge myself and still make the distinction between the necessity of water and the luxury of heating it."

"Well, what if a delivery man brought a pizza to the door?"

"I'd take it, and I'd enjoy it while it lasted, but I wouldn't lose sight of fundamentals. That's what a group like DEEPC's all about. It reminds people how dependent they are on the environment."

Libby drew from the deck and selected her discard—the three of spades. Josh was hard-pressed not to smile as he picked it up, but somehow he maintained his poker face even when she knitted her brows, considering the queen of diamonds he discarded.

This hand's in the bag, he told himself. A couple more rounds ought to do it! He angled toward the firelight and pretended to rearrange his cards, the picture of nonchalance as he said, "There's a difference between knowing you're dependent and feeling it in your gut. Until you feel it, you can't really appreciate the downside to technology."

Josh paused to watch Libby draw. Her frown inspired him to embellish his argument.

"We have cars, but we also have smog. We have telephones, and less privacy. We have satellite dishes that permit our television sets to receive a hundred and four channels, but we've forfeited the ability to be good neighbors. We have fine modern cities, and crime—"

Libby's nod cut him off in midsentence. He wondered if she had taken his reference to crime personally, until he saw that she was spreading her cards on the hearth.

"Gin," she said, in the friendliest possible tone.

He studied the cards, bemused. "Yep, that's gin, all right," he admitted, throwing in his own hand.

"Don't you want to tally the points?"

"What's your hurry. I thought we agreed we'd play for fun till you're comfortable with the strategy."

Libby's smile was serene and confident. "I think I've got the hang of it."

"To be completely fair, I should advise you to be more careful with your discards."

"Thank you, Josh. I will."

"This game can get really cutthroat," he persisted.

She shrugged off his warning. "We're only playing for a penny a point."

"But with bonuses and doubles, you'd be surprised how fast the points can add up. I wouldn't want you to get in over your head."

Libby began mixing the cards together. "It's nice of you to worry about me, Josh, but I assure you, I can take care of myself. Why don't we try a few hands? If the stakes get too high for either of us, we can stop keeping score."

Josh sat up straight and squared his shoulders. His eyes narrowed to slits. "What do you mean, for either of us?"

"Hasn't it occurred to you I might win?"

He stared at her, too indignant to answer.

Advertising was his life and success his mistress. But gin rummy was his passion!

His devotion to the game had begun when he was a kid and outlasted all his girlfriends and one or two significant affairs.

He loved everything about gin; its fast pace and simple rules, its subtle rituals and moments of suspense. He loved the impartiality of the cards. And over the years he had honed his skills at keeping track of the discards and calculating which cards were deadwood and whether it would be more profitable to knock or go for the shutout.

He played with a flair few opponents could equal and almost none could surpass. Yet Libby, a rank amateur, had the gall to presume she might beat him.

Not a chance! he thought. Not if I have anything to say about it.

The first hand had been an aberration. He'd been distracted by the conversation. She'd had the luck of the draw. But in the long run fortune favored the expert, and he wouldn't let himself be diverted again. From now on he'd give the game his undivided attention.

"Deal the cards," he told Libby, "and then you'd better hang onto your hat. It's going to be a bumpy night."

As it turned out, Josh was right. The night was extremely bumpy—for him.

Libby's grasp of the game was shaky, her style of play erratic, but she kept him guessing, off balance, unable to predict what she might do. She had a tendency to hoard face cards, but whenever he tried to capitalize on it, he found himself undercut.

At the end of the first game he owed her two dollars and thirty-two cents. The final score of the second was even more lopsided, and the third game came as close to a whitewash as he ever hoped to play.

"Are you sure you never played gin before?" he asked.

Libby insisted she hadn't.

"Then how do you explain your wins?"

"Beginner's luck," she replied.

He shook his head. "Beginner's luck might account for one game. Three would be incredible."

"But, Josh," she said softly, "you have to keep in mind I've had an excellent teacher."

As if to prove how good a teacher he was, she went gin the next two hands. And to add insult to injury, she started making excuses for him.

"It's late," she said. "You must be tired."

"Do I look tired?" he snapped.

Libby moistened her lips; her slight hesitation told him he looked churlish and intimidating. "Not at all. It's just that neither of us slept much last night. Maybe we ought to turn in."

She was so damned gracious, it was humiliating. "Very well, Libby. If you've had enough, we'll call it quits, but at least give me a chance to get even."

"Get even? How?"

"Let's play one last hand and up the ante. Make it double or nothing."

"No, Josh, I'd rather not."

"What's wrong? Afraid of losing?"

"Quite the contrary. I'm afraid of winning."

Libby replied in a small clear voice, and before Josh could think of a clever comeback, she rose and disappeared behind the privacy screen she had erected.

Dammit, she got to him, with her stiff-necked manner and touch-me-not-air. Nothing seemed to faze her. Not for long. And nothing seemed to crack her cool puritan reserve. The more he tried to impress her, the more awkward he felt—like a schoolboy showing off.

So why did he bother? If pride was her be-all and end-all, it was no skin off his nose. He'd tried threats of reprisals and demonstrations of courage and physical prowess. He'd talked himself blue in the face. He had *confided* in her, practically bared his soul, and she had yet to share one secret.

He had tried every approach he could think of to get her to open up with him. Well, almost every approach—

Josh's expression brightened as he gathered up the cards. He was totaling Libby's winnings when she reappeared, bundled into her sweater and poncho.

"Going somewhere?" he inquired.

"To bed," she said.

"Why the getup?"

"It's your turn to use the sleeping bag."

"Right," he said. "It's going to be a long, cold night."

Without looking in his direction, she lay down on her pallet and tucked the spare survival blanket around her.

He put the cards on the shelf for safekeeping, and yawning prodigiously, crawled into the sleeping bag. "In case you're interested, I owe you seven dollars and eighty-nine cents."

The pine boughs rustled as Libby turned her back on him. "Keep it."

He chuckled and swung his feet toward the hearth, wiggling his toes for warmth. "I imagine it gave you a great deal of pleasure to tell me that."

"About as much pleasure as it gave you to tell me how cold it's going to be tonight."

Josh didn't deny it. He yawned again and folded his hands behind his head, contemplating the patterns the firelight cast on the ceiling. "Seven dollars and eighty-nine cents won't buy much these days. You could go to the movies, maybe take a friend to the early show. Buy a bucket of popcorn and a couple of Cokes and—"

Libby flung back the blanket and sat up. "All right, Josh. You've got my attention. If you have a point to make, for heaven's sake make it so both of us can get some sleep."

"I just wanted to say, it seems a shame to let such a small amount of money come between us, especially on such a cold night."

"Money isn't the issue, Josh, and you know it."

"Well, whatever the issue, you're still way over there, away from the fire, with nothing but that thin little blanket to keep you warm. And here I am with the fire and the sleeping bag, but my conscience'll keep me awake. If we pooled our resources, we'd both be comfortable and I'd be able to sleep."

"Are you finished?" asked Libby.

"That's it—except I hope you understand I'm suggesting you join me for practical reasons. I promise you, I won't make any passes. It'd be strictly platonic."

Libby lay back down.

"Is that your answer?"

The pine boughs rustled as she flopped onto her stomach.

Josh zipped himself into the sleeping bag, conceding the game, set and match to her. But unless he missed his guess, before morning her victory would be cold comfort.

Oddly enough, this thought did not give him much satisfaction.

His feet were warm, and he swung them back onto the pallet, then stretched out his legs and sighed with exaggerated bliss. "'Night, Libby," he said. "If you change your mind, you know where to find me."

A PINECONE WAS DIGGING into her back, just beneath her left shoulder blade. Careful not to make a sound that would alert Josh to her predicament, Libby changed positions, searching for a smooth spot on the pallet. It seemed to take forever, but at last she found one. She was about to doze off when she became aware of the icy draft curling under the blanket, creeping along her spine.

She anchored one edge of the blanket beneath her hip and shifted this way and that, trying to form a seal against the cold. If the filmy synthetic fabric had been a foot or so wider and a few inches longer, she might have succeeded, but as it was, when she pulled the binding up to her chin, her feet stuck out, and when she covered her feet, the binding reached only to midchest.

She propped herself on one elbow and turned the blanket so that it lay on the diagonal, then slid down slowly until the envelope of fabric swathed her from head to toe. She lay immobile, without so much as a shiver. Minutes later she began to feel a tantalizing buildup of warmth, but she also felt the pinecone cutting into the same spot on her back.

For a while she lay still, but the more she tried to ignore the sharp bristles of the cone, the more they bruised her flesh. At last, resigned to going through her settling-down maneuvers all over again, she rolled onto her side and gazed longingly toward Josh.

He seemed to be sleeping, warmed by the embers on the hearth, and she stared at him, wondering if she had been too hasty about declining his invitation to share his pallet.

She'd been propositioned before, but never so unromantically. In one breath Josh had asked her to sleep with him, and in the next he had sworn that sex would not enter into it. Or words to that effect.

With those mixed signals, she wasn't sure how she should react, but the more she thought about it, the colder she felt, and the colder she felt, the more she realized that sharing the sleeping bag was the sensible thing to do. And because she always made every effort to behave sensibly, she found herself on her feet, cloaked in her silver blanket, trailing across the parlor to the fireplace.

Appearances notwithstanding, Josh was not asleep. When she bent over him, he opened his eyes.

"This blanket's too small. My bed's full of pinecones."

Josh grinned and unzipped the sleeping bag. Warmth encompassed her the moment she slipped inside. With the zipper fastened and the weight of his arm a welcome burden about her middle, she curled up on her side, so that their bodies spooned together.

"What took you so long?" he asked.

"I wasn't sure how to take your offer. I couldn't decide whether I should feel flattered or rejected."

Josh rested his chin against the crown of her head. "Do you do that often?"

Her spirits fell. She needed answers, not questions. "Do what?"

"Analyze your emotions. Decide how you should feel."

"Yes, fairly often. Don't you?"

"Not if I can help it. I prefer spontaneity."

"Even in business?"

"Uh-huh. Even there."

She thought this over, tongue-tied by inhibition. Finally she replied, "I can't honestly say I prefer restraint, but sometimes feelings can be overwhelming."

Especially if they're not reciprocated.

She bit her lip. A lump of tears filled her throat, and she swallowed to dislodge it. Her voice was surprisingly steady as she added, "It may not be healthy to stay in control, but sometimes it seems—safer."

"I know it does, honey. That's why I'm doing my best not to rush things."

Relief washed over her, so intense that it was dizzying. She drew in a breath and held it while her pulse resumed its normal rhythm, then exhaled on a sigh.

"I envy you, Josh. It must be wonderful to cut loose and let your emotions be your guide."

"Beats sleeping alone."

Josh brushed kisses along the side of her neck, from the base of her throat to the hollow behind her ear. The glide of his lips was mesmerizing; the scrape of his beard sweet torment. He nuzzled her earlobe and caught it gently between his teeth. His tongue darted out to tease and taste, and sensations she had never known existed clamored through her body.

Her lips felt fuller, riper, hungry for the press of his mouth. Her breasts seemed to swell, her bones to liquefy. Desire rioted through her veins, leaving ecstasy in its wake. Her hands ached to caress Josh, her arms to enfold him; deep in her womb something melted and yearned for him. But gradually, inevitably, the import of his last remark sank in.

Beats sleeping alone, he'd said.

"What about Blair?"

Libby barely breathed the words, but from Josh's response, she might have screamed them. He bolted to a sitting position, dragging Libby, the sleeping bag and a half a dozen pine boughs with him.

"What about her?" he demanded.

"Well, you seem awfully fond of her."

"She's my best friend's widow. Is there any reason I shouldn't be fond of her?"

"No, but I thought—that is, I wondered—"

Josh was tugging at the zipper on the sleeping bag. It snagged a third of the way down its track, and he muttered an oath as he squeezed through the opening. Arms akimbo, feet planted wide apart, he stood glaring down at her.

"For cryin' out loud, Libby! I know what you're wondering. It's obvious what you think. What I can't figure out is what gave you the notion that you have any right to question my relationship to Blair."

"Maybe it's because I care about you, Josh. More than I should. More than I want to."

His expression softened. "But you don't trust me."

"How can I trust you, when I don't understand you? One minute you're encouraging me to express my feelings, the next, you're yelling at me because I do, and you don't happen to approve of them."

"Whoa, there. I must have missed something. This is the first I've heard about feelings."

Libby shook her head miserably. "You might have heard it sooner if you'd stop talking and listen once in a while."

Josh dropped to one knee, hands clasped to his heart. "Forgive me, Ms. Pilgrim. A thousand, thousand pardons. I should be horsewhipped, tarred and feathered. My American Express card should be revoked. I'm the world's worst blabbermouth, unworthy to kiss your deck boots—"

"You also like to exaggerate."

"You can't fault me for that. It's my bread and butter. But I am a rotten sport."

"Only when you lose at gin."

Josh sobered. "Seriously, Libby, I'm sorry I came on too strong. I've been an insensitive clod. Overbearing, arrogant—I don't know what gets into me sometimes."

He looked so sheepish, she couldn't help smiling. "So tell me, Mr. Noon, with all your many flaws, why do I enjoy your company so much?"

"Well, nobody's perfect."

A hint of sadness clouded her smile. "That certainly includes me, Josh. Look what I've gotten us into."

"Don't blame yourself, honey. It's not as if you planned this."

"But I'm responsible!" She averted her gaze, fumbling with the end of her braid. "If I'd minded my own business, you'd be at the Windlass, out of danger—"

"And we might never have met. Do you think I'd give that up for anything?"

She shrank into the sleeping bag, mute with anguish.

"Well, do you?"

When she looked at Josh, the anxiety receded, sharpened, came into focus. "If anything happens to you—" She faltered into silence, reaching out for him, and he swept her into his arms.

"Hush, now. Nothing's going to happen to either of us. I won't let it."

"But what if we're never rescued?"

"Don't say that, Libby. Don't even think it. One way or another, we're going to be rescued. The coast guard must be searching for us by now, and tomorrow I'll hunt for our visitor. We'll keep the signal fires ready in case a plane flies over or a boat sails by, and before you know it, we'll be safe on the mainland and the shipwreck will seem like a bad dream."

She touched his cheek for reassurance. "What'll happen then, Josh? Will we see each other again?"

"As often as we can. I'd like to take you out to dinner—"

"I'd like that too, but where will we go?"

He rubbed his chin against her temple. "Someplace where the lights are low, the music's sweet, and the food's delicious. And afterward we'll go to the movies and sit in the balcony and neck. And after that we'll go dancing—"

She traced the outline of his mouth, and he kissed her fingertips. "That'd be lovely, Josh, only I never learned to dance."

"That's no problem. I'll teach you. I want to teach you lots of things—"

"The way you taught me gin?"

"What do you think?" His embrace tightened. "Have we got a date?"

She nodded. "It's a date."

A minute passed while Josh held her painfully, exquisitely close. And then he framed her face between his palms and kissed her, tenderly at first, exploring her mouth as if he would never know enough of her; then deeply, passionately, as if he were infusing her with his strength.

By the time the kiss ended, she almost believed they had a future.

Chapter Eleven

The days settled into a routine of sorts, bounded by dawn and dusk. Every morning Josh checked the signal fires, then went off to scour the island, determined to run their visitor to earth. And every evening he reported that once again the unseen occupant of Sagamore had eluded him.

In the course of his search he usually found something to supplement their diet—hazelnuts one day, wild onions the next, the day after that a variety of edible seaweed. It wasn't much, but every little bit helped, so his efforts were not a total loss.

For her part, Libby spent the mornings fishing. In the afternoons she combed the area adjoining the lighthouse for food. Toward sunset, she replenished their pallet of pine boughs, laid a fire on the grate and did a bit of housekeeping while she waited for Josh's return

Supper was their main meal—sometimes their *only* meal—and they prepared it together, surprising each other with the delicacies they'd found. The day she perfected the crab trap, she surprised Josh with her catch, and the next day, not to be outdone, Josh came home with a flounder clutched in his hands, pursued by an outraged seagull.

Despite these rare bonanzas she was constantly hungry, and although Josh never complained, she knew he must be ravenous. When she thought about the energy they expended looking for food and how little they got in return, she wasn't sure it was worth it.

If she'd been alone, she might have given up. But Josh was there from sunset to sunrise, offering the warmth of his pallet and the solace of his arms. He gave her hope. He gave her encouragement. He gave her the will to go on, but he didn't make love to her. He had sworn he wouldn't rush things, and he seemed determined to keep to this agreement.

Libby realized she should be grateful. Josh had neatly sidestepped her questions about Blair. For all she knew they might be much more than friends brought together by tragedy.

And she herself was physically drained, emotionally vulnerable. Just making it through the day taxed her resources to the limit. She couldn't cope with more complications. The last thing she needed was an affair with a man who might very well be involved with another woman.

But some treacherous part of Libby wished that Josh were a little less honorable and a lot less determined.

Neither of them slept much. After supper Josh gave her a dancing lesson, and she taught him to tie a few basic knots, and when the lessons were over they played cards far into the night. Hearts, draw poker, two-handed pinochle—anything but gin.

Sometimes, for a change of pace, they read articles from the old newspapers or made up stories about what might be happening in the outside world.

One evening she reminded him they were missing the end of the presidential campaign. He laughed and replied, "That's one hardship I don't mind at all."

But he missed basketball and cigarettes, onion bagels and his razor. "Two days without shaving was great," he said.

"But now I'm beginning to feel like a fungus has taken root on my face."

Libby missed *thirtysomething*, hot baths, clean clothes, the daily crossword, and she admitted she was worried about her parents. "The uncertainty must be hard for Mom and Dad," she said. "If only there were some way to let them know I'm all right."

"How about your brothers?" asked Josh.

"They're probably having the time of their lives. Not that they won't be concerned about me, but I expect they're preoccupied with the search."

Like Josh, her brothers seemed to thrive on crises. She envisioned Adam issuing orders, Ben plotting strategy, and Daniel, the charming coordinator, investigating her whereabouts with the utmost diplomacy.

And Caleb wouldn't stay on the beach and let the coast guard have all the adventure. He'd beg, borrow or rent a boat and look for her himself.

IN POINT OF FACT, Caleb had done exactly what Libby imagined he would do. On Wednesday he hitched a ride on one of Jacques Dubois's lobster boats, and while the boat island-hopped on Frenchman's bay, he monitored radio messages from Daniel to the rest of the fleet. But it didn't take long before the excitement surrounding his sister's disappearance began to pall.

All day Wednesday and Thursday he told himself, "No news is good news." On Thursday afternoon the boat began the homeward leg of its voyage, and Caleb acknowledged the likelihood that no news spelled disaster.

Libby had been missing for nearly a week. The last known contact with *Pilgrim's Progress* had occurred when she'd picked up Josh Noon. Adam had recruited a small armada. Dan had followed the slimmest leads. After a thorough sweep of the waters in the vicinity of Half-Moon Island, the coast guard had widened its search. Scores of private craft were on the alert. A number of possible sightings had trickled in, but none of them panned out. And by now the trail was cold as the weather—

Caleb stayed glued to the radio while the fishing smack approached the Day's Harbor breakwater. When the lights of the village were dead ahead, he grabbed his pea coat and made his way forward.

The temperature had plummeted along with the barometer. He could see his breath. A threat of snow drifted on the breeze. He pulled on his watch cap and stood by the bowline.

A crowd had assembled on the pier. From the size of it, he knew it wasn't a welcoming committee. He spotted Dan's patrol car, and a knot of apprehension gripped the pit of his stomach.

He tossed the line and leaped onto the dock without waiting to see who caught it. Before the boat had been made fast, he plunged into the midst of the throng.

He overheard someone say, "That's one of the Pilgrim boys." The buzz of conversation rose as this information was repeated, and there was an uneasy shuffling of feet as men jumped to the side, clearing a path for him.

"Dan," he said gruffly, hurrying toward his brother. "How's it goin'?"

"Not good, Caleb. Not good a'tall. One of Dubois's crews found some wreckage a few miles north of Seal Island. They brought this back with 'em."

Silently Dan held out a jagged chunk of wood. Caleb studied it, numb inside. His heart sank when he saw traces of black lettering on the fragment. His voice sounded hollow and faraway as he said, "It's from *Pilgrim's Progress*."

Dan bowed his head. His throat worked as he swallowed. "I was afraid of that."

"Does this mean MacAuley'll call off his men?"

Dan nodded. His expression was grim, almost angry. "As of seven o'clock this evening, the official search is over."

BY FRIDAY THEY HAD USED the last of their canned goods. The gulls had gotten wise to Josh's raiding and flown off to some other island, where their catch would remain unmolested.

Libby envied them. She wished she had the ability to leave Sagamore, and when she arrived at the shore that morning and found the crab trap ruined, she despaired.

The trap was a simple thing—a square of wire mesh weighted with sinkers and reinforced with wooden laths, with loops of fishing line strung from each corner, to which she tied the rope she used for raising and lowering the trap.

Using it was simple, too. All she'd had to do was fasten bait to the screen—by trial and error, she had discovered an empty sardine can was most effective—climb out onto the rocks, drop the trap in the water, wait a half hour or so and pull the trap out.

By then the sardine odor had usually attracted at least one rock crab, occasionally as many as two or three, and as she lifted the trap, the water pressure pinned them to the screen.

The trap was just that easy—and irreplaceable.

The supply of laths was endless. She had plenty of line and rope and sinkers. But she had spent an entire day sifting through the rubble before she'd come across a piece of wire mesh big enough for the trap that wasn't rusted or full of holes. Judging from that experience, she'd never find another one. And the screen had been cut to ribbons.

Angry tears filled her eyes as she surveyed the damage.

Someone had taken great pains to make it look as if the surf had smashed the trap, but she knew better. The surf might have splintered the laths and scattered them over the rocks, but only human hands could have slashed the wire mesh so thoroughly, so maliciously.

Libby gathered up the pieces and began the long climb to the top of the bluff. When Josh returned that evening, she dumped the evidence at his feet.

"We can thank our intruder for this!" she cried.

But despite the undeniable proof that their nocturnal visitor had sabotaged the trap, Josh refused to abandon the hunt.

"We need his help," Josh argued. "Now more than ever."

"If you still think he'll help us after this, you're as crazy as he is!"

Josh regarded her coolly. "You're upset, Libby, so I'm giving you the benefit of the doubt. I'll pretend you never said that."

But the harsh words came between them. They ate the last of the crackers and drank watery cups of cocoa in strained silence. For the rest of that night Josh didn't smile at her. He didn't tease her, and even though necessity forced them to share the sleeping bag, they were careful not to touch.

Libby felt bereft. Lonely. She tried to think of something she could say, something she might do to bridge the distance between them, but since she wasn't sure how to go about it, she did nothing.

When she woke the following morning, Josh was gone. Her first thought was that he must have left for the day, without even saying goodbye. She dragged herself out of bed, more miserable then before—until she heard him running across the porch.

"Rise and shine, sleepyhead. We've got snow!"

"Perfect," she muttered. "Just what we needed."

"Get yourself out here," he called. "There's something you've got to see."

She dug her spare socks out of the duffel bag, and sat on the hearth to put them on.

"You coming out, or do I have to come in and get you?"

"Give me a minute to get myself together," she answered, wondering why Josh sounded so pleased.

She heard his impatient pacing and hastily stamped into her boots. She was only halfway into her poncho when she joined him on the porch, but he gave her barely enough time to pull the hood over her head before he grabbed her arm and dragged her toward the stairs.

"Take a look at this," he said, pointing at the parallel tracks that plowed through the two-inch snowfall, up to, then away from the house.

"Footprints," she murmured. "Are they yours?"

"Nope. Too small." Josh planted one foot next to a print, comparing the difference in sizes. "Our intruder's paid us another visit. My guess is, within the last half hour."

Libby rubbed her hand across her forehead. "He had to know he was leaving tracks."

"Yes. I suppose he must have."

"Well, why do you think he did it?"

"I don't know, Libby. I don't care. What's important is, this time he's left me a trail to follow."

"And naturally you're going to follow it."

"You bet I am."

"What if he's leading you into some kind of trap?"

"That's a chance I have to take."

"Then I'm going with you." Libby set off along the trail before Josh could object, but she didn't get far before he fell into step beside her.

"I really don't think there's much risk involved. From the depth of these prints, this guy's a bantamweight, and God knows, if he intended to harm us, he's had plenty of opportunities."

Libby scuffed a print with the toe of her boot. "Has it occurred to you he might've left the trail, hoping to separate us?"

"Sure it has, but for the life of me, I can't figure out why. We've gone our own ways the past several days, so what would be the point?"

"I couldn't begin to guess, but after what he did to the crab trap, I wouldn't put anything past him."

"Neither would I. That's why, just to be on the safe side, I'd rather you'd stay here."

Libby swung around to face him. "I'll stay if you will, Josh. The choice is up to you."

Josh frowned and smoothed a strand of hair away from her cheek. His expression grew gentle as he blended the wispy tendrils into her braid. At last he replied, "We'll stick together, then. But *I'll* take the lead."

Chapter Twelve

Libby's first trek across the island had been difficult. The second was a nightmare.

They were unencumbered by supply packs, and Josh had the trail to guide him, so they didn't have to backtrack. Her blisters had healed, her muscles didn't ache, and instead of being dazed from lack of sleep, she was wide-awake. After a week without central heating she scarcely noticed the cold. In fact, they hadn't hiked a quarter of a mile before she warmed up enough to dispense with the poncho.

But fear dogged her heels. She couldn't shake the feeling that they were walking into an ambush, and with every step they took the feeling grew.

The footprints led them through the woods, then made a slippery climb to the ridge that bisected the island. When they reached the summit, Josh paused for a backward glance at the rough terrain.

With an admiring shake of his head, he remarked, ''This guy must be part mountain goat.''

Libby nodded, too breathless to speak, and followed Josh along the ridge. The going was easier for the next half mile, and he lengthened his stride. Now and again she had to take a few skipping steps to keep up with him.

They were nearing the leeward side of the island when the prints left the ridge and wound through a stand of pines. The tracks were fainter here, partially drifted over. Before they had hiked a hundred yards into the trees, a gust of wind completely obliterated the prints.

Josh zigzagged, trying to pick up the trail, and Libby lagged some distance behind. She was praying they had reached a dead end, when suddenly he turned to her and grinned.

"I smell smoke."

She licked her lips as the wind carried a more delectable aroma her way. "Bacon!"

Josh broke into a trot, and she kept pace with him, following her nose toward the homey fragrance. Her mouth was watering and she forgot her fears, until they stepped out of the pines into the dooryard of a snug cabin.

Josh slowed to a walk, and Libby stopped at the edge of the woods when the front door opened and a woman emerged.

Dressed in well-worn slacks and a shapeless pullover, she was thin as a wraith, tough as whipcord. Her face was as seamed and stony as the granite cliffs of Sagamore.

"Took you long enough to find me," she snapped.

"You were expecting us?" said Josh.

"Why else do you think I'd blaze you a trail broad as a four-lane highway?"

A fierce glare accompanied the woman's answer. In spite of her advanced age, her appearance was so forbidding that Libby's first impulse was to turn around and run back the way she had come. But Josh, as usual, chose to take a congenial approach.

He strode toward the woman, smiling, holding out one hand. "You're the ghost of Sagamore Island, I presume. Allow me to introduce—"

"Never mind the introductions. If I can believe your driver's licenses, your name's Joshua and the scared rabbit yonder is Elizabeth."

Rankled by the woman's derisive tone, Libby moved a few feet closer. "And you are—"

"Etta Cassidy. As if you didn't know."

"We didn't," said Libby. "We thought the island was deserted."

"Well, now you've seen it isn't, what the dickens are you doing here?"

"Trying to survive," said Josh. "How about you?"

"The same."

Josh shoved his hands into his hip pockets. "From the smell of that bacon, you're surviving a lot better than we are."

"Yes, well, long as you're here, you might as well come on in and have some breakfast."

The invitation was issued with unmistakable belligerence, but pangs of hunger drove Libby onto the stoop and through a cozy pine-paneled living room into the cabin's kitchen. And once she was seated at the table with Etta and Josh, warmed by the glow of a Franklin stove and by the first decent meal she'd had since they'd left Mount Desert Island, Libby realized her fears were groundless.

Etta Cassidy was not a gracious hostess. She barked questions at them as if they were on trial and she had already found them guilty. But by the time Libby had finished hearty portions of bacon and eggs and hash browns, she began to suspect Etta's bark was worse than her bite.

There was a lull in the questions when Etta got up to refill the serving platters, but even while she urged Josh to have another rasher of bacon she asked, "What brings you to Sagamore?"

"A nor'easter," he said. "We had the option of running aground or sinking in the Atlantic—"

"You expect me to believe that?"

"Why shouldn't you believe it?" Libby replied. "You must've seen our boat go down. You were up on the bluffs watching us, the morning after we came ashore. You followed us to the lighthouse, and you've been spying on us ever since."

Etta didn't bother with denials; she simply resumed her interrogation, and if their answers were less than satisfactory, she became downright hostile. But for reasons of her own she had chosen to ply them with food, and she was a terrific cook.

"Eat up," she said, offering them a plate of cinnamon rolls. "There's plenty more where this came from."

"Oh? Where's that?" said Josh.

Etta studied him with hooded eyes. "That's for me to know and you to find out."

Josh met her gaze without flinching. "We've been honest with you, Etta."

"If that's true, we'll get along fine."

"It's true," he insisted, "and whether you accept that or not, you can afford to explain why you're suspicious of us."

Etta's eyebrows shot to incredulous peaks. "You mean Lester didn't fill you in?"

Libby and Josh exchanged puzzled glances. In unison they asked, "Who's Lester?"

"My no-good parasite of a nephew."

"If he's your nephew, why do you call him a parasite?"

"Well, now, that's a long story—"

"Please," said Libby. "We'd like to hear it."

"Have another cinnamon bun, stop interrupting, and you will."

This was one admonition Libby was happy to obey. She helped herself to seconds of everything, and listened while Etta went on.

"Lester hasn't always been a parasite—least not so's you'd notice. He could spot an opportunity quicker 'n gravel goes through a goose, but I never thought of him as a con man till Rollie retired."

"Rollie?" said Josh.

"My husband."

Josh leaned back in his chair and peered into the living room. "Does he live here, too?"

"I'm a widow," Etta replied. "Rollie was an investment banker. He dealt in commodities—very successfully, I might add—but he reached a point where picking winners wasn't the thrill it used to be. He had a nice, fat portfolio, but his personal life had gotten thin. His health wasn't the greatest, either. He had two heart attacks before he was fifty, and after the second one his doctor laid down the law. 'Rollie,' he said, 'you better get your act together, or you'll never make it to sixty.' Rollie wasn't afraid of much, but that really spooked him."

Josh nodded. "I can relate to that."

Etta shrugged and refilled their coffee cups. "Anyway, that's when we decided to move back home."

"To Sagamore?"

"No, to Monhegan. No place like it. That's where we both grew up. My daddy was the lighthouse keeper, and Rollie's folks ran the general store. After his father died, Rollie couldn't bear to let the property go. He'd always planned on reopening the store someday, only someday came sooner than either of us expected."

"How long did you live on Monhegan?" Libby inquired.

"Like I said, we grew up on the island. More often than not we spent our vacations there, and after Rollie's retirement we were there another sixteen years."

"Where did Lester come in?" asked Josh.

Etta grimaced. "He used to stay with us summers, when we needed extra help in the store."

"Sounds like an ideal arrangement."

"It seemed like one at first. The tourists had a place to buy their souvenirs, Rollie and I had our evenings off, and Lester had his salary, plus commissions. Sales were up, business was booming. Everybody was happy till I began to wonder why profits weren't as good as they ought to be. I started paying closer attention to daily receipts, and after a while I noticed peculiar fluctuations in the sales figures. Whenever Lester worked the store alone, a smaller percentage of customers settled their accounts with cash."

"Lester had one hand in the till," said Josh.

Etta gave him a stern parody of a smile. "You're one step ahead of me. Two steps, actually. Rollie and I were fond of the boy. He was family—like the son we never had. So I made excuses for him. It took me a long time to admit he was stealing from us, and I never did tell Rollie."

"Never?" said Libby.

"No, never," Etta replied. "I couldn't bring myself to disillusion him. Not as long as Lester didn't get too greedy. Besides, by the time I discovered what was going on, Lester was about to graduate from law school. I talked to the boy, let him know I'd found out what he was up to. I warned him I had proof he'd been cooking the books, and I told him, if he ever took another cent that wasn't rightfully his, I'd show my proof to his uncle. I figured the threat of being revealed for the slimy little leech he was would keep the boy honest, and it did until a couple of years ago, when Rollie died and I had a stroke, and Lester started making noises about my giving him power of attorney. Just while I recuperated, he claimed. But Lester doesn't give two pins about my welfare. All he cares about is having me declared incompetent, so he can control Rollie's estate."

"So you came here," said Libby.

"That's right, with several detours along the way. Before I managed to give him the slip, Lester traced me to Portland and Bangor and Orono. But he'd never think to look for me here, so here I'll stay."

"Don't you get lonely?"

"'Course I do," Etta answered. "But I'd rather be lonely than shut up in a nursing home—"

"And if Lester can't find you, he can't put you away," said Josh.

"That's it in a nutshell."

Etta's tone made it clear that she was adamantly opposed to relinquishing her independence. It was also apparent that she didn't trust Libby and Josh. While they polished off the last of the cinnamon rolls, she admitted she had been keeping an eye on them.

"I know you've been through the mill," she said, "and I apologize for being standoffish, but for all I know, you're in cahoots with Lester."

"We're not," said Libby. "All we want is to get back to the mainland."

"I only have your word for that, don't I?" Etta responded cautiously. "Maybe you're telling the truth, but I can't be too careful. If you're lying—Well, it wouldn't be the first time my nephew's sent his goons after me."

Josh pushed his plate aside and crossed his forearms on the table. "Listen, Etta, let's cut to the chase. It's obvious you couldn't have managed out here on your own. You've got to have some way of getting supplies. Either you have access to a boat or you're in contact with someone who does, which means you're in a position to help us get off the island, and I'm prepared to make it worth your while—"

"If it's money you're offering, save your breath. I've got pots of money—more than I could ever hope to spend—and look where it's landed me."

Josh shook his head. "I had something more personal in mind."

"Such as?"

"Getting your nephew off your back. You can't be deprived of your rights without due process. Just say the word, and I'll see to it that you're represented by an attorney who'll put Lester on the defensive and keep him there."

"Hmph! You don't know Lester. He's got more angles than a spiderweb, and he's a lawyer himself. He has connections."

"He's not the only one," said Libby. "My brother Dan is chief of police in Day's Harbor. My brother Ben is on the faculty at Harvard Law, and one of my uncles is a superior court judge."

Josh gave Etta a triumphant grin. "With that much influence on your side, Lester will be hamstrung by so many writs and injunctions and restraining orders, your case'll never come to trial."

"Well, I have to admit that's a tempting offer. I'll have to give it some thought."

"Do that," said Josh, "and while you're thinking about it, you can notify your contact we're here."

A hint of craftiness darkened Etta's face. "Didn't I make myself clear? I can't let anyone know you're here till I'm sure you and Elizabeth are what you claim to be."

The woman's certifiable! thought Libby. She bit her tongue to keep from blurting out the possibility that Lester had a point. At that moment she found herself sympathizing with the notion that his aunt needed a keeper.

Josh's grin faded, but his response was measured. "How can we convince you?" he inquired.

Etta looked at him with something akin to amusement. "If you've had enough to eat, you can start by giving me a hand with my chores."

Chapter Thirteen

Libby made several attempts to speak to Josh alone that morning. The sooner they could decide what strategy to take with Etta Cassidy, the better. But Etta had her own strategy. She kept them busy and separate.

While Libby cleared the table, Josh chopped wood.

While she washed the dishes, he chopped more wood.

While she swept the floors, sticks of cordwood gathered, numerous as snowflakes, about his feet. And Etta shadowed Josh wherever he went and asked a stream of questions.

When Libby went outside to sweep the snow off the stoop, she overhead Etta quizzing Josh about Healey and Noon and his plans for relocation to Mount Desert Island. She swept very slowly, admiring the lithe power of Josh's movements, and eavesdropping for all she was worth.

"I've always liked Chicago," Etta said. "There's nothing phony about it, if you know what I mean."

"I do." Josh swung the ax, and grunted as the blade bit into the wood. "Like the song says, it's my kind of town."

"And you say you've been successful there?"

Another swing, and two more chunks of firewood hit the ground.

"Well, why'd you decide to leave?"

"After my partner died, it seemed like a good idea." Josh hefted a foot-and-a-half slab of pine onto the chopping block and shortened his grip on the ax. "I wanted to simplify my life, and the most logical way to go about it was to shut down operations in Chicago and start a new agency with a select, more manageable client list."

"That makes sense," Etta allowed, "but why Maine?"

Josh squared his shoulders and glanced at the snowy woods, at the picturesque cabin, caught between sky and sea. "Why not?" he answered carelessly. "This is where everyone wants to spend their summer vacations."

"It's also about as far away from Chicago as a body can get without leaving the continental U.S."

"To my way of thinking that's a definite plus."

"Then you admit you're running away."

"No, just trying to mend my ways."

Libby gave up the pretense of sweeping and leaned on the handle of her broom, watching Josh turn the pinewood on end and shave off strips of kindling.

"You see, Etta," he said, "Walt and I worked in the same pressure cooker, only in my case, the pressures have been more extreme because I haven't found a safety valve—"

"There's no escaping death, boy."

"I'm not trying to escape it, but I wouldn't mind living long enough to reap the rewards of my labor."

Etta propped her hands on her hips and looked Josh up and down. "You look mighty healthy to me."

"Walt looked healthy, too."

"But his time was up. Yours isn't."

"Maybe not, but I can't help thinking 'There, but for the grace of God, go I.'"

"So you're happy to be alive, even though Walt's dead. What of it? It's a natural reaction—certainly nothing to feel guilty about. And take it from one who's been there. All the guilt in the world won't bring your partner back.''

"No," said Josh. "Nothing can do that. But I can pay tribute to his memory.''

"That'd be the camp you were telling me about.''

Josh nodded.

"How does Mrs. Healey feel about it?''

"Blair approves. I wouldn't have pursued the project if she didn't.''

"And does Blair approve of your leaving Chicago?''

Libby swept the stoop a millimeter at a time, waiting for Josh's reply, but before he could answer, Etta's eagle eye saw that she was loafing. "You're gonna wear out that broom," she scolded. "If you're finished there, you can peel some potatoes for stew.''

Resigned, nonplussed, annoyed that once again her efforts to learn more about Blair Healey had been stymied, even more annoyed that she had been caught eavesdropping, Libby swept her way into the cabin and slammed the door behind her.

"Of all the nerve!" she sputtered, stamping toward the kitchen.

Etta Cassidy had no right to criticize. Not when her probing and prying confirmed the surmise that she had been spying on them all week.

"She's invaded our privacy. She knows things about Josh he hasn't told me! Who the hell does she think she is?''

Libby flung the broom into the pantry and pressed her hands to her cheeks. Her face was hot with embarrassment, but that didn't stop her from climbing onto a step stool, looking through a high, narrow window and discovering, if she stood on tiptoe and craned her neck, she had an excellent view of Etta and Josh.

She watched them moving back and forth between the chopping block and the lean-to at the far corner of the cabin, stacking the firewood Josh had chopped, and talking as they worked. She released the latch and opened the window a crack, so that she could hear snatches of what they said.

Josh was telling Etta about his feud with DEEPC, recounting the sequence of events that had brought him to Sagamore. Although his voice was pitched low, confiding, and the noise he made stacking the wood drowned out most of the conversation, Libby heard Margaret Ogilvie's name and Sally Gillette's, and finally, distinctly, she heard Etta's summary of his story.

"Elizabeth's a kidnapper," Etta declared. "That's what it all boils down to."

It's true what they say about eavesdroppers, Libby thought. They don't hear anything good about themselves. Especially when the thuds of firewood striking the cabin wall created such an awful din.

She sank back on her heels, away from the window, before it dawned on her that Josh seemed to be defending her. He said something about *Pilgrim's Progress*, then added some bit of nonsense about a Lansford's clam chowder mermaid that made Etta chuckle.

"You're a trusting sort," she remarked, "but I'm surprised you're so charitable."

"It's not a question of charity," Josh replied.

"Then why are you so forgiving? I don't mind telling you, if someone hoodwinked me the way Elizabeth did you, I'd be cranky as Billy-be-damned."

"So was I at first, but there were extenuating circumstances. Now I've had time to cool off, I can see why Libby went along with the plan. She's devoted to DEEPC's cause, and her devotion clouded her judgment. When you think about it, there's a strong similarity between what she did and my own reaction when Walt told me he'd decided to leave H and N. The moment he mentioned selling, years of friendship went out the window. All I cared about was preserving the agency, so how can I condemn Libby for wanting to preserve Half-Moon?''

"In other words, you've got the hots for her."

An armload of firewood crashed against the wall. Footsteps crunched through the snow, away from the cabin, growing fainter as they crossed the yard.

"Don't go away mad," Etta chided.

The footsteps stopped. "I'm not," Josh answered evenly.

"Well, where are you going in such an all-fire hurry?"

"Back to the lighthouse to pick up our gear. If I leave now, I should be back before dark."

"That's a fine idea, as long as Elizabeth stays here. I'll tidy up the guest room while you're gone."

"Don't go to any trouble on my account."

"It's no trouble, I assure you." The footsteps started again, and Etta's voice became more distant as she called, "Just one thing— The room has bunk beds, and I'd like to know if you object to sharing with Elizabeth."

That makes two of us, Libby thought.

But the footsteps had receded into the pines. She couldn't hear Josh's answer.

Minutes later, Etta brought a supply of firewood into the cabin to fill the wood box. By the time she arrived in the kitchen, Libby was at the sink, peeling potatoes.

Etta shivered, and after a suspicious glance at Libby, went into the pantry, closed the window and latched it, then stood in the doorway, unbuttoning her parka.

"You were listening," she said.

Libby tossed her head defiantly. "Desperate situations call for desperate measures."

"What's that? The latest activist shinola?"

"No, just one woman's opinion."

Etta removed her parka and hung it on a hook beside the pantry door. "What's so desperate about your situation?"

"I'm a hostage, aren't I?"

"Hah! Some hostage! You're warm. You've got a roof over your head, food in your belly, and an honest-to-God feather mattress to sleep on tonight. Compared to the way you've been living, your life's taken a turn for the better."

Libby rinsed the potato she was peeling and put it on the counter. "What's that? The latest hermit shinola?"

Much to her astonishment, Etta grinned. "If you're hoping to win my confidence, you're going about it the wrong way."

"Well, if you had an ounce of human decency, I wouldn't have to win your confidence. You wouldn't put any conditions on helping Josh and me get back to the mainland. You'd help us because it's the right thing to do."

Etta sighed and slumped against the doorjamb. "Bear with me, Elizabeth. It's not often I have company, so my social skills tend to get rusty. My precautions may seem eccentric. No doubt you find them offensive, but I can't let my nephew get the upper hand. All I need is a few days to check you out."

"A few days?" Libby repeated dubiously.

"A week at most. Is that asking too much?"

"Do I have a choice?"

"No, and neither do I."

"But you do, Etta. You could stop hiding out and come with us—"

"That's easy for you to say. You don't know Lester."

Arguing with the woman was a waste of time! Libby pressed her lips together, considering this impasse. A week wasn't much to her, but to her family it would seem endless. If only she could get a message to her parents, let them know they needn't worry—But without Etta's cooperation, there was no way she could communicate with the mainland.

I might as well give in gracefully. Try not to alienate Etta, and pray she doesn't change her mind.

Libby swallowed her frustration and reached for another potato. "It's your game, Etta. You hold all the trumps. We'll play by your rules."

Etta patted her on the shoulder. "Girl," she said, "as long as you understand that, we'll get along fine."

THE REST OF THE DAY passed companionably enough. Libby prepared the vegetables for the stew, Etta browned the beef in a big Dutch oven and put together an apple pie, and while they worked they pumped each other for information. Etta asked Libby about her influential relatives, and Libby asked Etta what she had learned about Blair.

"Not a lot," Etta replied thoughtfully, directing her attention to trimming the excess pastry from the edges of the piecrust. "From what Josh says, she sounds like kind of a space cadet."

"But how does he *feel* about her?"

"He claims he feels responsible."

"Responsible? In what way?"

Etta glanced at Libby with bright, expectant eyes. "So it's like that, is it? You're jealous of Blair."

"Why should I be jealous? Josh and I aren't—well, he hasn't—that is, we've never—"

"Don't give me your haves and have-nots," Etta snorted. "You could conjugate verbs all day and it wouldn't change a thing. You're in love with him."

"Whatever gave you that idea? To tell you the truth, I'm not even sure he's my type."

"Oh? What type is that? Smart? Good-looking? Sexy?"

Aware that any response to this gambit might be used against her, Libby changed the subject.

Once the pie was in the oven and the stew was simmering, they made up the beds in the spare room, and when that job was finished, Etta showed her the rest of the cabin.

It wasn't very big—just the two bedrooms, the living room and kitchen—but it was solidly built and comfortably furnished, and after more than a week of roughing it, the place seemed palatial to Libby.

A floor-to-ceiling cabinet in Etta's room held an interesting variety of books. Novels by Dickens and Austen were scattered among recent bestsellers, and there were nonfiction titles on an array of subjects from anthropology to sports.

Libby leafed through a copy of *A Tree Grows in Brooklyn*, pausing to skim a passage or two that Etta had underlined. "You must do a lot of reading," she observed.

"As much as I can," Etta replied. "That's one of the advantages of being a hermit."

She went on to explain that the cabin was equipped with a generator. "But mostly I get by with lanterns," she said. "They're more soothing than electric lights."

The Franklin stove and a huge stone fireplace provided heat, the cook stove was fueled by bottled gas, and there was hot and cold running water.

But in Libby's estimation, the greatest luxury of all was the bathroom. As she took stock of the modern fixtures and thick velvety towels, she murmured, "Have you any idea how much I've longed for a shower?"

"Go ahead," Etta told her. "Be my guest. There's soap and shampoo in the stall, and you'll find extra toothbrushes and combs on the top shelf of the linen cupboard. If you'd like to wash your clothes—"

"Would I!"

Libby didn't need any coaxing. She had already kicked off her boots, and grinning at her eagerness, Etta said, "I'll find you something to wear till your own things are dry."

Left alone, Libby quickly undressed, adjusted the taps and stepped into the stall. For a while she simply stood beneath the spray and let the water course over her body.

It was heaven! It was bliss! It was better than she had dreamed it would be.

She undid her braid and shampooed and rinsed, and when the last particle of sand went swirling down the drain, she shampooed and rinsed again. Then she found the soap and worked up a lather and scrubbed herself till her skin tingled.

The day's tensions seemed to wash away along with nine days' accumulation of grit. Feeling carefree and euphoric, she splashed and played and blew soap bubbles and belted out the chorus of "My Kind of Town."

She enjoyed herself immensely. She didn't leave the shower until the water started to cool, and by then she had forgiven Etta's high-handed tactics. She had forgotten her need to speak privately with Josh, and it never occurred to her to wonder why Etta should be so well prepared for guests.

When Josh got back with their gear shortly after sunset that evening, she was drying her hair by the fire.

"You look cozy," he remarked.

She ducked her head and turned away from him, wishing that Etta's green chenille bathrobe was more flattering.

Josh dropped the duffel bag and bedding pack beside the door, just as Etta appeared from the kitchen.

"You can haul that stuff to the spare room. Elizabeth'll show you where it is. And mind you don't track snow."

Josh knelt down to take off his shoes. "Something smells good enough to eat," he said.

"That's my rum-runner stew. It'll be ready soon as the dumplings are done."

"In that case, I guess I'd better wash up."

Libby was already leading the way toward the bedroom, and he picked up the packs and followed her, closing the door behind him. He paused there, easing the packs to the floor while his eyes grew accustomed to the darkness, but she went directly to the bureau and lighted a lantern.

"You seem to have made yourself at home," he said.

Libby opened a connecting door and motioned Josh toward it with a jubilant wave of her hand. "Wait'll you see the bathroom."

"In a minute," he said, his voice falling to a whisper. "First I want to know if you've seen any signs of a radio."

"No, I haven't."

"Are you sure you saw the whole place?"

"Yes, Josh. I'm positive. Etta gave me the grand tour."

"Then she must have it hidden. Any idea where?"

Libby shook her head, fumbling with the belt on the robe, as Josh strode toward her.

"Think, Libby!" he urged. "Try to remember anything unusual."

She knitted her brows. "There was one thing," she answered, and without prompting, went on to tell Josh about the toothbrushes and combs.

"There, you see!" he said. "You noticed more than you realize, and since Etta's got to have a radio somewhere—a closet or drawer, maybe one of the cupboards—you must have some suggestion where we could look for it. You've been with her all day."

"Yes, of course. Except—"

Libby faltered into conscience-stricken silence, and Josh grabbed her by the shoulders.

"Except what?"

"Well, I did take a shower."

"You mean you let her out of your sight?"

"Y-yes, for a little while."

Josh scowled. His grip on her hardened. "How long?"

"Fifteen or twenty minutes. Maybe half an hour—P-please, Josh. You're hurting me."

Still scowling, he released her. "I don't believe this," he growled. "Etta's our passport out of here. I thought I could rely on you to keep an eye on her. For God's sake, Libby! I was only gone a few hours. Couldn't you have waited to take a shower till I got back?"

"I—I'm sorry, Josh. I didn't stop to think—"

He rolled his eyes toward the ceiling. "Do you ever?"

Josh was furious. If his rough behavior hadn't made that obvious, his sarcasm did. He'd depended on her to keep tabs on Etta, and she had disappointed him.

She had also disappointed herself. She wanted to cringe at the recollection that if she had stopped to think in the first place, neither of them would be here.

The truth hurt, and as she confronted it, she studied her stockinged toes peeking out from beneath the hem of the robe. She felt dispirited, crestfallen, utterly miserable. She must have looked it, too, because Josh murmured a hoarse endearment and folded her into his arms.

He kissed her forehead, her eyelids, the corners of her mouth, and between kisses he whispered, "It'll be all right. There's two of us and only one of Etta. She has to sleep sometime. All we have to do is keep our eyes peeled, and eventually she'll give herself away."

"Or she might even decide to help us."

"That's true. She might. But if she doesn't, there'll be other chances. We're not beaten yet. Not by a long shot."

Libby drew in a long, shuddering breath, and moved closer to him. "I won't let you down again, Josh."

"I know you won't, honey." He kissed her once more for reassurance, then glanced down at her and grinned. "I better wash up now, before Etta comes in to check up on us, but as soon as supper's over, I'll have a shower. And while I'm at it, I'll search her bedroom. The radio might not be in there, but it's as good a place as any to start."

Libby nodded agreement. "While you're checking out the bedroom, I'll keep Etta occupied."

"That might not be easy."

"Easy or not, you can count on me."

Josh gave her a searching look. "I do," he said quietly. "More than you realize."

Chapter Fourteen

Etta's radio was in her room. Josh found it in her closet. But, as he informed Libby later that night, when they were lying wakeful in their beds, "The CB won't do us any good. Etta's removed the batteries."

"If you can plug it in, we can still use it," said Libby. "Etta told me she has a generator."

"That won't help without an adaptor."

"You mean Etta's taken that, too?"

"Yes, and Lord knows where she's hidden it. Could be she keeps it with her."

Libby tucked the covers beneath her chin and settled deeper into the goose down mattress, trying to get warm. It was strange, having the top bunk to herself. Without Josh to share it, the narrow bed felt vast and empty. When she stretched her arms and legs, the crisp percale sheets seemed to go on forever.

She drew her knees up to her chest and asked, "What's our next move?"

"I suppose we do whatever it takes to convince Etta we're harmless."

"That could take a while."

"You're telling me?" Josh replied with bitter irony. "This is the second time in less than two weeks that I've fallen victim to the same tactic. First you with the dory, now Etta and the CB. I should've seen it coming."

Libby's throat ached with loneliness. Josh was less than four feet away, yet he sounded remote. "I didn't tamper with the outboard," she said.

"Somebody did," he insisted. "Probably another female."

"No. No, it wasn't."

"Then who was your accomplice?"

"Do you remember the old man at the landing?"

"Uh-huh. He suggested the motor might be flooded and pointed out your boat."

"He also disconnected the spark plugs."

"So *that's* how you managed it." The bedsprings creaked as Josh sat up. "What's this guy's name?"

"Why do you ask?"

"No reason."

"You swore you'd get even."

"I was angry. Now I'm not, and pressing charges seems like a waste of energy. If I have anything to say about it, there won't be any legal repercussions."

"Do I have your word on that?"

"Sure, Libby. Word of honor."

"All right, then. His name's Homer Trask."

Josh reached up and touched her lightly on the shoulder. The back of his hand brushed her cheek. "Thanks for appeasing my curiosity, honey. I appreciate your trusting me."

"Your thanks are premature, Josh. Not that I don't trust you, because I do. But I have to admit I'm curious, too."

"About what?"

"Blair Healey."

Josh heaved a sigh. "I'm not romantically involved with her, if that's what you're wondering, but somebody has to watch out for her. Walt left her a bundle, and she's kind of an easy mark."

"And you feel obligated to see to it that she's not victimized."

"Yeah, I do. But more than that, I care about Blair. She's one of the kindest people I've ever known. It's impossible not to like her. The truth is, I probably feel about her the way your brothers feel about you—only she really needs someone to run interference for her."

Josh yawned and lay down again, and Libby hugged her pillow, chastened, yet relieved.

"You must be tired," she said. "Why don't you get some sleep and let me worry about Etta?"

The bedsprings creaked again beneath Josh's weight as he shifted about. "Libby," he replied, "that's the best offer I've had all day."

But half an hour later he still hadn't settled down, and Libby began to wonder why he should be so restless. After a week of sharing her pallet, was he making the most of having the bunk to himself, or did he miss her as much as she missed him?

I wish—she closed her eyes tightly, concentrating with every atom of her being on her unspoken prayer. *I wish he'd kiss me. I want him to hold me. I wish he'd speak to me...say my name. Only my name. If he says my name before I can count to one hundred, everything will be all right.*

Willing him to give her this small omen, she began counting slowly, and when she reached fifty, even more slowly. By the time she reached sixty, she couldn't bear the silence any longer.

"Josh," she said in an urgent whisper. "Are you awake?"

There was no response, and Libby wondered whether his interest in her was genuine. Would it survive their return to the mainland, or was she just a passing fancy?

The obvious answer was that once they got back to civilization they'd go their separate ways. If Josh went through with his move to Mount Desert Island, now and again she might run into him on the street, and he'd say, "Hello, how are you?" And she'd say, "Fine. How are you?" Then they'd pass each other and walk on as if they were strangers, and he would never know how much she loved him.

If only she could turn back the clock, go back to the night Josh had invited her into his sleeping bag, she would make love with him and never count the cost. That way at least she'd have some memories to dull the pangs of separation.

But no matter how much she mourned lost opportunities, there was no going back.

The pragmatist in Libby acknowledged this, and knew the sooner she accepted it, the better off she'd be. But the dreamer in her rebelled against reality.

It's not too late she argued. *We're not off Sagamore yet.*

When some small sound woke her just before daybreak, she had scarcely closed her eyes. She was burrowing under her pillow, courting sleep, when it occurred to her that the sound she'd heard had been the front door closing, and in the same instant she realized that Etta had left the cabin, Libby recalled her promised to Josh.

"You can count on me," she'd told him. "I won't let you down again."

Galvanized by this recollection, Libby climbed out of bed and crossed to the window. When she pushed back the curtains, she saw Etta striding along the trail to the shore.

If she didn't hurry, Etta would give her the slip.

Libby threw on the green chenille robe and scurried to the living room to look for the dungarees she had left drying on a rack by the fireplace.

Her clothes were gone. So was the rack. By the time she found them, squirreled away in the pantry, the chug of a diesel engine broke the early-morning silence.

The dungarees were still damp, but she pulled them on, anyway. She got into her boots, grabbed a mackinaw from the coatrack and threw it on over the robe. And then she was running, out the door and along the trail, skidding occasionally on the icy spots.

Pine boughs lashed at her, twigs snarled in her hair. A vine snaked across the path to trip her. She stumbled and lost her footing, landing on all fours. When she picked herself up, her ankle gave way beneath her and she realized she had twisted it, but still she rushed on.

Finally the trees thinned enough that she caught a glimpse of a lobster boat, riding at anchor in a sheltered inlet some distance below. After a few more steps she saw an inflatable dinghy with Etta and a companion aboard, skimming across the water toward the boat.

"Wait! Don't leave!" Libby waved her arms and hopped up and down on her one good ankle, trying to attract the lobsterman's attention, but neither he nor Etta glanced her way, and if either of them heard her shouts, they gave no indication.

She picked up a fist-size stone beside the trail, and pitched it as far as she was able. It clattered downhill, dragging other rocks with it, launching a miniature landslide before it bounced to a stop at the foot of the hill, but even that commotion got no response.

"They're too far away," Libby cried. "They can't hear me."

If she had stopped to think, if she had brought the flare gun, she'd have a foolproof way of signaling—but the flare gun was back at the cabin at the bottom of Josh's duffel bag, and all she could do was watch helplessly while Etta's companion helped her climb aboard his boat.

Within a matter of minutes the anchor was up, the engine revving, and the lobster boat was churning toward the mouth of the inlet. Libby could have wept with frustration as it rounded the point and vanished from sight.

To have the possibility of rescue so near that she could almost identify the face of her rescuer, and then to have the possibility snatched away, was more than she could bear.

"They'll be back," she quavered. "There'll be other chances."

But this thought offered little consolation. She felt defeated as she limped up the trail, and she dreaded the moment Josh learned what had happened.

How could she confess that she had let him down again? What would he say when she told him Etta was gone?

Libby imagined him taking the news with grace and forbearance. She imagined him furious, flying into a rage, and she knew that she had to make a clean breast of things before she built the situation out of proportion.

She peeked in at Josh as soon as she got back to the cabin. He was still sleeping. She debated waking him, but he looked so peaceful, so relaxed and carefree, she hadn't the heart to disturb him.

Etta was gone, and there was nothing he could do about it. Besides, for all she knew, Etta wouldn't travel very far. Perhaps she was making a quick trip to Monhegan to check up on them and restock her supply of Vick's Vap-o-rub. If that were the case, she could return in a few hours. She might even return before Josh woke up.

By this evening we could be home.

This thought should have been heartening. But as Libby closed the bedroom door and hobbled toward the kitchen, she felt more dejected than ever.

IT WAS ALMOST NOON before Josh wandered into the living room. By then Libby had made a systematic search of the cabin, looking for spare batteries for the radio.

She had also done a lot of thinking, and had resolved to make the most of whatever time they had left. But they couldn't make the most of anything until she had told him about Etta's departure, so she broke the news bluntly, without offering excuses or sparing herself.

Josh's reaction was surprisingly sympathetic. "Don't feel bad," he said. "Etta's a hard one to pin down."

"But if I'd been more alert—"

"It wouldn't have made any difference. Believe me, Libby. This island is Etta's turf. She knows it like the back of her hand, and she's a master at hide-and-seek. How else do you think she managed to elude me all week?"

Libby glumly admitted she hadn't considered that, but Josh hardly listened. He seemed more interested in her ankle, which she had soaked and bandaged and propped on a hassock, than he was in their elusive hostess.

He sat on the edge of the hassock and eased her foot onto his lap. "What've you done to your ankle?"

"I twisted it, chasing Etta."

He flattened his palm against the sole of her foot and applied gentle pressure. "Can you put your weight on it?"

Libby nodded. "I walked back to the cabin."

He caught her little toe between his thumb and index finger. "Let's see you wiggle 'em."

His hold was light enough to tickle, and she laughed as she complied. But Josh wasn't satisfied. When she tried to pull away, he gave her a repressive scowl and began unwinding the bandage.

"It's nothing serious," she said. "The main thing I damaged was my pride."

"Then you won't mind if I take a look."

"It's not that I mind, but it's not necessary—"

"Don't worry, honey. This won't hurt a bit." His expression had softened. So had his voice. He seemed almost bemused as he unwound the last few wraps in the bandage and laid it aside. "There doesn't appear to be any swelling."

"Of course there isn't. I told you, it's perfectly fine."

Josh ran his fingers over her instep, tracing the pattern of fine blue veins. "It's perfect, all right. So's the other one. And your legs aren't bad, either."

"Not bad?" she echoed, resisting the impulse to pull the hem of Etta's bathrobe over her knees. "Is that supposed to be a compliment?"

"Well, actually they're gorgeous. You should always wear skirts, you know. It's criminal to hide legs as terrific as yours."

Libby flushed and looked away from him. "Thank you," she answered modestly, "and if I may return the flattery—"

"Please do!"

Josh's hand was making a skin-tingling foray along her ankle, his touch so electrifying that the fine downy hairs on her calf stood on end.

The color in her face brightened, partly with pleasure and partly with self-consciousness at what she was about to do. She was keenly aware of her inexperience as she raised her gaze to his and, with what she hoped was a coquettish flutter of lashes, murmured, "I think your legs are terrific, too."

Josh's fingers halted halfway to her knee. "Do you really?"

"Cross my heart."

For emphasis, she slid her toes along the inside of his thigh. She felt him tense, felt his muscles bunch and quiver, and decided she wasn't doing at all badly for an amateur. Might as well go for broke, she thought, and she lay back against the sofa cushions and gave him a languid, sidelong glance.

"I could do without the beard, though."

Josh cocked an eyebrow at her. "What's wrong with my beard?"

"I don't mean to be critical, but whiskers are rough on the skin—"

"And you prefer your men clean-shaven."

"I knew you'd understand." She smiled the way she thought a temptress would, warming to the role she was playing.

He rubbed his jaw. "Doesn't my five o'clock shadow remind you of Don Johnson?"

"There's no comparison, Josh." She touched his cheek, and to make her intentions crystal clear, moved her toes higher on his thigh. "You're much sexier than Don Johnson."

Josh drew in a ragged breath and shot her a speculative look. "Is this a come-on?"

Her eyes widened innocently, but her toes inched higher. "What do you think?"

"I think you're up to something."

"I'm not the only one."

Josh's throat worked as he suppressed a groan. He grabbed her foot, putting an end to her explorations, but not before she had felt the telltale stirrings of arousal.

"Don't do this to me, Libby. Not unless you're serious."

She smiled again, without pretense, and endless nights of yearning for him leaped into her eyes. "Do I look as if I'm teasing?"

She barely got the words out before Josh's arms closed around her and his lips were trailing kisses over her face, her throat, her shoulders. Her own lips were stinging from the raspiness of stubble, but it was worth it. She would gladly risk impalement on his ten-day growth of beard to plant hot, possessive kisses on whatever part of his anatomy happened to be within her reach. And when his mouth intercepted hers, she returned the bold feint and parry of his tongue with undisguised eagerness.

Her arms held him fiercely and her hands were slippery with perspiration as they tunneled beneath his shirt and caressed the smooth hard skin at the small of his back. She felt feverish, desirous, and her body arched provocatively, responding to his slightest movement.

"Easy, love. Easy," he whispered against her lips. "There's no need to rush things. We have plenty of time—"

"At least until Etta gets back."

Josh nuzzled her earlobe. A tremor of anticipation shook her as he untied the belt of her robe. "Any idea when that'll be?"

"None, but we should be able to hear the boat."

He raised his head and grinned down at her. "Then we might as well do this right."

"R-right," she echoed, torn between desire and dismay.

She had made the advances. She'd practically thrown herself at Josh, and suddenly she felt inadequate, overwhelmed by shyness. He was getting out of his clothing, fumbling with buttons and zippers, and she felt too self-conscious to help him. All she could think of was how awkward it would be, trying to make love on a lumpy sofa in a stranger's cabin, in an alien environment.

"If only—"

Josh gave up struggling with the buttons, and pulled his shirt off over his head. "What, sweetheart?"

She brushed the tousled hair away from his forehead. "It just this minute dawned on me, you've never seen me in a dress."

His jeans joined his shirt in the middle of the floor. "This is the first time I've seen your *legs*, and look what that's done to me. I get turned-on just thinking about the treats I have to look forward to."

"Have you ever pictured me wearing lipstick, and eye shadow, and maybe perfume?"

"Maybe once or twice. But I happen to like the way you smell, and that other stuff—the wardrobe and makeup—they're props, honey. You don't need them."

Her fingers plucked nervously at the high neckline of her long-sleeved singlet. "But thermal underwear is—Well, it's—"

"It leaves a lot to the imagination," Josh finished dryly. "But that's not what I'd call a drawback, because it also enhances the mystery."

Libby shook her head. "Go on. Say it. I must look a sight!"

Josh wadded up his crew socks and banked them off the corner of a lamp table, so that they landed in one of his shoes. "You're beautiful, Libby, no matter what you're wearing. Don't you realize how desirable you are? Why, the first time I saw you, I knew I'd found the ideal mermaid for the Lansford's clam chowder account."

She studied him from beneath her lashes. "I heard you say something about that to Etta, but you never mentioned it to me."

"I assumed you wouldn't be interested. In fact I was afraid, if I approached you about the campaign, you'd be insulted."

"Whatever gave you that idea? I did some modeling before—"

Josh silenced her with a kiss. Now that he'd gotten rid of his clothes, his busy hands were unfastening the row of snaps on her singlet. "The point is, you're plenty feminine and sexy without trying to be."

Libby sighed. "Oh, Josh, I'd like to believe you, but you're such a romantic."

"Only when I'm with you."

He eased the singlet away from her shoulders and bosom carefully, almost reverently, as if he were unveiling a priceless work of art, and her heartbeat accelerated as he traced the demarcation line between her tan and the pale, creamy skin the sun had not touched with small, biting kisses.

But still she was worried. Josh had such high expectations. How could she hope to live up to them?

"What if you're disappointed?"

"I won't be," Josh answered, his voice thick with passion. "But if your underwear offends you, take it off. That's how I'd most like to see you, you know. Wearing nothing but a smile."

He slid one arm beneath her, lifting her off the sofa and angling her toward him as he removed the singlet completely. The crush of his naked chest against her breasts sent eddies of excitement through her, and when he claimed her mouth yet again, her last remnant of doubt evaporated in the slow fire of his kiss.

She surrendered to sensation, to the sorcery of his fingertips as they discovered secret untouched places, to the taste of his kisses and the sleekness of his skin and the potent rippling of muscles across his back, and she marveled that he should be capable of great strength and, at the same time, exquisite gentleness.

Desire escalated to frenzied awareness as his hands charted a course to the pleasure points of her body. And then his mouth embarked on the quest, and she felt the tip of his tongue—now probing her ears, now burning hotly across her shoulders, now invading the hollow of her navel, now drawing feathery patterns on her breasts—and she relished his kisses and wove her fingers through his hair, clinging to him without reservation as his caresses created a delicious new tension within her.

There was no part of her that escaped his attention. There was no part of him she did not adore.

Her body was delicately rounded where his was angular, all womanly softness where his was hard and masculine, yet they meshed together perfectly, blissfully, consumed by the same need.

As their embrace became more intimate, she met his demands with her own, and when at last they reached the peak, the awesome splendor of release was revealed to her— so blinding in its perfection that when she closed her eyes to savor its brilliance, she saw it still, and felt herself dissolving in the crucible of love.

"Beautiful," Josh murmured. "So beautiful."

He whispered something else. It could have been "I love you." But he breathed the words so softly that she might have imagined them.

Spent and replete she lay in his arms with the warm weight of his body blanketing hers.

She wanted to tell him how much she cared for him. She wanted to tell him that making love with him was the most glorious thing that had ever happened to her. But she was too contented to speak, and so instead of talking she rejoiced in his closeness, while languor replaced passion and her limbs grew heavy with drowsiness.

Her only regret was that she had wasted precious time.

Ever since the storm had brought them to Sagamore she had been poised on the brink, reluctant to admit her love for Josh, and now she was sorry that she hadn't taken the plunge sooner.

Her hesitation had made her feelings for him appear complex; making love with him had shown her they were really very simple. And now she knew, whatever tomorrow might bring, she would always cherish today.

Chapter Fifteen

They had thirty-six hours together. A day and a half of solitude to explore the boundaries of love. And in that time they spoke of many things, but neither of them said, "I love you."

More than once, Libby was tempted to tell Josh how she felt about him. She longed to ask how he felt about her, but deep inside, something wise and intuitive told her she didn't have to.

A kiss, a smile, a glance, a touch expressed their feelings more eloquently than words.

The following evening Etta returned, arms laden with shopping bags. She walked through the door just as they were getting ready for supper.

"Did you miss me?" she called.

Ever the diplomat, Josh replied, "Of course we did."

Libby simply set another place at the table.

"I expected to find the two of you keeping watch on the shore," Etta said.

"We would have," said Josh, "if we'd known exactly where you'd land."

Etta chuckled and rubbed her hands together. "Ah, yes. That's the beauty of a two-man raft."

Libby put the bean pot on the table and pulled off her oven mitts. "Who's your friend?"

Etta's expression soured. "If you're talking about the lobsterman, Wyatt's not a friend. He's just someone I pay to bring me supplies and ferry me back and forth to the mainland."

"How do you know you can trust him?" asked Josh.

"Two reasons. I make it worth his while to keep my whereabouts a secret, and he has a grudge of his own against Lester."

"What kind of grudge?"

"Seems my nephew represented Wyatt's wife when they were divorced. His ex got the house, the car, the lion's share of the lobster boat and custody of the savings, and Wyatt, poor guy, got the shaft."

"So there's no love lost between him and Lester."

"None whatsoever. Wyatt wouldn't give Lester the time of day."

Etta ladled baked beans onto her plate and reached for the salad bowl, and with a glance at each other, Libby and Josh silently agreed to defer further questions until the meal was over. But when Libby got up to pour the coffee, Etta spoke up without prompting.

"I went to Day's Harbor," she said, "by way of Mount Desert Island."

"Then you must know we've told you the truth," said Josh.

"That's for sure. You two are famous. You're on TV, the radio, all over the papers." Etta waved a hand toward her purchases. "The *Day's Harbor Packet* is in one of those sacks. Take a gander at it and you'll see for yourselves."

Josh moved the parcels onto the table. "What else is in these?"

"This 'n that. I got each of you a change of clothes."

Libby frowned. "You didn't inform the authorities we're here?"

"I didn't tell anyone. Couldn't risk it. Not while there's so much publicity. You'll have to stay here till the ruckus dies down."

"But my parents—"

"No need to fuss about your folks, girl. They're doing fine, according to the piece in the paper."

Josh found the newspaper and, with an anxious Libby leaning over his shoulder, folded it open. The first thing he saw was the headline, "Tragic Find Ends Coast Guard Search." The next was his photograph, and the lead, "Plans for Retreat Gain Support." An accompanying article featured interviews with Sally Gillette, Blair Healey and, curiously enough, Margaret Ogilvie who, he noted with some satisfaction, was referred to as "the former president of DEEPC."

A quick scan of the article revealed another startling fact. "Good Lord! Ogilvie's facing criminal charges."

"She's not the only one," said Libby, pointing to an article about the search her brothers had mounted. It began with a quote from her father, "I'm certain my daughter is alive," and ended with the statement, "If Ms. Pilgrim has survived, there is a possibility she will be arrested as an accomplice in the abduction of Joshua Noon."

Josh muttered a curse. "That's ridiculous. The most you're guilty of is choosing the wrong friends."

Libby appreciated his vote of confidence, but privately she disagreed. She had been mistaken about so many things, she couldn't keep track of them all.

She had listened to Margaret, turned a deaf ear to the dictates of her own conscience, and persistently jumped to the wrong conclusions.

She had thought of herself as a law-abiding citizen, yet she had taken the law into her own hands.

She had considered herself charitable, yet had shown a flagrant disregard for Josh's safety.

She was supposed to be smart—she had the grades and degrees to prove it—yet she had used her intellect to rationalize her actions.

And she had behaved as if the conservationists' cause was more important than the people involved, when the truth was that there was no comparison.

She saw that now, saw it so clearly; she was appalled by her foolishness.

While Josh pored over the sports page and Etta had a second cup of coffee, Libby made her excuses and escaped to the bedroom, overwhelmed by remorse. She spent a sleepless night, but by morning she had regained her sense of perspective.

The crucial thing about mistakes was to learn from them, and she had learned her lesson well.

If she was arrested, she would take whatever punishment the court meted out, and try to minimize its impact on those she loved. If she was not arrested, she would find some constructive way to make amends for her crime. But she would keep her penance to herself. She wouldn't let it destroy her, nor would she succumb to self-pity.

Moving quietly so that she wouldn't wake Josh, Libby showered and dressed in the slacks and sweater Etta had bought for her, then gathered up her old clothes, planning to launder them. She left the bedroom, filled with a sense of purpose, and with gratitude that her dark mood had lifted without Josh's becoming aware of it.

AFTER LUNCH THAT DAY, Josh announced he was going to check the signal fires. "Care to come with me?" he inquired.

The invitation was meant for Libby, but his gaze never strayed from Etta, who was standing at the sink, washing dishes.

"I'd love to," Libby replied with quiet enthusiasm. "It'd be nice to get out for a while." With Etta the length of the island away, it would also give her the perfect opportunity to be alone with Josh.

Or so she thought, until Josh dispelled the notion.

"How about you, Etta? Will you join us?" he asked.

"Why bother? In a week or so you'll be yesterday's news, and I'll arrange for Wyatt to take you home."

"To borrow a quote from my favorite hostess, I only have your word for that."

"You don't believe me?" Etta shot Josh an irate glance, but he defused her hostility with a wink.

"I believe in hedging my bets," he said.

Etta pursed her lips to keep from smiling. "What's the point? Those fires are useless as a barrelful of bungholes."

"If they're useless, you can't possibly object to my tending them," Josh countered. "Besides, it's a beautiful afternoon for a walk."

"For you youngsters, maybe. Not for me. You've kept me hopping ever since you got here. Haven't give me a moment's peace."

Josh pantomimed strumming "Hearts and Flowers" on a make-believe violin. "Poor defenseless Etta," he teased. "She's just a weak, helpless old lady."

"Hmph! You know damned well I'm not helpless and I'm sure as shootin' not weak. You and Libby haven't seen the day you could outhike me, but when a person's on the shady side of sixty, it begins to take longer to recover from a marathon, so I don't mind admitting these old bones are tired.''

''Is that why you ruined the crab trap?'' Libby asked.

Etta stared at her, mouth agape. ''What the dickens are you talking about?''

''The crab trap,'' said Libby. ''You've been honest enough to admit you're tired, and I can understand why you felt you had to keep us under surveillance. But as long as we were camped at the far end of the island, you had to cover a lot of extra miles. So, as one means of inducing us to move closer, you wrecked the trap.''

''Girl, I've heard my share of nonsense in my day, but that has got to be the silliest story I ever heard.''

Etta stiffened her spine and began scouring the countertop with furious swipes of her sponge, and Libby folded her dish towel neatly over the rack.

''Please, Etta,'' she coaxed. ''Why don't you admit you did it? No one's going to hold it against you.''

''I should hope not, 'cause I never touched your stupid crab trap.''

''Then who did?''

''How should I know? Unless maybe it was Lorna.''

''Who's Lorna?'' asked Josh. ''Do you mean there's someone else on the island?''

''Nope. No one human, anyway.''

Libby paled. ''Lorna's the ghost, isn't she?''

''There's some who claim she is.''

Josh glanced from Libby's ashen face to Etta's, bright with mischief. ''Tell her you're joking,'' he instructed the older woman.

''I can't say I'm joking, 'cause I'm not.''

''Tell her,'' Josh insisted, slipping his arm about Libby's waist. ''Can't you see she's frightened?''

"'Course I can. My eyes aren't what they used to be, but I'm not blind. I'm not stupid either, and that's why I won't insult Lorna's memory by denying her existence."

"Obviously you'd rather insult my intelligence—"

Etta held up one finger, indicating she wasn't through. The grin she gave Libby was meant to be reassuring. "I will say that personally I don't believe in ghosts. If I did, I wouldn't be afraid of Lorna. She's prankish, but not malicious. She doesn't mean any harm."

"Sounds like another resident of Sagamore," Josh muttered.

Etta dried her hands on her apron. "Now that you mention it, Lorna and I do have certain things in common."

"What things?" asked Libby.

Josh couldn't suppress a groan. "For God's sake, honey, don't encourage her."

"I'm sorry, Josh," Libby said contritely. "I appreciate your concern, but I really have to know." Turning to Etta, she repeated, "What things?"

"To begin with, we both grew up on islands. Lorna's daddy was a lighthouse keeper, too. She was born while he was stationed on Nantucket."

Etta hesitated, staring absently out the window. When she spoke again, her manner was distant, as if she were caught up in the past.

"People tend to romanticize lighthouses and the lives of the men who kept 'em, but as I recall, there wasn't much romantic about my family's life. Dad was responsible for maintenance and repairs. He polished the brass and kept the lantern in apple-pie order, and now and again he'd man the lifeboat and rescue some sailor in distress. He worked like a Trojan, and so did the rest of us. We helped with everything, you see. Not only was it expected of us. It was part of the tradition, and it helped to relieve the boredom."

"You must've been lonely," said Libby.

"We were," said Etta. "Our only regular contact with the outside world was with the telegraph, and let me tell you, we used to scrap over whose turn it was to monitor it."

"I noticed the telegraph key in your bedroom," said Josh.

Etta nodded. "I found it here, in the keeper's house."

"Is it functional?"

"Not without wires."

"Even if it were wired, it wouldn't be much use," said Libby. "Telegraphy's a dying art."

"That it is, except for a few old-timers like me. Many's the night I've spent tapping out messages, brushing up on Morse code. It's one of those skills you either use or you lose."

"I suppose Lorna was a telegrapher, too," said Josh.

"It just so happens she was. And that's another thing we have in common." Etta sighed and sat across from Josh at the table, determined to draw him into her story. "I'm not exaggerating when I say that part of me identifies with Lorna. She died before I was born, but we're sisters under the skin. I know her, and I know her family. I know what they thought and how they felt, and I can tell you, like most islanders, they were rugged individualists. Proud, independent—sometimes to a fault."

"For instance?" Libby prompted.

"Refusing to ask for help from the mainland, no matter how much they needed it—or in the case of Lorna's mother, even when it was a matter of life and death."

"Why? What happened to her mother?"

"She got a splinter, and it got infected, and the infection spread. It could be she was a diabetic. Or maybe her resistance was low. Anyway, home remedies weren't effective. Lorna's daddy wanted to fetch the doctor. Mama wouldn't hear of it. Then her fever went up and she became delirious. That scared him, so he sent for the doctor anyway, but by the time the doctor got there, gangrene had set in."

"Did he manage to save her?"

Etta shook her head. "Lorna was only eight, but her childhood was over. Her daddy was out of his mind with grief. There were days he scarcely got out of bed, and somebody had to hold the family together. She had meals to cook and clothes to wash and two little brothers to take care of, and when she finished her chores, there was her father's work to do."

"God," Libby murmured. It sounded like a prayer. "How long did that go on?"

"For the rest of her life."

"She never married?"

"No, never."

"How'd she wind up here?" asked Josh.

"Her father got to drinking and lost his station. This was after Lorna had covered for him for several years. Evidently, being suspended was enough to sober him up. Not permanently, mind you, but long enough to file an appeal with a representative of the Lighthouse Board. He pleaded hardship. He promised to reform. He threw himself on the mercy of the Board, and since this was during World War I and there was a shortage of manpower, he wound up with a transfer."

"To Sagamore?" said Libby.

"That's right," Etta replied. "And as soon as they were settled, he went off on a toot—"

"Leaving Lorna in charge."

"Right again. And while he was gone to the mainland, a squall blew in. It was a freakish storm, very localized, almost like a tornado. One minute the ocean was quiet as a millpond, the next the ripples had turned to whitecaps and the whitecaps to breakers, and the breakers to waterspouts that sounded loud as thunder as they roared across the water. Lorna sent a message to her dad, begging him to get the first passage home, but the storm never reached the mainland, so he figured she was crying wolf, and he told himself 'I'll show my daughter a thing or two. I'm not going to let her spoil my fun.' And he went on with his bender till he ran out of money—which, considering how small his salary was, didn't take long."

Etta paused and glanced from Libby to Josh. "Lorna's daddy got back to Sagamore a week later, and what do you think he found?"

"The place in a shambles," said Josh. "His children sick—"

"Or dying," said Libby. "Already dead."

Etta shook her head. "You're not even warm."

"Well, what then?" they demanded.

"Nothing. Absolutely nothing."

"No storm damage?" said Josh.

"Some, but it was minor. The wind had uprooted a tree or two, and the house was kind of waterlogged because part of the roof had blown off. Apart from that, though, everything was normal—with one exception. Lorna and her brothers were gone."

"Maybe they got fed up with their father and took off," said Josh.

"They may have, but from the evidence, it doesn't seem likely they planned to leave."

"What evidence?"

"Their clothes were in their bureaus. Breakfast was on the table—"

"Any signs of a struggle?"

"None at all. They just disappeared. No one ever saw them again. Not in this life."

It was warm in the kitchen, but Libby shivered. "What do you think happened to them?"

"I suspect they were washed out to sea. That wouldn't have been unusual, you know. But that's only one person's opinion. Some say Lorna's daddy did her in. Some say a German U-boat surfaced off Sagamore, and one of the children saw it. The captain of the U-boat couldn't afford to leave any witnesses, so he kidnapped the three of them. Then again, there are those who believe Lorna's mind finally snapped and she took her own life."

"That wouldn't explain her brothers' disappearance," said Libby.

"No, it wouldn't," said Etta.

"What happened to the father?"

"He stayed on here another thirty years, tending the light, waiting for his children to turn up. If he left Sagamore, he said, they wouldn't know where to find him."

"That makes sense," said Josh, "in a wacky kind of way."

"Wait," Etta told him. "It gets better. As her daddy got on in years, he claimed Lorna was using the telegraph to communicate with him. Next thing he started acting as if she were around. He talked to her constantly and kept her room ready, as if she were living there. He set a place for her at the table, fixed meals for her, served a plate for her—"

"Did he eat for her as well?"

Etta chuckled. "I haven't a clue what became of the food. Maybe he used it to grow penicillin. What's more important is, he never touched another drop of liquor, yet he carried on that way until the day he died. So I ask you, was he tortured by guilt, or did Lorna's ghost come back to haunt him?"

"I'd say Lorna's father was a brick shy," Libby answered.

"I'd say you're right," Etta allowed. "But when you've been around as long as I have, you begin to realize that truth is stranger than fiction."

Josh shrugged and got to his feet. "True or false, it's quite a tale. I'd say it's the stuff legends are made of."

Although Libby nodded agreement, she was more convinced than ever that Etta had destroyed the crab trap. Otherwise, why would she invent such an elaborate pack of lies?

I might be superstitious, Libby thought, *but I'm not an idiot.*

She had fallen for the ghost stories once; she was not about to fall for them again. But whether or not she believed Etta, discussing ghosts and hauntings made her feel uneasy, so she kept her doubts to herself and let the subject drop.

HALF AN HOUR LATER, the three of them were walking single file along the trail to the far end of the island, with Libby in the lead and Etta bringing up the rear.

Hiking between the women, Josh kept to a leisurely pace, stopping every so often to enjoy the view or to soak up the tranquility of a sun-dappled glade, offering Etta the chance to catch her breath.

They were beginning the descent from the ridge to the keeper's bungalow when he expressed an interest in the technical aspects of lighthouses, and Etta responded at some length.

She seemed happy to display her considerable knowledge of beacons and lamps and reflectors, and Libby was delighted to listen. She led the way downhill, relieved that neither Josh nor Etta seemed inclined to revive the topic of Lorna.

Instead of dwelling on the supernatural, Etta gave Josh a capsule history of navigational lights, from primitive signal fires to the ancient Tower of Pharos to the eighteenth-century tower on Little Brewster Island that guided square-riggers to the entrance of Boston Harbor.

"There's been a steady evolution from the early days of lighthouse operations," Etta declared by way of summary. "Whale oil lamps gave way to kerosene lanterns, and lanterns gave way to electric light bulbs, and nowadays I've heard tell there are lights powered by solar energy."

Josh climbed onto a fallen log that blocked the trail, and turned to help Etta over the obstacle. "What kind of candlepower are we talking about?"

"Not nearly as much as you might think. With a Fresnel lens, even a modest light source gives off an intense beam. Here, I'll show you." Twig in hand, Etta sketched a beveled sphere in a patch of snow beside the trail. "I'm no artist, but you can imagine this is a beehive of precision-ground prisms, hinged on one side to permit access to the light—"

"I see what you're driving at. It's basically a matter of refraction and magnification."

"Absolutely. The Fresnel is so efficient, it made the old-fashioned lenses obsolete."

Josh glanced toward the glass-domed lantern deck, just visible above the pines. "Does Sagamore have one?"

"It used to," Etta replied, following the direction of Josh's gaze. "From the condition of the tower, it's hard to say whether the lens is still intact."

"Would the coast guard have removed it?"

"They might have, although it'd be quite a job. Those lenses must weigh half a ton or more. But don't forget, this station's been abandoned a good many years, so if the coast guard didn't take the lens, there's a passel of others who might've taken it.''

"But if the lens is there—"

"Then there it'll stay till the lighthouse falls down. The state that building's in, a body'd have to be crazy to try to get to the lantern deck. If you ask me, he'd be taking his life in his hands!''

Chapter Sixteen

Crazy, Etta called it.

Probably she was right.

But taking his life in his hands?

Maybe she was exaggerating. Then again, maybe not. Josh intended to assess the danger himself, but he had to postpone his assessment until he'd checked the signal fires.

Above all else, he mustn't arouse suspicion.

Libby was frantic with worry about her parents. The more she tried to hide it, the more he realized how distraught she was. Last night, aware of her insomnia, he had felt her anguish as sharply as if it were his own, and he'd recognized that somehow or other he had to get her home.

But the last thing he wanted was to add to her distress, so he bided his time and waited till she and Etta wandered into the woods to gather hazelnuts. Only then did he approach the lighthouse, studying the bank of windows at the top.

The glare of sunlight off the glass prevented his seeing much, aside from blue reflections of sky. He couldn't determine whether the lens had been removed, but this evening he'd have another look, before he made the climb.

If he made it.

Hands on hips he surveyed the tower, tipping his head to one side to compensate for the structure's off-center slant.

The exterior was as bad as he'd remembered. In fact it was even worse. The wrought-iron walkway that skirted the windows had fallen away from the crumbling brick walls, reinforcing his impression that the lighthouse might topple in the next gust of wind.

At first glance it appeared hopeless. He didn't have to examine the stairs inside to know they were impassable, and there was no way he could scale the outside walls, but when he opened the door and saw the sturdy central column rising from the concrete floor to the lantern deck, he felt a resurgence of optimism.

Josh drummed the heel of his palm against the column, and a hollow echo filled the tower. He nodded, satisfied that the details Etta had given him were accurate.

With his belt and a hank of rope, the column would serve as his stairway.

Made of welded steel tubes about fifteen inches in diameter, its function, Etta had explained, was to house the system of weights and pulleys that had once turned the lens. It was a simple device, really—Etta had compared it to the mechanism of a grandfather clock—and if he had known about it two weeks ago, he and Libby wouldn't have been stranded on Sagamore for more than a night or two.

Even now, if he had someone to help him, it would be a cinch getting to the lens. All he'd have to do is find a hacksaw, cut a hole in the pipe, and haul his assistant to the lantern deck with the cable.

The irony was, he had discovered this escape hatch when his feelings for Libby made it impossible to use it. Now that he'd gotten to know her, now that he'd fallen in love with her, he would not under any circumstances jeopardize her safety. And while using the cable as a hoist seemed comparatively foolproof, there were still some unknowns.

The lantern deck, for instance—

Josh took a backward step away from the column, peering up at the point more than twenty feet overhead where the floor of the deck joined the staircase landing.

The joists looked solid. So did the landing. And he didn't see any rust, which seemed a reliable indicator that the joists had been forged from the same steel as the column.

If the lens was up there, and if it was as heavy as Etta claimed, the joists had supported its weight all these years. Therefore, with any luck at all, they would support him.

But what if he wasn't lucky?

That's all the more reason to keep this from Libby, he decided. If his climb was successful, she'd find out about it soon enough. And if it wasn't successful—

Josh shook his head. He refused to contemplate failure.

It'll work, he told himself. It has to. All it'll take is careful planning.

He thought about the climb all the way back to Etta's place, but if he was uncommunicative, Libby was too preoccupied to notice.

Etta wasn't, though. Once or twice he caught her watching him, as if she were baffled by his silence. To throw her off the scent, he asked how she coped with isolation.

"It's not easy," she replied. "You might not believe it, seeing me now, but when Rollie and I lived in the city, I was quite the social butterfly—"

With Etta warming to her anecdote, Josh returned to planning his climb. By the time they reached the cabin, he had worked out most of the logistics. He even had a timetable. Five minutes to collect the equipment he would need, another five to make himself some sort of backpack, an hour and a quarter for the round-trip to and from the lighthouse, fifteen minutes to assemble a climbing harness and sling, ten to shinny up the tube to the landing, ten to clean the lens and install the lantern, ten more to either slide down the pipe or belay a rope and rappel to ground level.

Once he'd factored in a few extra minutes here and there, just to be on the safe side, he figured he'd be gone or otherwise occupied for a grand total of two and a half hours, and he had no idea how he was going to account for that long an absence—unless he borrowed a page from Lorna's book and simply disappeared.

But the whole point of this exercise was to ease Libby's mind, and if he were to vanish, she'd certainly be upset, which made a disappearance unacceptable.

Josh was trying to think of an alternative, when Libby walked into the bedroom and caught him stuffing the last of his supplies into a pillowcase.

She stopped, dismayed, just inside the room. "What are you doing? Are you going somewhere?"

He snatched up his pack and brushed past her, into the living room and through the front door. "I thought I'd spend the night at the keeper's house."

"Wait! I'll come with you."

"Sorry," he answered stiffly. "I'd rather be alone."

The door slammed shut behind him, but not before he caught a glimpse of Libby's face.

She looked desolate. He wanted to rush back inside and comfort her, hold her in his arms and take her into his confidence. But he didn't have time for explanations. Not if he hoped to make it to the lighthouse before the sun went down. Already the shadows were lengthening—

Josh swung the supply pack over his shoulder and trotted across the clearing, settling into an easy lope when he reached the path to the ridge.

The hour and a quarter he'd allotted himself was cutting it close. If he kept to his timetable, he couldn't afford to waste a minute, especially considering he'd be making the return trip after dark.

But the trail was familiar. So was the topography, and while the daylight lasted, he took a few shortcuts that got him to his destination in the brief golden minutes before sunset.

He felt a sense of triumph as he approached the lighthouse for the second time that day. Not only had he conquered Sagamore's rocky terrain, he'd also conquered his pack-a-day habit. He hadn't even thought of cigarettes since—

Well, to be honest, he'd thought of them last night, when Etta walked in with her shopping bags. For a split second he'd been tempted to ask whether she'd brought him any Marlboros.

So okay. Maybe it was too soon to claim he'd given up smoking, but he deserved a pat on the back for making it from Etta's cabin to the lighthouse in record time.

Two weeks ago, he'd never have been able to run that far without stopping to rest. Or if he had, he'd have been so winded, it would've taken him at least five minutes to recuperate.

But now he felt invigorated, rarin' to go—except that he was thirsty.

He made a detour to the spring for a drink of water, and knelt beside the pool, scanning the tower.

Years of neglect had left a layer of grime on the lantern deck windows, but behind this murky patina he saw a darker silhouette—

The lens was up there. No doubt about it. And tonight, thanks to him, it would send out a beacon that anyone within twenty miles of the island would see.

Josh sat back on his heels and opened the pillowcase, running down his mental checklist of supplies. Lantern, matches, flashlight, sheath knife, rope, a hand towel, filched from Etta's bathroom, to clean the lens—

Everything appeared to be in order.

He removed the knife and a coil of nylon line from the case, then stood up and took off his belt. Working quickly, he assembled his climbing harness and fastened one end to the belt buckle and the other to the eyelet he'd punched through the leather. That done, he returned the knife to his supply pack, tied a knot in the pillowcase and strapped it around his middle with what remained of the nylon line.

He spread the harness on the ground, and after testing the knots, stepped into it and pulled it up over the pack, extending the belt in front of him.

It wasn't pretty, but it ought to get the job done.

For safety's sake, he had taken the precaution of giving himself three release points. Untying one would permit him enough mobility to make the transfer from the pipe to the landing, while the other two kept him from falling. If he elected to use the harness to slide back down the pipe, he'd leave the knot nearest the buckle, which was attached to the rope on his pack.

Josh squared his shoulders and started toward the lighthouse, visualizing himself scaling the pipe with the sure-footed grace of a lineman climbing a telephone pole.

In the shadow of the tower he shot a final look at the windows, and his step faltered. Dry-mouthed, heart-pounding, he stared up at the dome.

Was it his imagination, or had he seen a hint of motion on the lantern deck?

"Is anybody up there?"

The cry of a passing seagull answered his call, and he decided his eyes had been playing tricks on him.

He pushed through the door into the dusky interior.

The wind sighed through the tower, setting off a penetrating, high-pitched whistle that piped him on his way, and as he approached the central column he thought the only thing moving around up there was the gull's reflection in the glass.

Josh sucked in his breath and unhooked the belt buckle. He slipped the belt around the pipe, then secured the buckle again.

"So far, so good," he told himself. "You're right on schedule. Who says you're out of your element here?"

His voice was steady, restoring his confidence. The next few minutes would tell the tale, but for now he felt invincible.

He slid the belt up and down the pipe a couple of times, just to get the feel of it, and then he started to climb.

AT FIRST LIBBY WAS HURT.

She sat on the stoop, face buried in her hands, thinking *I've lost Josh. Was it something I did? Something I said? Where did I go wrong?*

Then she was defensive.

She raised her head and glared at the woods.

Josh had made it abundantly clear that he didn't want to be with her. Well, she didn't want to be with him, either. What was more, she didn't need him. She'd gotten along without him for twenty-six years; she could get along without him from now on.

She sprang to her feet and paced about the dooryard, working herself into a fine, self-righteous anger.

So she wasn't perfect. Neither was he. He was mule-headed, impatient, impetuous, shallow. He talked too much. He was fickle, self-centered. All he cared about was himself... and gin rummy... and basketball... and adver-

tising...and Sally...and Blair...and Walt...and the retreat.... And for a time she'd thought he cared about her....

Libby's anger burned out, leaving a cold ache inside.

Josh had his faults, but he was the least temperamental
person she'd ever met. It wasn't like him to go off in a huff.
If she'd offended him, why hadn't he told her about it?
Wouldn't it be more characteristic for him to speak his
mind?

He's up to something, she realized. *But what?*

Should she follow him?

Her heart said yes. She started running toward the pines.
But at the edge of the woods she stumbled to a stop.

Josh had promised he'd get even with her for abducting
him. Was this his way of balancing the books?

"No!" she cried. "He was furious when he made that
threat. It was resentment talking. He didn't mean it."

Josh was sweet and considerate. He was honorable,
compassionate, tremendously loyal— There wasn't a vin-
dictive bone in his body.

And even if there was, she still loved him. Nothing could
change that.

Which meant she had to trust him. She had no other
choice.

But it wasn't easy.

Libby slumped against the chopping block, completely
befuddled.

What if I'm wrong? she wondered. *What if I've lost
Josh? Was it something I did? Something I said?*

THE CLIMB WAS physically taxing. It required coordination
and strength, but it wasn't particularly hazardous—not for
the guy who'd been champion of the rope climb at Lincoln
Junior High.

Of course, he was a whole lot heavier now, and the rope had been quite a bit narrower than the pipe. Instead of straddling it, you could either hold onto it with your knees or, if you were inclined to show off, you could use the method he'd preferred and go up hand over hand.

This climb demanded a different technique. He had to grip the pipe with the soles of his Topsiders, rest his weight against the column to create some slack in the belt, then flip the belt upward, pull himself after it, establish a new grip, and lean back to keep from losing the few inches he'd gained.

Sometimes this worked. Sometimes it didn't. Even with perfect timing he made slow progress.

Too slow.

Josh saw that the light was fading faster than he could climb, and wished he'd had the foresight to keep the flashlight handy. He peered up at the lantern deck, trying to memorize the position of the staircase relative to the column.

He closed his eyes and visualized the layout. Could he swing from the pipe to the landing in the dark?

I can try, he thought, redoubling his efforts. He hoped it wouldn't come to that.

He was halfway to his goal when he encountered a seam where the pipe had been welded. It took precious minutes and several tries before he managed to work the belt over the obstacle and haul himself upward.

By the time he made it to a perch above the seam, fatigue had set in. He had cramps in his legs, and his arms were beginning to feel like worn-out rubber bands. He flexed his hands to restore the circulation, but he couldn't afford to rest.

"Keep going," he told himself. "The hardest part's behind you. Things can't get any worse."

But they did.

The higher he climbed, the darker it got. Only willpower kept him going. He negotiated the last few feet, fighting the tendency to lean into the column and ease the strain on his arms and legs. But if he relaxed, even for a moment, he'd slide back down the pipe. Making the climb once was bad enough. He couldn't do it again.

He reached the top in a haze of exhaustion, in a twilight so dense, he could scarcely see his hand in front of his face. But in his mind's eye he reconstructed the smallest details of the landing.

He lay back against his harness, braced one foot against the column and kicked out blindly with the other. His toes glanced off metal. The landing was closer than he'd anticipated.

It's about time something came easy, he thought.

He propped both feet against the column, and traced the ropes of his harness, feeling for the release knot. He found it and hesitated, plotting his next move.

He had better grab the landing on the first swing. Once he had committed himself, he wouldn't get a second chance.

He tensed, preparing to propel himself toward the staircase, then simultaneously arched to the side, released the knot and pushed off, reaching for the landing with his toes, one hand stretched toward the rim of the deck. His foot missed the target, but his fingertips connected with something cool and gritty and metallic. He identified the handrail the instant his hand closed around it, and knew he had overshot the mark.

Instinct guided his reaction. He let go of the railing, lunged for the pipe and locked his arms and legs around it. He felt something give, felt a slackness in his harness and realized the second release knot must have snapped. Then he was slipping, clutching the pipe, trying desperately to brake his slide. But the closer he hugged the column, the less resistance he offered.

Now, ignoring his instincts, he forced himself to push away from the pipe.

You've still got the harness, he thought. Let it work for you.

The harness and sling might have done the trick, if the belt hadn't snagged on the weld. Josh remembered the seam in the pipe too late, after the jolting stop dragged him into the column.

His jaw collided with cold, hard steel. His head pitched back, and his teeth cut into his tongue. The safety harness became a trap as he swung in a deadly arc, bouncing off the pipe again and again, like a human pendulum.

He was suspended head down, dazed and disoriented, and the more he struggled to right himself, the more the ropes dug into his middle.

I can't breathe, he thought. I've had it.

He felt a sudden gouge from the belt buckle. Then, just as suddenly, it was gone.

God, Libby! Why does it have to end this way?

He saw an explosion of stars as he rebounded off the pipe. He felt himself falling . . . falling. . . .

And then, mercifully, he felt nothing.

Chapter Seventeen

A breeze sprang up about sunset. It made Libby even more uneasy. She returned to the cabin, but couldn't stop pacing.

She roamed aimlessly through the living room to the kitchen, then back to the living room, pausing at the door to Etta's bedroom. She raised her hand to knock, then thought better of it and wandered toward the kitchen.

If Josh was up to something, he might not appreciate her alerting Etta.

A fire crackled in the Franklin stove, dispensing warmth and cheer, but the dancing flames did nothing to lift Libby's mood. She stood at the sink and watched the evening gather outside the window.

Etta found her there half an hour later.

"Where's Josh?" she demanded, her voice shrill with excitement.

Libby studied the older woman's image in the windowpane. "Why do you ask?"

"Because I'm worried about him, that's why!"

Libby fumbled with the end of her braid. "I'm worried too—"

"No!" said Etta. "You don't understand and I don't have time to explain. You better come with me."

Her tone discouraged argument. When she spun on her heel and left the kitchen, Libby followed.

"What's happening?" she inquired. "What's this all about?"

"You'll see," Etta replied, continuing through the living room.

An odd tapping noise came from her bedroom—the imperious staccato of the telegraph key. Libby frowned, astonished by the rapid-fire striking of the key lever against the anvil, until the lever held at a neutral position and the clatter stopped.

Her frown shifted to Etta. "If this is your idea of a joke, I don't think it's very funny."

Etta shook her head. "Believe me, girl, it's no joke."

As if to affirm her statement, the key swung into motion again, rattling off dots and dashes with practiced authority. Faster and faster it bobbed, picking up speed until the clicking sounds ran together and the lever seemed to blur.

Both women watched until, all at once, it stopped.

Etta held up her hands, spreading them wide. "No strings," she declared flatly, "and you can see for yourself, I'm nowhere near that thing."

Libby stared at the key, horrified. "Then how do you account for it?"

"I can't."

"You mean it started sending on its own?"

"No, not quite. I was practicing, and after a while—it was the darnedest thing. The key just sort of—took over."

Libby wet her lips. "Can you make out what it's sending?"

"Not all of it. It goes too fast. All I could spell out was Josh's name and one word. *Help.*"

Libby's scalp prickled with fear. She started toward the door, but managed only two wobbly steps before Etta grabbed her arm. She twisted her wrist this way and that, trying to break Etta's hold.

"Let me go! I have to go to him."

"Where is he?"

"The keeper's house. He wanted to spend the night there."

"I'll come with you, but for heaven's sake, girl, use your noggin. It's black as pitch out. We won't get far without flashlights, and if we're going to do this right we ought to take some bedrolls and the first aid kit—"

"Oh, God, Etta! What if he's hurt?"

"If he is, it's even more important that you don't go off half-cocked. You'll be no damned good to anyone unless you get a grip on yourself." After giving Libby a sobering shake, Etta set her free. "Now you get us some blankets, and give me a hand rounding up the rest of the gear. The quicker that's done, the quicker we'll see whether there's any truth to that message."

A BRITTLE CALM possessed Libby. One wrong move might shatter it.

She found the blankets and helped Etta load a knapsack with medical supplies, and when Etta was satisfied that their preparations were complete, she obediently got into her poncho, feigning composure.

She followed the older woman away from the cabin like a sleepwalker. But they hadn't gone far before panic returned and threatened to spin out of control.

Libby wanted to run. Etta would not be rushed.

"We don't know for sure that Josh made it to the keeper's house," she reasoned.

Dear God! Libby thought. What if Etta's right? What if Josh had an accident on the trail? What if he fell? What if he's unconscious? What if he can't hear us calling him?

What if he hears, but can't answer? What if we miss him in the dark?

On the other hand, what if Etta was wrong? What if Josh was at the keeper's house? He might be lying there, injured, in pain—

Why didn't I go with him? Libby thought. If only I'd followed him, stayed with him, kept him in sight, I'd be with him now, when he needs me.

"Maybe I should go on ahead while you scout the trail," she suggested.

"Not on your life," Etta replied. "The state you're in, you'd get yourself lost, and I'd wind up hunting for both of you."

The wind rose and the temperature fell. Libby could see her breath. As the cold intensified, she discovered another cause for alarm.

"Josh wasn't wearing his coat," she said.

Etta swept the underbrush with her flashlight, considering this. "Didn't that strike you as strange?"

"It does now," said Libby. "He didn't take the sleeping bag either, or his duffel, or the survival blankets—"

The beam of Etta's torch froze on the gnarled branches of a pitch pine. "What did he take?"

Libby bit her lip, trying to remember. "Some matches. Some rope. A hand towel—and I think he took one of the lanterns."

"That's it?"

"That was all I saw. He was putting things into a pillow slip."

"Appears as if he wanted to travel light."

Libby nodded. "It does seem that way."

"But he told you he'd be gone all night?"

"Yes," said Libby. "Or words to that effect."

"And you believed him?"

Libby frowned at how easily she'd been deceived. "I did at first, but after Josh left I began to wonder if he had something else on his mind."

"Any idea what?"

"No," said Libby. "I wish I did."

Etta sighed. "Whatever he's up to, let's hope he's doing it at the house. If he's not there, we won't know where to look for him."

THE FIRST FLAKES OF SNOW fell while they were making the descent from the ridge. When they were halfway down the slope, Libby bolted. They were almost at the bluff now, and neither the darkness nor the danger could stop her mad scramble down the hill.

"Slow down, girl," Etta cautioned. "Watch where you're going or you'll break your fool neck."

The warning fell on deaf ears.

When Libby reached level ground, she ran faster, across the clearing to the house. She took the porch stairs in a single stride, calling out to Josh.

Please, God, let him be here, she prayed as she raced inside.

She hurried toward the parlor, dodging the jumble of fallen roof beams and gaps in the floor, pausing to shine her flashlight on the ruins that branched from the hallway.

By the time Etta reached the house, Libby was waiting on the stoop.

"He's not here!" she cried. "I've looked *everywhere*."

Etta switched off her flashlight. "Give me a minute to catch my breath, and we'll decide where to look next."

She sank down on the porch steps, and Libby sat beside her, but after a minute's rest, Libby succumbed to impatience.

"I can't just sit here, doing nothing. I'm going to search the outbuildings."

She was gone before Etta could protest, hurrying toward the toolsheds. She searched each of them carefully and each of the supply shacks, as well. She was picking her way through the rubble surrounding the oil hut when Etta caught up with her.

"I've been thinking 'bout this afternoon," Etta said. "When the three of us were hiking over here—"

Libby nodded anxiously. "What about it?"

"Well, it occurred to me, Josh asked a heap of questions about the lighthouse."

With that reminder Libby remembered the questions. With a guilty start she also recalled that she had paid them scant attention.

If only she had listened.

She thought of the items Josh had packed in the pillow slip, and suddenly they made sense. The matches, rope and lantern—even the towel! The clues had been there all along, and she'd been too absorbed in her own concerns to notice.

"He was going to climb the tower," she said. "That's what he was up to."

THEY FOUND JOSH on the floor of the lighthouse, enmeshed in a tangle of nylon rope. His belt lay nearby, its broken buckle testimony to the events that had preceded his fall. One side of his face was swollen and bleeding. Dried blood matted his hair. His forehead was clammy, he was unnaturally pale and so very still. He hardly seemed to breathe.

A sob welled up in Libby's throat. Tears misted her eyes, but she made herself blink them back.

She would cry later—after she had tended Josh's injuries. For as long as his survival depended on her, she didn't have time for tears.

She dropped to her knees beside him, feeling for his pulse. "Shine that light over here," she called.

Etta remained rooted to her spot near the doorway. Devastated by remorse, obviously shaken, she had to hold the torch with both hands to keep the light trained upon Josh.

"He's lost an awful lot of blood," she quavered.

"But the bleeding's stopped," said Libby. And most of his cuts seemed superficial, except for a lump the size of a goose egg behind his right ear.

"Why is he so quiet? Is he—?"

Libby silenced the older woman with a glare. "He's alive," she said firmly. Inside she was quaking, but she kept her voice steady—as steady as Josh's pulse. Surely that must be a favorable sign!

Her hands were numb. They trembled with apprehension. She blew on her fingers to warm them, and set to work loosening the knot in the pillow slip.

"Where are those blankets?"

Etta shrugged the bedding pack off her shoulders and unrolled the blankets. As she folded them around Josh, her movements were clumsy and disjointed, as if she had lost the ability to control her own body. Through chattering teeth, she said, "It's cold in here. Maybe we should rig up a stretcher and carry him to the house."

"I don't think we should do that," said Libby. "Not till we're sure he's not seriously hurt."

Keeping the patient immobile had been rule number one in the Girl Scout first aid course she had taken. If she and Etta attempted to move Josh, they risked aggravating his injuries. And if they didn't move him, they risked exposure, hypothermia, pneumonia.

We've got to have help, Libby thought. *That's the only solution.*

She gave up trying to untie the knot and ripped an opening along the seam of the pillow slip. Seconds later she had retrieved the lantern. Once she had a decent light, she'd be able to get a better idea of Josh's condition.

She primed the lantern, found a match and struck it against the floor—

"I always wondered what's up there." Etta spoke in an absent singsong, scowling into the darkness at the top of the column. "Do you s'pose Josh made it all the way to the deck?"

Libby stared at Etta aghast until the match burned her fingers. When she dropped it the flame went out, and she reached for another one.

"Etta," she said quietly, "I could use some water."

For a moment the older woman gazed at her with the vacant, unseeing eyes of a shock victim, and then she made a visible effort to pull herself together.

"I'll get some," she replied feebly, starting toward the door.

With Etta out of the way, Libby adjusted the valve so that the lantern gave off an even glow. She pulled off the knapsack, removed the first aid kit and scooted closer to Josh.

"Please, God, let him be all right. He's a good man, and I love him so much. Don't let him be seriously hurt."

Bending over Josh, she pushed back her sleeves and began gently palpating his head and neck, his shoulders and rib cage, and finally his limbs.

So far as she could tell, he hadn't broken any bones, and aside from facial contusions and the livid bruise on his scalp, she found no other wounds.

She wrapped the blankets more snugly around him, then topped the blankets with her poncho, and when Etta brought her a canteen of water, she bathed Josh's face and staunched the trickles of blood. She treated his cuts with antiseptic and applied a cold compress to his head. She made him as comfortable as possible, and when she had done everything she could, she sat beside him, holding his hand, willing him to come to.

"Open your eyes," she whispered. "Please, darling, try to respond."

At regular intervals she changed the compress, but after the fourth change, Josh still had not regained consciousness.

Etta left to refill the canteen, and returned dusted with snowflakes. "His color's better," she observed. "Here's hoping it's only a concussion."

Libby stroked Josh's hand. "I'm worried about internal injuries."

"You and me both."

"He needs medical attention. One of us has to go back to the cabin and radio the coast guard."

Etta slumped forward and ducked her head. In the last few hours she seemed to have aged twenty years. "You want me to do it?"

Libby was tempted to go along with Etta's offer, but common sense prevailed. Of the two of them, she was the one who could make better time. Hard as it was to leave Josh, she tucked his hand under the blankets and rose.

"I'll go," she said.

"Right now?"

"Of course now. This minute. Before the weather gets any worse."

Etta looked at Libby as if she had taken leave of her senses. "The coast guard won't be able to land a copter here before daylight."

"I know they won't, but if they had advance notice it should expedite matters."

At a loss, Etta watched while Libby switched on the flashlights and selected the brighter of the two to take with her.

"That trail will be tricky enough after this snow without trying to hike it in the dark."

"I'll make it," said Libby. "I have to."

"What if you don't?"

"That's a chance I have to take."

Libby didn't actually say that every second counted, but her tone made it clear that she considered the discussion closed. Etta was beaten and she knew it. The only thing left to do was offer reluctant approval.

"Since I can't talk you out of this, will you at least wear my coat?"

"It'd slow me down," said Libby. "Thanks, anyway."

Etta followed her to the door. "Do you know how to work the radio?"

"Not without the batteries."

Although Etta remained dubious, she fished the batteries from the pocket of her mackinaw.

Libby accepted them gratefully. "I appreciate this, and I want you to know your secret's safe with me. I won't tell anyone you're living here."

Etta cleared her throat. "Whether you tell or not, this is the least I can do. If I hadn't been a selfish old fool, you and Josh'd be safe on the mainland."

"Don't blame yourself," said Libby. "If I hadn't been so blasted stupid, none of this would have happened."

The two women shared a brief, fierce hug, acknowledging their common guilt.

"Take care of him, Etta."

"Don't you worry about Josh. I won't leave him for a minute." Etta moved away, avoiding Libby's eyes. "Now go on, girl! Get out of here before I change my mind."

Chapter Eighteen

The coast guard helicopter arrived shortly after daybreak the next morning. Josh came to while the paramedic was examining him. He remained conscious long enough to ask what had happened and answer a few questions, then drifted off and slept all the way back to Southwest Harbor.

"He has a severe headache," the medic told Libby, "and no recollection of the accident. That may or may not change, but it's nothing to worry about. Limited amnesia is fairly typical with this degree of trauma. What's significant is that he was alert and oriented and responding appropriately."

"Does that mean he'll be all right?"

"You'll have to save that one for the doctors," said the medic. "They'll need lab tests and skull films and a neurology consult before they'll be willing to predict whether there'll be any residual. But I can tell you this much. His vital signs are stable and his sense of humor's intact. The first thing he said to me was, 'If you think I look bad, you should see the other guy.'"

"What about his face?" said Libby.

"He won't win any beauty contests for a while, but I wouldn't anticipate any scars." The paramedic paused to supervise the crewmen who were loading Josh's stretcher into the belly of the copter. His patient taken care of, he said, "One thing has me stumped. Maybe you can explain it."

"I can try," said Libby.

"When you called in last night, you told the dispatcher there were three people on Sagamore. Yourself, Joshua Noon and Etta Cassidy—"

"I'd appreciate it if you'd keep Mrs. Cassidy's name confidential. She's publicity-shy, and it would be extremely painful for her if the newspapers revealed her whereabouts."

"Sure," said the medic. "No problem. But Josh kept talking about someone named Lorna, and I wondered how she figures into all this."

"That's a coincidence," Libby murmured. "I've been wondering about that myself."

The medic folded his stethoscope into a pocket of his flight jacket. "Is their relationship that complicated?"

"No, not complicated. Just hard to understand. But I think it's safe to say that she's a friend."

"Will she be making the trip back with us?"

Libby broke into a smile. "I can promise you she won't."

"Then she lives on the island."

"In spirit," said Libby. "Only in spirit."

The crewman hopped down from the cabin just then and hustled them aboard, sparing Libby further explanations. She strapped herself into a seat near the stretcher, where she could keep an eye on Josh. He was sleeping peacefully, naturally, his ruddy-bronze beard a sharp contrast to the stark white bandages on his face.

She wanted to hold his hand, but the upper half of his body was hemmed in by medical paraphernalia, so she had to be content with looking at him.

"All set back there?" the pilot called.

The medic checked the monitors and adjusted the IV drip, then gave the pilot a vehement thumbs-up. "Let's get this show on the road."

The engine roared to life, and the huge rotor blades slapped the air. The noise was deafening. Libby marveled that Josh could sleep through it.

The pilot was about to take off when one of the crewmen pointed toward the lighthouse. "Looks like we've got another passenger."

He left the cockpit to open the cargo door, and Libby saw Etta struggling across the clearing toward the copter, doubled over to make headway against the force of the draft.

The crewman jumped out to hurry her along, and the paramedic held out a helping hand. Etta shouted her thanks as they hauled her aboard, and as they guided her to the seat next to Libby's she inquired, "How's our patient?"

"A-okay," said the medic. "Resting comfortably."

The crewman secured the door, and Etta sat back and buckled her seat belt. "I decided I'd come along for the ride."

"I'm glad you did," said Libby. "Friends are hard to come by."

"Yeah, they are," Etta replied, meeting Libby's gaze. "Talking with Josh, hearing what he's been through, what with his partner's death and trying to relocate and the heat he's taken from the Coalition, made me realize it's time I confronted my problems instead of running away from them."

"Well, you won't have to face Lester alone. I'll help. So will Josh."

Etta reached over the armrest to clasp Libby's hand. "Bless you, girl, you've already given me more help than you know."

The whirring thump of the rotors had accelerated to takeoff speed, and the whine of the engine made conversation impossible as the copter lifted off.

This is it, thought Libby. *We're on our way.*

As the pilot banked the craft and brought it onto a westward heading, she turned to the window for a last look at the lighthouse. The sunrise washed the dome with a warm pink glow and threw long violet shadows onto the ground. The tower seemed radiant, less dilapidated. As their altitude increased, it even seemed to stand straighter.

Libby pressed her nose to the glass, entranced by the bird's-eye view. From that perspective, Sagamore was picturesque and not at all intimidating, and she watched the island recede until the sparkle of its snow-dappled cliffs blended into the glitter of the sea.

Etta tapped her on the shoulder. "Never look back, girl. You've gotta look forward."

She merely mouthed the words, but Libby caught their meaning. She nodded and faced forward, wondering what the future would hold.

I'll be home soon she thought. *I'll see Mom and Dad and my brothers. By now I must be an aunt, and I'll probably see the baby.*

But, after today, would she see Josh again?

Her vision blurred, and she blinked her eyes and rubbed the bridge of her nose.

Etta gave her a suspicious glance. "Not crying, are you?"

"No," said Libby, shaking her head. "The sun glare hurt my eyes."

Somehow she managed to smile.

WITH THE SERIES of misadventures Josh and Libby encountered, their voyage from Frenchman's Bay to Sagamore Island had taken two and a half days. The return trip took thirty-five minutes.

It was barely eight o'clock when the helicopter approached the landing pad on Mount Desert Island, but a good-size crowd had assembled despite the early hour.

There were housewives and club women, merchants and business people, curiosity seekers, tourists, and a contingent of schoolchildren who had been ferried over from Day's Harbor. Newspaper and television reporters ranged through the throng, vying for scoops and human interest stories. Politicians kissed babies and shook hands with well-wishers while they waited for the chance to be photographed with a friend or relative of the castaways—or better yet, with the castaways themselves.

Homer Trask was there with the delegation from DEEPC, and Margaret Ogilvie made her first public appearance since her arrest. She was considered a "hot" interview, which guaranteed her popularity with the press, but her former colleagues from the Coalition made it a point to shun her.

As DEEPC's new president told the *Packet*'s society columnist, "After her scandalous behavior, after the outrageous way she courted publicity just to build membership in the Coalition, I'm shocked Margaret would show up."

"I'm shocked, too," the columnist agreed, "but I'll say this much for Margaret. She certainly dresses well."

Unlike her successor, who was as dowdy as she was long-winded, the columnist thought to herself.

While DEEPC's new president outlined her plans for revamping the organization, the columnist scanned the crowd, her tight-lipped expression registering distaste for the lumberjack shirts and blue jeans that were the uniform of the day.

In the midst of so much denim, Margaret's well-cut tweeds and perfectly matched pearls seemed the pinnacle of sophistication.

"Last night's meeting was most productive in that we established a number of goals. The first, obviously, is to distance ourselves from the former executive and repudiate her tactics. That may seem ruthless, but it's the only way to salvage our credibility. DEEPC's reputation is at stake!"

The monologue droned on, with the president ticking off priorities on her fingers. She had used all the fingers on her left hand and was up to the middle finger on her right when the columnist spied a pair of newcomers in the crowd.

Her eyes narrowed. She licked her lips. Her nostrils flared like a hound's on the trail of a hare.

Sally Gillette had arrived, accompanied by a fashion plate whose outfit had graced a recent cover of *Vogue*.

"...honesty, honesty, honesty!" said the president. "I cannot stress this enough—"

"Excuse me, dear. This has been very enlightening, but there's someone I must speak to."

Niceties observed, the columnist plowed into the crowd, nose twitching, notebook at the ready. "Yoo-hoo, Mrs. Gillette!"

The familiar trill set Sally's teeth on edge. From the corner of her eye she spotted the society columnist bearing down on them.

"Don't look now," she groaned, clutching Blair Healey's elbow. "We're about to be waylaid by one of the local journalists."

Blair grinned good-naturedly. "Take it easy, Sal. I can handle reporters. In the past ten days I've discovered I can handle lots of things."

"I'm delighted by your confidence, but you don't know what you're letting yourself in for. That woman is a world-class snob, and when it comes to gossip, she's in a class by herself.''

"Well, if it's gossip she wants, I'll give her an earful—and while I'm at it, I'll work in a plug for Walt's memorial. If we're going to see the retreat established, it wouldn't hurt to have someone with media connections in our corner."

Sally was skeptical and it showed. But as it turned out, she needn't have worried. She had scarcely performed the introductions when a sober young policeman appeared.

"Mrs. Gillette?"

Sally nodded and linked her arm through Blair's. "This is Mrs. Healey," she said.

"Pleasure to meet you, ma'am."

"Any news about the helicopter?" Sally inquired.

"It's due any minute, ma'am. In the meantime, Chief Pilgrim sends his compliments. He wonders if you and Mrs. Healey would care to join him in Commander MacAuley's office."

"Is that where they'll bring Josh?" asked Blair.

"No ma'am. I believe they'll be takin' him directly to the hospital, but the ambulance is parked in back of the building. The driver'll be movin' out soon to the edge of the landin' pad, and you can ride out with him."

"I think we should accept the chief's invitation," said Sally. "This crowd'll go wild once that copter arrives."

Blair favored the columnist with her most vivacious smile. "You'll forgive us for deserting you?"

"But of course, my dear. That goes without saying. You'll be much more comfortable out of the crush. With your permission though, I'd like a rain check on an interview."

"Why don't you call me later at the Windlass? We'll see what we can work out."

Thoroughly charmed, the columnist gushed, "My dear Mrs. Healey, you're much too kind."

You can say that again, Sally thought.

But as the officer escorted them off the field, Blair turned to her and said, "Better a pesky ally than a powerful foe."

Sally smiled to herself, and shook her head. Was it possible she had underestimated Blair?

THE COPTER CAME IN over Bass Harbor Head, and a spasm of excitement shook Libby. All of Mount Desert Island was spread out below her, a sun-drenched patchwork of gold and blue. There was Brown Mountain, and Acadia, and the narrow inlet between them that led to Somes Sound.

A crosshatch of rooftops marked the village of Southwest Harbor, and the pilot began his descent.

Libby stared out the window as the helicopter skimmed the treetops, pursuing its own shadow toward the leeward shore. The boat basin came into view and beyond that the landing pad, ringed by a cordon of police cars.

She watched an ambulance draw up to the tarmac and the attendants leap out and unlatch the back doors, and as the copter hovered a dozen feet off the ground, she noticed a swarm of upturned faces.

"Look at all the people. What are they doing here?"

Etta shrugged. "I expect they turned out to welcome you and Josh home."

"But there are so many of them!"

"I told you, you're celebrities. And that was when most everyone assumed you were dead. Now you've been resurrected, you'll be even more famous."

In my case infamous, thought Libby. *The infamous kidnapper of Joshua Noon.*

Etta unbuckled her lap belt, preparing to make her getaway the moment they touched down, but Libby remained seated, searching the crowd. She saw Homer and Margaret and other acquaintances from DEEPC. She also identified several people from work, but with those exceptions she saw only strangers.

Where were her parents? Her brothers? Her sister-in-law?

A cheer went up as the cargo doors opened and the crewmen lifted Josh's stretcher out. Photographers rushed onto the tarmac, cameras clicking. Then a phalanx of police formed a wedge around the stretcher, and with the paramedic carrying the IV stand, the crewmen trundled Josh toward the ambulance.

Two women were waiting inside the vehicle. Libby recognized one of them as Sally Gillette; the other undoubtedly was Blair. She was just as Josh had described her; sweet-faced, angelic, adoring—and ecstatic at his return.

Libby saw Blair smile as she bent over the stretcher, then the crowd surged around them, cutting off her view.

She stood on tiptoe and stretched as tall as she was able, which permitted her to see the attendants positioning the stretcher in the back of the ambulance. And then a squad car careened to a stop beside the helicopter, the passenger door opened, and a blond giant of a man got out—

"Caleb! Oh, Cal, it's good to see you!"

She threw out her arms and was caught in a bear hug, just as Adam appeared from the driver's side of the car.

"How 'bout a hug for me, Sis?"

"And me," said Ben.

"Out of the way, boys. You'll have to wait till your mother and me have a look at 'er."

An older version of her brothers elbowed a path in Libby's direction. She saw her parents through a rush of tears, then suddenly she was surrounded, and everyone was hugging her and kissing her and talking at once.

"You look great, Sis! Doesn't she look great?"

"A little peaked maybe, but some of your mom's home cookin'll put roses in her cheeks."

"And meat on her bones!"

"Takes more than a shipwreck to keep a Pilgrim down!"

"Speaking of ships—"

"Not now, Cal."

Caleb glared at Adam. "I just wanted to find out how that Noon feller treated her."

"There'll be time for that later," said Daniel, who had been keeping a wary eye on the crowd. "I hate to break this up, folks, but the ambulance is leaving. We'd better get Libby out of here before the reporters gang up on her."

Adam hurried Libby to the police car and put her inside. Her mother leaned down and kissed her cheek.

"Aren't you and Dad coming with us?" asked Libby.

"They'll follow in my car," said Ben.

Her mother said, "Buckle your seat belt," and Dan got behind the wheel. He radioed in to report they were leaving as he guided the car through the crowd, and once they reached the highway, he drove away from the coast guard station with breathtaking speed.

"It'll be nice to get home," Libby said.

"We're not going home. Not right away."

Dan hunched over the wheel, gaze fixed on the road, and Libby choked back a cry as they barreled toward a pickup. She felt the car sway as the truck hurtled by, and cast a pleading glance at her brother.

"Wherever we're going, I'd like to get there in one piece."

Dan sighed and straightened his shoulders. "Meaning?"

"I'd appreciate it if you wouldn't drive so fast."

"We're only doing forty," he said, but he eased back on the accelerator.

She clung to the armrest, studying him, thinking how solemn he looked. They had left Southwest Harbor several miles behind before it occurred to her that he hadn't welcomed her home. While the rest of her family had greeted her with affection, her youngest brother had held back.

"How are things at home?" she asked.

"Okay, I guess. Janie sends her love."

"No baby yet?"

"Not yet." Dan shrugged. "It'll come when it's ready."

He must be worried about the delivery, thought Libby. Perhaps that explained his reserve. "Is the doctor still talking cesarean?"

"Nope. Now he's talking about inducing labor."

"But Janie's feeling all right?"

"She's fine. Tired of waiting."

And so, apparently, was Dan. Unless his grumpiness had nothing to do with his wife's pregnancy. What if it was connected to his work? Or to her?

"You seem very official, Dan."

"I'm on duty."

The gruff reply told Libby she was on the right track. "Am I under arrest?"

Dan spared her the briefest glance. "You probably should be, but I've got no case. As of this minute, all I have is Margaret Ogilvie's confession, and for all I know, that could be nothing more than a pipe dream."

"But you'll look into it."

"Naturally I will. That's my job. As soon as I have medical clearance I'll interview Josh Noon. If he corroborates Margaret's story, you'll be in deep trouble. If he doesn't, there'll be no proof a crime was committed—and maybe I can get a decent night's sleep."

Feeling chastened, Libby folded her hands in her lap. "What happens in the meantime?"

"You spend the morning at the hospital and let the doctors check you out, and if you know what's good for you, you'll keep your mouth shut. You won't discuss this with anyone."

"Including you?"

"Especially me!" Dan pounded one fist against the wheel. "Dammit, Libby, if you ever do anything like this again—"

"I won't, Dan. I swear it."

"Have you any idea what you put us through?"

"I'm sorry you were worried." She pressed her palms together, steepled her fingers. "About the boat—I imagine Caleb is furious."

"He was. He got over it."

"Will you, Dan? Do you think you can ever forgive me?"

Dan's cool demeanor thawed. He looked at her and grinned. "You betcha. You're my sister."

"Well, is it too soon to ask a favor?"

"Not if you want to press your luck."

For Etta's sake, Libby decided to risk it. "It's not for me. It's for a friend."

"What friend?"

"I can't tell you her name till you give me your word this conversation is off the record."

"What the—?"

"Please, Dan. This is important."

"Oh, all right. I promise."

"Well, her name's Etta Cassidy, and for the past year she's been living on Sagamore."

Daniel's grin became a smirk. "You're putting me on. Everybody knows that island's deserted."

"Everybody's wrong!"

The smirk slipped a notch. "What is she? Some kind of hermit?"

"What if she is? There's no law against it, and it's not as if she's become one voluntarily."

"Hey, hold on! Are you saying someone's twisting her arm, forcing her to live out there all alone?"

"Yes, Dan. That's exactly what I'm saying."

After that shaky beginning, Libby went on to tell her brother about Lester's attempts to gain control of his uncle's estate. She told Dan how Lester had persecuted Etta, accused her of incompetence, driven her into hiding.

"He destroyed her trust," said Libby, "but he couldn't destroy *her*."

"She must be one tough lady," Dan remarked, encouraging Libby to go on.

By the time they reached the hospital, she had brought him up-to-date, and extracted a promise that he would try to find Etta.

"You say she was at the coast guard station?"

"She flew in with us on the copter," Libby answered. "She told me she was going to confront her nephew, but when she saw all those reporters, she must've changed her mind. One minute she was there, and the next she was gone."

"She just blended into the crowd?"

Libby nodded. "She was terrified of publicity."

"Can't say I blame her. That mob at the landing field would give anyone cold feet."

"There's more to it than that, Dan. You see Lester's a lawyer. Etta was convinced if he got her into court, she wouldn't have a prayer of coming out on top."

Daniel lapsed into a reflective silence while he followed the hospital driveway to the back of the building and parked near the loading dock. He sneaked Libby through an employees' entrance, through a maze of corridors to the emergency room, and after a hurried conference with the receptionist, a nurse appeared and led them to a visitors' lounge.

"I'll page Dr. Metcalfe and let him know you're here," said the nurse. "You shouldn't have too long a wait."

She waved them toward a sofa and bustled away down the hall, the rubber soles of her oxfords squeaking against the tile floor.

Libby ignored the sofa in favor of a bench, which offered a view of the white-curtained examining cubicles. Was Josh in one of them, or had he already been taken to his room?

"You know, Sis, if Etta's as fond of Noon as you seem to think, she'll probably get in touch with the hospital to find out how he's doing."

"Or she might contact you, Dan. She's aware you're Chief of Police."

Dan sat on the bench beside Libby, a notebook on his knee. "In case Etta doesn't surface, what's Lester's last name?"

"Cassidy, I assume. Etta never mentioned it."

"Did she say where he lives?"

"Not that I recall."

Dan glanced up from his notebook, pencil poised. "So he might be from away."

"I suppose that's possible. Etta did say he used to visit them on Monhegan, but that was quite a while ago, before her husband passed away."

"Do you know when he died?"

"Unfortunately I don't, but from the way Etta described him, he was quite a prominent man."

"Then there should be an obituary."

"That's right! You might find Lester's full name there."

Dan made a note to himself to check the *Packet*'s morgue, and bracketed the note with question marks. "Did Etta ever mention any friends?"

"No, I'm afraid she didn't."

"Well, where do you think she'd go?"

"You might try bookstores and libraries. She really loves to read."

"Where else?"

Libby studied the spatter design on the floor tiles, considering this. "I'm sorry," she apologized. "That's all that comes to mind. I realize it's not much to go on."

Daniel shook his head. "I can tell you right now, this won't be easy, but I'll do what I can."

He closed the notebook and returned it to his shirt pocket as the nurse reappeared with the doctor in tow.

Libby went to meet them, intending to ask for news of Josh, but Daniel beat her to it.

"Mr. Noon's doing remarkably well," said the doctor, "although he's not what I'd call a model patient."

"No, indeed," said the nurse. "When I left him he was threatening to sign himself out, because we won't let him go gadding about the hospital and we won't give him breakfast."

"Why won't you?" asked Libby.

"Strictly a precaution," the doctor explained. "We're running some tests, which I expect will be normal. To show you how confident I am, I've already written orders to discontinue Mr. Noon's IV as soon as the results are back from the lab. By this evening he should be on a regular diet, and if he tolerates that, I'll release him tomorrow."

"I need to talk to him, Doc," Daniel said. "Is he up to answering questions?"

"Well, there's no doubt he's lucid, but you'll have to be brief. He's scheduled for a CAT scan in about half an hour."

"What room is he in?"

"Two-fourteen. I'll come with you if you like."

But Daniel was already rushing toward the elevator. "Thanks, anyway," he called. "I'm sure I can find it. Just take good care of my sister while I'm gone."

"That's what we're here for," the nurse assured him, and taking a firm grip on Libby's arm, she added, "Now, Miss Pilgrim. if you'll come with me."

Do I have a choice? Libby wondered, as the nurse steered her into an examining room. "All this fuss isn't necessary," she said.

"Nonsense," the nurse countered, handing Libby a hospital gown. "You've been through an awful ordeal, and take it from one who knows. Where your health is concerned, it's better to be safe than sorry."

Libby insisted that she felt fine, but her protests did no good. For the remainder of the morning she was poked and prodded and subjected to a variety of tests.

The rest of the Pilgrims came trooping in while Dr. Metcalfe was examining her, but she saw them only in passing, when the nurse wheeled her down to the radiology department.

While the x–rays were being processed, Dan stopped by the emergency room and left a message that she was in the clear. Josh's statement made it evident he had asked for a lift to Southwest Harbor, she had obliged, and fate had intervened.

Caleb walked Dan to his squad car so that he could get an eyewitness report on Josh's character. "What's Noon like?" he asked.

"He's a Bulls fan," Dan replied.

Caleb frowned. "I guess you gotta expect that, him bein' from Chicago."

"Right," said Daniel, "but aside from that, he's a nice enough feller."

Twelve o'clock came and went. Libby was weak with hunger. Except for half a stale donut and a cup of coffee the helicopter crew had given her, she'd had nothing to eat or drink since lunch the day before.

And her brothers were getting restless. They had long since thumbed through the outdated magazines in the visitors' lounge. Adam began pacing the halls. Ben went off to investigate the computer room. Caleb flirted with the nurses. All of them dodged reporters and became increasingly bored.

When Libby's parents inquired how long it would be before she could go home, the doctor told them, "Be patient. Give us another fifteen minutes and she'll have a clean bill of health."

"That's what you said an hour ago," Adam replied.

"And an hour before that," Ben argued.

"He's been sayin' that all mornin'," said Caleb.

Outnumbered, Dr. Metcalfe had to admit there had been unforeseen delays. "We've been invaded by the press, and it's led to one complication after another. But we have the results of her blood work. All that's left is the report on her chest x–ray, and even as we speak the radiologist should be reading the films."

But when the report arrived, Dr. Metcalfe said, "It seems we have a problem."

"Not another one!" Libby groaned.

"Yes, my dear, I'm afraid the radiologist saw something. No doubt it's insignificant—an artifact of processing. But it could be pneumonitis."

The Pilgrim family responded to this announcement with tight-lipped silence. Dr. Metcalfe shuffled stacks of paper from his In basket to his Out basket and looked acutely embarrassed.

"What I propose," he advised Libby, "is that we find you a room and repeat the films at our leisure."

"You want me to check into the hospital?"

"Only till we've ruled out pneumonia."

"Would I be able to have lunch?"

"Well, the lunch hour's over, but I'm sure I could persuade the dietitian to send up a snack."

"Make it a double cheeseburger and I'll stay."

"Traitor!" Caleb grumbled. "You'd swap your birthright for a Big Mac."

If Caleb expected Libby to deny his accusation, he was disappointed.

While Dr. Metcalfe made arrangements for her admission, she said her farewells to her mother and father and promised she would call them the moment she was released. And once her parents had left, while a candy striper guided her to her room, Libby acknowledged there must be a kernel of truth in Caleb's observation.

She had traded an evening with her family for the chance to see Josh. If that made her a traitor, so be it.

Chapter Nineteen

Libby was just finishing lunch when Sally Gillette came by. She said, "We haven't met, but I feel as if I know you. Caleb's told me so much about you."

"I hope you don't believe everything Caleb says."

Sally laughed. "Spoken like a true sister."

Libby laid her napkin on her tray and asked the question that was uppermost in her mind. "How's Josh?"

"Grouchy. Ornery. Not fit to be around."

"But he's usually so good-natured."

"True," said Sally. "But he's not accustomed to physical discomfort.

"He's in pain?"

"He must be. Not that he's complained, but he's covered with bruises, and he's trying to hide how much he's hurting because he hates being confined. You'd be doing me a favor if you'd stop by for a visit."

"I'd like that," said Libby. "When would be a good time?"

"What's wrong with now?"

Not a thing, thought Libby. Now's perfect.

She was tempted to make a run for the door. It was all she could do to restrain herself for the minute it took to slip into the surgical gown she'd been given to use as a robe and run a comb through her bangs; once she had made herself presentable, she couldn't conceal her eagerness.

"This has been the longest morning of my life," she confessed as she followed Sally along the hall. "Dr. Metcalfe told me not to worry. He said Josh would be fine, but I can't tell you how hard it's been, not being able to see for myself."

Sally opened the door to two-fourteen. "Now's your chance," she said, motioning Libby into the room.

Josh was on the phone, but the moment Libby walked in he broke off his conversation. In the last few hours his bruises had darkened and his right eye had swollen shut. Combined with his beard, his battered features gave him a bold, piratical look, especially when he grinned.

"You found her, Sally. Good job."

"Thanks, boss. I also lined up that cassette recorder for you. It'll be delivered this afternoon."

Josh removed a briefcase from the visitor's chair. "Sit here," he said to Libby. "Sally's about to leave."

"But first I want to make sure I've got my assignments straight." Sally collected a pencil and steno pad from the nightstand and stood at the foot of the bed, reading through a hastily scrawled agenda. "What did you decide about the plane tickets?"

"Nothing," said Josh. "Better hold off on those till tomorrow."

Sally made a check mark on her list. "Staff meeting?" she prompted.

"Monday morning. Nine o'clock, sharp."

"When do you want to schedule the presentation to Lansford?"

"If Gordie's as antsy as you say, we'd better do it as soon as possible."

"Tuesday, then," said Sally. "And if it's all right with you, I'd like to set up interviews with the administrative assistant applicants for tomorrow."

"Tomorrow's okay, but you'd better make it late in the day. Otherwise I'll have to see them here."

"Gotcha, boss. Now, about the press conference—"

"Don't bother with that. I'm leaving it to Blair."

Sally's eyes grew round and incredulous. "But you've always—"

"Don't say it, Sally. I know what I've done. I made the same mistake Walt did. For all the time they were together he treated Blair as if she were made of spun glass—and now I find out she resented it. She informed me this morning that unless she's allowed more input into the plans for Walt's memorial, she'll withdraw her financial support."

"I can't say I blame her, boss. She'll never develop strengths until she has to depend on herself. But that doesn't change the fact that she picked a heck of a time to put her foot down. The situation with the retreat is tricky. Public opinion could go either way."

"Blair's as cognizant of that as we are. She realizes we're not out of the woods yet, but Walt was her husband, and as she rightly pointed out, she has to begin somewhere."

"Well," said Sally, shaking her head, "mine not to reason why. Mine but to do what I can to help."

"Blair's relying on that," said Josh, "almost as much as I am."

"Which means I've got my work cut out for me. But it's kind of nice to be needed."

With a rueful smile, Sally gathered up her belongings and left the room. As the door swung shut behind her, Josh sighed and lay back against the pillows, but Libby sat on the edge of her chair.

Alone with Josh in these surroundings, she felt awkward—almost shy. She crossed her legs and smoothed her palms over the surgical gown, trying to appear at ease.

"Sally's quite a dynamo," she ventured.

"She's an invaluable employee," said Josh. "Things piled up while I was gone, but Sally has 'em organized. If she keeps this up, I'll have to make her a partner."

Libby linked her hands about her knees and stole a glance at Josh. "Would you mind?"

"Actually I wouldn't. I enjoy the creative end of advertising, but it'd be a relief not to have to worry about the details of day-to-day administration."

Josh didn't look the least bit worried. With his bandage skewed to a rakish tilt, he looked as if he was having fun. And the instructions he'd given Sally made it obvious he couldn't wait to get back to work.

"Dr. Metcalfe says he'll probably release you tomorrow."

"He'd better. If he doesn't, I'll go AWOL."

Josh issued this threat in a monotone that told her the subject was closed. She got up and wandered about the room, searching for a new topic of conversation.

"You have some lovely plants," she said. "Two azaleas—"

"The pink one's from Blair; the other one's from the gang at the Windlass."

"They're gorgeous! And this African violet's blooming its little heart out."

"It's from Sally."

"The jade tree?"

"Margaret Ogilvie."

"Ooh, Josh! The flowers on this one look like orchids."

"That's what they are. Your parents sent them."

Josh held out his hand, beckoning Libby to the bedside, but she bent over the fragile white blossoms and pretended not to notice.

"They're beautiful," she murmured. "Absolutely exquisite."

"Listen," Josh scolded, "if you won't come here and give me a kiss, would you at least sit where I can see you?"

"I'd be happy to, as soon as I've had a closer look at the ficus—"

"The ficus can wait. I can't. For God's sake, Libby! With all the things we could be talking about, why are we talking about plants?"

Libby heard the scowl in Josh's voice. She wanted to look at him but couldn't meet his gaze. She focused on the shiny green foliage of the rubber plant. "Maybe we're trying to avoid mentioning things we'd rather not discuss."

"Such as?"

"Your trip to Chicago."

"So you picked up on Sally's question about the plane tickets. I was afraid you might have, but I can explain—"

"You don't need to explain, Josh. I understand. I've known all along that you'd never go through with the relocation."

"What gave you the idea I won't go through with it?"

"Well, it's obvious. You love the excitement of the city. You thrive on it!"

"I won't deny I enjoy being at the hub of things, but the only reason I'm going to Chicago is to let my clients see that I'm still kicking. I put off answering Sally's question about reservations till I could find out whether you'd care to come along."

Libby stared at Josh through the greenery. "You want me to come with you?"

Josh winked at her with his one good eye. "There's nothing I'd like better."

"How long would we be gone?"

"A week or ten days to take care of business, another two weeks for a honeymoon, and then we'll come back here. You'll be home in time for Christmas."

Honeymoon? Dear God, he was proposing! And her first inclination was to accept. Through no small effort she resisted the impulse, but her emotions went into a tailspin.

"J-Josh," she answered, faltering over his name, "you never cease to amaze me. I don't know what to say."

"Try 'Yes, Josh, I'll marry you.'"

"I—I'm sorry. I can't."

"Well, if you can't manage that, a simple yes will do."

"I can't say that, either." But, oh, how she wished she could!

Josh grinned, unabashed. "I realize we haven't known each other long—"

"We're barely acquainted!"

"Speak for yourself, love. I'm not in the habit of sleeping with acquaintances. After all we've been through and the intimacies we've enjoyed, I'd recognize you anywhere."

"I'd recognize you too, Josh—on Sagamore, under extraordinary circumstances. But on the mainland, in the normal world, we're strangers."

"So what you're saying is, 'This is so sudden. Give me some realism to go with the romance.'"

"I'm saying more than that. I'm saying let's not rush into anything till we've figured out where we're going, and whether we're traveling the same direction. To begin with, I think you should reconsider leaving Chicago—"

"Dammit, Libby! Are we back to that again?"

"You asked what I was saying! The least you can do is listen."

A muscle leaped along the line of his jaw. "Very well. I'm listening."

"And I'm telling you, there's no need to go to extremes. If you leave Chicago, it won't bring back Walt. It won't accomplish a thing."

Josh turned onto his side, facing her, and the movement made him wince. "I'm trying very hard to be patient, Libby, but I wish you'd make up your mind. You say you don't know me, yet you presume to hand out advice."

She touched his shoulder. "You're offended and I'm sorry, but I don't regret speaking out. Every time I look at you, I see a man who's talented, courageous and incredibly generous, making the biggest mistake of his life."

"And when I look at you, I see a woman who's independent as all get out, stubborn, overly cautious, and afraid to reveal how much she cares." Smiling with newfound tolerance, Josh covered her hand with his. "You see, sweetheart, I do know you, and I love you to distraction, so I'm going to give you the time you need to get accustomed to the idea of marriage."

Libby stared at Josh, mute with astonishment, waiting for him to revert to type. And she was not disappointed. After a moment's silence, he added, "I just hope to God it doesn't take too long."

AN HOUR LATER, in the privacy of her hospital room, Libby regretted the things she had left unsaid.

She hadn't mentioned Etta.

She hadn't thanked Josh for clearing her with Dan.

And she hadn't told Josh she loved him.

The press conference was televised that evening. Blair's arrangements must have been satisfactory, because it went off without a hitch. Dr. Metcalfe issued a medical bulletin, then introduced his star patient.

Josh's statement made it apparent that his harrowing experience had not dampened his enthusiasm for the Walter Healey memorial. "Just the opposite," he said. "In my time on Sagamore, I developed a reverence for the island. I learned that some things are worth waiting for, and some should not be postponed. And I'd like to think I've learned to make the distinction between the two. I am totally convinced that work on the retreat should go forward, and I'm totally committed to the project."

Josh went on to express his appreciation to the coast guard, and he particularly thanked the Pilgrim brothers for carrying on the search when the evidence indicated that neither he nor Libby could have survived.

He presented an appealing image on television. Even on the antiquated set in Libby's room his sincerity was clear.

In the hours since she'd seen him he had gotten rid of the beard, and with it gone, he'd also lost his brigand's air. Clean-shaven he looked heroic, dashing, candid, adorable, sexy.

And he loves me, she thought. *He wants to marry me.*

But Josh's proposal seemed unreal—almost like a fantasy. She couldn't believe he'd made it any more than she could believe she had not accepted.

Was she that unselfish? Did she care for him so much that his welfare meant more to her than her own?

Or was she frightened, overcautious, too timid to grab her chance at happiness and never let it go?

Libby couldn't decide, and she resolved not to think about it. Some questions, she told herself, have no answer. And over the next few weeks she discovered that the whys and wherefores of her actions weren't important. What mattered were the consequences, and the major consequence of what she had done was that she was miserable without Josh.

The Saturday after she left the hospital, he phoned her from Chicago. He asked how she was doing, and she told him she was fine. She asked about the Lansford campaign, and whether Blair was making progress with the retreat.

Before he hung up, Josh told her he'd given some thought to her comments about the relocation. "Nothing's definite yet," he told her, "but it could be you were right on the mark."

Josh said he missed her, and her spirits soared. He asked if she missed him, and she admitted she did. But she didn't realize how much until the call ended and her spirits sagged, leaving her more miserable than before.

She missed Josh's teasing and his taunting and his aw-shucks grin. She missed his easy laughter, the sound of his voice, his endless supply of stories. She missed playing cards with him, walking through the woods with him, sitting by the fire with him, lying in his arms. She missed his kisses, his lovemaking, the way he'd made her feel.

She missed him waking and sleeping, and as the days drifted by, she began to lose touch with the woman she had become with Josh.

What had happened to that Libby? Where had she gone? She had shown so much promise, so much warmth and affection. She had been joyful, approachable, a better person in every way than Elizabeth the archivist, who took life too seriously, whether she was preserving the environment, wallpapering her kitchen or fulfilling her responsibilities as an aunt.

Dan's wife went into labor the Monday before Thanksgiving. "It was the longest pregnancy in history, but it was worth it," Janie declared, cuddling her infant daughter.

"She's like a darling little doll," said Libby, awestruck by the baby's shell-like ears, her tiny fingers and toes. "They're so delicate. So perfect." But the most fantastic thing about her niece was the speed of her transformation from blissful contentment to red-faced tantrum, and once her needs had been taken care of, just as swiftly back again.

"This little girl's got a great set of lungs," said Daniel.

"That's babies for you," Janie replied. "They don't bottle up their feelings. Whatever makes 'em feel good *is* good."

Libby marveled at her sister-in-law's wisdom, and she was enchanted by her niece's capacity for pleasure.

When visiting hours were over, she remarked to Caleb, "That baby's less than a day old, but she's already smarter than I am." And of course Caleb agreed with her, which was why she seldom confided in him.

November became December, and Libby returned to work. She arrived at the college before sunup and by the time she left her basement office, evening had set in.

She could have been the Lansford chowder mermaid, and she had chosen to become a mole. She felt trapped in eternal gloom, and she lived for the brightness of the weekend and the occasional call from Josh.

On the night he announced he would be staying in Chicago, she told her parents, "I'm in a rut, and I can't seem to find my way out."

Her mother suggested a new job might help, and her ever practical father said, "Either that or an office with a window."

To Libby this made a lot of sense. She decided to take their advice.

She was crossing the campus the next afternoon, bundled to the eyes against the blustery wind, hurrying to keep an appointment at the personnel office, when she ran into Etta.

"I've been terribly worried about you," she told the older woman, "but now I can see I needn't have been. You're looking great."

"I guess that's what success does for a person," Etta replied.

"Where are you staying? What have you been up to?"

"I've been living out at the Windlass, working with Blair Healey."

"On the retreat?"

"Yep. Right now we're in the planning phase, but come April we'll start building. When the camp opens, I'm gonna manage it."

"That's wonderful, Etta! But why didn't you tell me?"

"I am tellin' you. Now."

"And Lester?"

"He's no problem. I haven't heard a peep out of him since me and my lawyer showed him another kind of power of attorney."

Libby went on to her interview with a spring in her step and a promise from Etta to keep in touch, but by the time the meeting ended, her good mood had evaporated.

The moment she got home, she placed a call to Josh. His phone rang one...twice...three times, and the answering machine clicked in.

She could have wept with frustration. Despair prompted the message she left.

"Help! I'm a marooned in a three-room apartment in Rockport, Maine. The roof keeps the snow out. There's food in the cupboards, but I'm starving for your company. I love you, Josh Noon. I need you. If you don't rescue me, I don't know how much longer I can survive."

For the rest of that night Libby sat by the phone, waiting for Josh's response. But she waited in vain. The phone mocked her with its silence.

By midnight she had resolved to rescue herself. If Josh would not come to her, she would go to him.

She called United Airlines' toll-free number and reserved a seat on the seven a.m. flight from Bangor to Chicago, then threw some clothes into a suitcase and sat at her desk, writing notes to her parents, her landlady, her department chief at the college, explaining her abrupt departure.

The letter of resignation was hardest to compose. She wrote several drafts, and finally acknowledged there was no excuse for what she was about to do. Her conscience chided her for her irresponsible behavior, but she chose to think of it as spontaneous.

She addressed her letters and propped them on top of the mailbox in the vestibule, where the postman would find them. She slid the note to the landlady under her door, then returned to her apartment to shower and change into a skirt and sweater.

She braided her hair with one eye on the clock. It was five thirty-five when she finished, past the time she should have left for the airport. She buttoned her coat, grabbed her suitcase and tote bag and literally raced out the door, praying that luck would be with her.

If the weather cooperated and the roads were clear, she should make her flight with minutes to spare.

She tossed the luggage into her Toyota, brushed last night's snowfall off the windows and climbed behind the wheel. Her hands were shaking as she fitted the key into the ignition. She patted her coat pockets, making sure she hadn't forgotten her gloves, then shifted into neutral and turned the key.

Nothing happened.

"Start," she implored the engine. "Please, please start."

She pumped the gas pedal, and tried the key a second time.

Again nothing.

And then she heard the laughter.

She peered through the windshield toward a late-model sedan, which was parked at the curb beneath a street lamp.

She had never seen the car before, but the man who stepped out of it was familiar. He was bareheaded despite the cold, and although the light at his back cast his face into shadow, she recognized him immediately.

"Josh?"

She scarcely got his name out before her breath lodged in her throat.

She opened the driver's door, and he laughed again and held up a round piece of metal with hoses dangling from the side. She started toward him, staring at the object with dawning comprehension.

The distributor cap. No question about it. No wonder her car wouldn't start.

Her heart did a crazy flip-flop. She felt buoyant, lighter than air, as she broke into a trot. "Can you take a passenger?"

Still laughing, Josh held out his arms to her. "That depends. Are you going my way?"

"Always," Libby vowed, and she ran into his embrace.

COMING NEXT MONTH

SOMEBODY'S BABY
Marilyn Pappano

Daniel Ryan never even knew that he had a
daughter — until the day a lawyer presented him
with tiny, adorable Katie and a contract for one
year's custody. Now the year was almost up and
Katie's mother would be coming to take her back.

Daniel remembered Sarah Lawson all too well.
She had seemed warm, sensuous, the answer to all
his lonely prayers. So how could she have given up
her child?

GLASS HOUSES
Anne Stuart

Laura de Kelsey Winston had fire. She had spirit.
She also had the colossal gall to challenge the most
powerful and feared man in Manhattan.

Michael Dubrovnik thrived on challenges and
welcomed a battle of wills. He was looking forward
to doing battle with Laura!

COMING NEXT MONTH

CATCH OF THE DAY
Marion Smith Collins

Katie John's heart stood still as the sound of her pursuer's footsteps grew closer. The docks were deserted and dark; the light at the end of the pier seemed so far away. Relief flooded through her at the sight of a dangerously sexy charter-boat captain.

Joe Ryder was all that stood between Katie and disaster; he wanted to keep his distance because of his past, but he couldn't ignore her need.

HOME TO THE COWBOY
Bobby Hutchinson

Mitch Carter was a professional cowboy, at home on the back of a stallion, a hero in the rodeo ring. So why did he envy the new vet in town, Sara Wingate?

Sara was fast gaining the respect of the community, making friends and putting down roots. Watching Sara, Mitch felt his heart stir with the unaccustomed need to belong to someplace, to someone ...

Silhouette

A Free Silhouette novel for you!

At Silhouette we always do our best to ensure that our books are just what you want to read. To do this we need your help! Please spare a few minutes to answer the questions below and overleaf and, as a special thank you, we will send you a FREE Silhouette romance when you return your completed questionnaire.

Don't forget to fill in your name and address so we know where to send your FREE BOOK.

Please tick the appropriate boxes to indicate your answers. ✔

1 **How long have you been reading Silhouette novels?**

	Less than 1 year	1-2 years	3-5 years	More than 5 years	I don't read this series
Special Edition	❑	❑	❑	❑	❑
Desire	❑	❑	❑	❑	❑
Sensation	❑	❑	❑	❑	❑

2 **How often do you read each series?**

	Every month	Every 2-3 months	Every 6 months	Once a yr or less	I don't read this series
Special Edition	❑	❑	❑	❑	❑
Desire	❑	❑	❑	❑	❑
Sensation	❑	❑	❑	❑	❑

3 **Which of the series, if any, is your favourite?**

Special Edition	❑	Desire	❑
Sensation	❑	Like them all equally	❑

4 **Why is this your favourite?**_____

_____

_____

5 **Do you read historical romances** Yes ❑ No ❑ **Please complete overleaf**

6. How often, if at all, do you read any of the following Mills & Boon novels?

	Every month	2-3 months	Every 6 months	Once a yr or less	I don't read this series
M&B Romance	☐	☐	☐	☐	☐
M&B Temptation	☐	☐	☐	☐	☐
M&B Medical Romance	☐	☐	☐	☐	☐
M&B Best Seller	☐	☐	☐	☐	☐
M&B Collection	☐	☐	☐	☐	☐

7. Where do you get your Silhouette books from?

	Special Edition	Desire	Sensation
Reader Service	☐	☐	☐
Buy new from the shops	☐	☐	☐
Buy secondhand	☐	☐	☐
Borrow from library	☐	☐	☐
Borrow from a friend / relation / colleague	☐	☐	☐

8. So that we know a bit about you please tick the boxes that apply to you:

Age group Under 25 ☐ 25-34 ☐ 35-44 ☐ 45-54 ☐ 55-64 ☐ 65+ ☐

Employment	Marital status	Children
Student ☐	Single ☐	No children ☐
Work part-time ☐	Divorced ☐	Children of pre-school age ☐
Work full-time ☐	Married ☐	Children of school age ☐
Full-time housewife ☐	Co-habitating ☐	Children have left home ☐
Unemployed ☐	Widowed ☐	
Retired ☐		

9. Do you think you might be interested in taking part in any future research that we carry out on Silhouette books?

Yes, I might be interested in any research by post ☐

Yes, I might be interested in any research discussions ☐

No thank-you, I am not interested in any further research ☐

Thank you for your help. We hope that you enjoy your FREE book.

Post this page TODAY TO: Silhouette Survey FREEPOST, P.O. Box 236, Croydon CR9 9EL.

Mrs/Ms/Miss/Mr_____ SILQ

Address_____

_____

_____

Postcode _____